SONG IN THE
KEY OF MADELEINE

SONG IN THE
KEY OF MADELEINE

Pauline Crame

The Book Guild Ltd

First published in Great Britain in 2021 by
The Book Guild Ltd
9 Priory Business Park
Wistow Road, Kibworth
Leicestershire, LE8 0RX
Freephone: 0800 999 2982
www.bookguild.co.uk
Email: info@bookguild.co.uk
Twitter: @bookguild

Typeset in 11pt Minion Pro

Printed on FSC accredited paper
Printed and bound in Great Britain by 4edge Limited

ISBN 978 1913913 151

British Library Cataloguing in Publication Data.
A catalogue record for this book is available from the British Library.

Thank you to Elizabeth Simpson and Matt Wood for all the time you invested and the detailed and helpful comments you provided.
And
Thank you to John Byrne for turning my dream of being published into a reality.

Prologue

Forty Years Later

The house matched his memory perfectly. It had been almost forty years, but it seemed the changes were no more than superficial. Seeing the house now was like having his conscience laid bare before him; the ghost of the former time vibrated from the very foundations and teased from behind the curtains. Shibu gently opened the small, iron gate, which creaked still, like an echo from the past. He stood at the foot of the steps, looking up at the front door. The same brass knocker dressed it and seemed to mock him, like a gargoyle, as if in warning of the significance of entry to the house. He delayed by creeping down the side and into the back garden.

Gravel crunched under his feet, noisy and sharp. Fearing early detection, he remained still and observed from where he was. In contrast to the front everything was different here, reduced to the practical level. In place of the jungle-like foliage, in which a mirror, a Buddha and an old gramophone once hid; there were large, easy to manage pots. Around the one remaining feature, the beech tree, gravel lay, like crystallised tears, in place of the daisy-rich lawn. The garden, once wild and contradictory like Madeleine, was now plain and functional.

Returning to the foot of the front steps Shibu hesitated once more; he could so easily just turn and walk away without need for confrontation with the past, but he had promised. He feigned confidence in the knock that would take him over the threshold from present to past. The door opened to reveal an even bigger leap than he could ever have imagined.

"Hi," the woman said, a little too cheerfully for the circumstances. "I guess you must be Shibu. I'm Jasmine."

Chapter One

Shibu paused and checked the address. There was no number on the door, so he strolled up to the neighbouring house to be sure, before entering through the small iron gate, which creaked as he opened then closed it. He climbed the three steps to the front door, raised his hand to the large brass knocker, which bore a face inside a symbol of the sun, and was about to knock when the door was opened by a woman, who said, "Hi, can't keep your arrival secret, I'm afraid."

Shibu frowned and pouted in puzzlement.

"I heard the gate." The woman was dressed in denim dungarees; her tawny hair was just long enough for the band that tied it back from her face, but one loose ringlet teased her cheek. In her left hand she held a paintbrush, wet with fresh paint; she extended the other to Shibu.

"I'm Madeleine. You found me alright then?"

Madeleine felt his energy even before their hands met.

"Shibu. Was easy, but you don't have number."

"Don't need it. My friends know where I live and the postman is my boyfriend." She giggled. "I'm just finishing off painting the room," she said, waving the brush gently. "Just let me put this in some white spirit and I'll be with you."

While she was gone Shibu took in his surroundings. The hallway was painted deep red and magnolia. On a small, dark wood table stood a glass vase of yellow flowers. Just inside the door there was a rack for coats and another wooden one for shoes, a variety of which were lined in pairs. Shibu turned towards Madeleine as she returned and caught a glimpse of himself in the mirror that hung above the table; realising he looked as worried as a dog in the midst of a family row, he adjusted his expression to a smile.

"Okay, I'll show you the room, follow me," Madeleine said.

Shibu looked away from her gaze, finding it a little too intense.

"Here we are – mind, the door is still wet. I've only just put the furniture back. Of course you're free to move it around."

The room was large, the ceiling high enough to make Shibu wonder how anyone, leave alone a woman not even as tall as him, could have painted it. The walls were pale mushroom-coloured and at the large sash window a pair of heavy cream curtains hung. The bed was double, with a chest of drawers on one side and a small table on the other, on which stood a portable radio and compact disc player. There was an old large wardrobe in one corner

2

and in the other a desk and chair. All of which pleased him, but most appealing of all was the warm atmosphere. Warmth, in any respect, was so lacking in his current lodgings.

Madeleine led him over to the window. "You're looking out onto the garden so it's quite private, but I can put a net up if you like."

"Means?"

"Um! A thin curtain to protect privacy."

"No, is not necessary." Shibu looked out at the garden. There was a tree, from which hung a bird feeder. From the dense foliage in the far corner a gramophone horn protruded; next to it a half-length mirror glinted in the autumn sun. Prayer flags ran between the tree and the guttering of a white-brick shed. Yet neither these nor the large stone Buddha reminded him as much of home as did the brightness of the washing waving in the breeze.

"How much is rent?"

"How much do you pay at the moment?" Madeleine propped herself against the chest of drawers.

"Four hundred pound." Shibu had hoped to spend less here but feared this room would be expensive.

Madeleine raised her eyes upwards in thought; she knew a little of his circumstances from her friend Carol, with whom he worked. "Can you afford all that?"

He shrugged.

"Can you afford three hundred?"

"I think is not enough."

"It's enough! So, I'll show you the rest of the house."

There were two more bedrooms on that floor, one

belonging to Madeleine and the other to her father, who, Shibu learnt, was also the owner of the property.

"He has a place in Spain, he's hardly ever here, but he likes his room saved so that he can come whenever he chooses. It was my grandparents' house. It'll belong to me, eventually. That room up there is sort of a studio." Madeleine indicated a room at the top of another small staircase. "I make a bit of jewellery and I paint. Let's go down, I'll show you the kitchen and living room."

Shibu looked a bit confused.

Too many words, Madeleine thought. *Why do I gabble on so when I'm nervous?*

Both rooms were big and immaculately kept.

"D'you want some tea?" Madeleine had let her hair down now and it fell unevenly on her cheeks, taking the length out of her face and softening her chin.

"No, I don't like."

"You're from India and you don't like tea!" Madeleine teased. "That's like being French and not liking wine. Would you like something else? Coffee?"

"Yes, please, I have."

"Sugar? Milk? Okay. So, d'you want the room?"

"Yes, please."

"Good. I've already cleared this cupboard out for you." Madeleine opened it by way of demonstration. "If you need more space I can probably find some. You can use these plates, pots and pans here. I sorted them out especially." She opened cupboards to demonstrate the contents and illustrate her words.

They sat at the round wooden table as they drank their drinks. "Have you ever been India?" Shibu asked.

4

"No, but I'd like to. I hear Kerala is a beautiful place, with a climate that would suit me. I'm not fond of the cold. What d'you think of the English weather?"

"English peoples always ask about weather." He laughed. Then he remembered last winter in the house without heating. The snow and ice had made it necessary to spend his days off sitting in bed watching television, even though he hated it, because if he slept in the day he couldn't sleep at night, and if he walked the shops without spending, he was eyed with suspicion. "I don't like winter, but I can adjust. Spring and summer is better than India, is too hot there."

"No such thing as too hot for me."

"I think Kerala summer too hot for anyone."

"Maybe. I'd like the chance to find out, but if I ever go it'll probably be in winter."

As he walked away from the house Shibu felt happy. Madeleine seemed as bright as her washing, and the room was more than he had hoped for. He would be glad to leave the cramped and clinical one he currently inhabited. His own home in India was spacious and hummed harmoniously with the stories of his family. He expected that in Madeleine's old house there would be the echo of many voices and many tales to inspire his dreams. He thought now of his parents and sister, sleeping under the warm black night, their ears as deaf to the familiar snores of animals and each other, as to the insect chorus. Shibu's own ears had only just grown accustomed to the night sounds of his English home: the constant drone of electricity, the goose-like sound of occupants vacating pubs, the occasional swish of a passing car. Now they would have to learn anew.

Madeleine stood for a while watching her soon-to-be lodger walk down the road, as she smoked her second cigarette of the day. He wasn't going to be any trouble, she was sure; he seemed so gentle and genuine; even without Carol's recommendation she would have taken him.

As soon as Madeleine mentioned her intention to get a lodger Carol had suggested Shibu.

"He's just started a couple of weeks ago and I know he's looking for somewhere closer to stay. At the moment he's got two hours each end of the day travelling – can you imagine? He doesn't get home until ten and he has to leave at six the next morning. What a life: work, eat sleep."

As she replaced the tobacco taste with toothpaste Madeleine remembered all her concerns in response to Sean's suggestion that she take in a lodger. Although she knew it made sense, she loved the house too much to happily share it. Unless her father was there it was as much her haven now as when she'd been a child. She'd worried over future messes in the kitchen, queues for the bathroom, unfamiliar noises and smells over which she had no control, but worst of all she feared confrontations and the need for explanations over lifestyles. Now that she had met Shibu, however, Madeleine was reassured.

He moved in on a Friday evening, arriving with his friend, one suitcase and a small box. Madeleine offered drinks and biscuits, which both men refused, so she returned to the living room and her emails, leaving the door ajar to make it clear communication was allowed but none was sought. There was comfort in the sound of the male voices drifting through the ceiling, because they sounded solid. Yet, those same qualities also induced anxiety, in case they heralded future control.

Soon there were footsteps on the stairs, the sound of the door opening and closing, as Shibu's friend left without saying goodbye, and then silence. The silence seemed even more profound because there was another person in the house.

Madeleine was in the kitchen clearing up after her meal. The noise from the running water prevented her from hearing Shibu, so she jumped as he said, "Hi Madeleine." Then, "Oh, I sorry." His voice was baritone and tended towards the minor chords.

"My fault. I was lost in thought. Is there something I can do for you?"

"I need shop or department store. Is near?"

"For groceries? Fifteen-minute walk – I'll show you."

"Is not necessary, you can explain."

"It's okay, the walk will do me good. D'you want to go now?"

Shibu shrugged. "It depends upon you."

"Give me a minute to brush my teeth and I'll be with you."

She timed; half a minute for the top back, half a minute bottom back, half a minute each for the front top and bottom.

In the hallway Shibu waited, with an attitude of resignation.

"Don't you want a jacket?" Madeleine asked, grabbing her own.

"Is not necessary." He noticed that Madeleine smelt fresh from toothpaste yet stale from tobacco.

Shibu paid attention to where they were going, which was difficult sometimes because Madeleine kept talking. They walked over a small arched bridge that took them to a housing estate, through a park with a pond and a fenced-off children's playground, then an industrial estate, at the end of which was the supermarket.

"I'll wait here, I don't need anything," said Madeleine.

"You can go. I find my way back."

"Well, if you're sure."

She went home via Carol's so that she could tell her of Shibu's arrival. Together they went to the local pub, where a live band was playing, and one beer soon turned into three so that it was almost midnight when Madeleine arrived home. She checked the fridge and saw that it was full of Shibu's stuff so she knew he'd found his way back. She went quietly to the bathroom, performed her routine then went to bed.

Chapter Two

The alarm rang, seven o'clock. Madeleine opened her eyes on a bright morning, but the dark cloud was hovering. She turned onto her side, closed her eyes again and snuggled into the pillow. Then remembered two things: it was her Saturday off – the cloud came closer, it would win for a while – but then, Shibu, there was much to do so she needed to get to the bathroom before him. She sighed, pushed the duvet aside and the cloud with it, although it stayed close behind her as she made her way downstairs.

There was no sign of Shibu, and nothing to indicate whether or not he was in. She'd carry on as normal with her routine and hope he wasn't in the bathroom when she wanted to be.

Frankincense was required in the oil burner this morning, she decided, for its comforting qualities. For the same reason, and because she hoped it would stop her hurrying to get done before Shibu put in an appearance, she put the relaxation music on. Despite counting through each pose the same number of times as always, she did feel rushed and self-satisfaction eluded her.

Now it was seven forty and there was still no sign of Shibu, so Madeleine made for the bathroom.

I must remember to check with him every day whether he's working or not, she thought.

In the shower she counted to twenty as she wet her hair, ten as she rubbed in the shampoo and twenty-five as she rinsed it. She massaged in the conditioner to the count of ten, leaving it to soak in while she performed her washing ritual, applying soap to each body part to the count of twenty, rinsing then applying shower gel, rinsing and applying twice more. Finally, she counted to fifty whilst she enjoyed the feel of warm water rinsing her hair and cleansing her body.

The safety of the routine was threatened by the risk of a knock from Shibu, and momentarily she was transported back in time.

It seemed as if the pounding hand would penetrate the door. In her imagination she saw the panels warp and split, as first the fist then the face, then the whole man came into her space, shaming her with his stares at her naked body. From panic she hurried, but that same emotion made her feel clammy and her hands were clumsy with speed.

"Will you for God's sake get out of there?"

The aggression in Philip's voice left no doubt about what was coming, so she delayed opening the door. But then she heard the other noises: a sharp slap against soft flesh, a gasp, a whimper and then the words, "You've got your sister to thank for that."

Now Madeleine opened the door, cautiously, and was greeted by Philip leaning over Tom and hissing through gritted teeth. "Stop grizzling, you wimp!"

"About bloody time," he said when he saw her. Then he grabbed the back of her dressing gown, shook her and pushed her towards Tom, who was folded forwards into himself. "You're lucky this time, he got what you had coming."

Madeleine fell into her brother as Philip let go of her and slammed his way into the bathroom, and she snapped, "Get off," at Tom's attempts to comfort her. Immediately, and forever afterwards, she felt ashamed that before compassion for Tom had come fear for herself.

As she dressed in the bedroom she felt her face curl into a sneer, so like Philip's she wanted to rip it off and tear out her heart. From behind the bathroom door she heard Philip crying. When he emerged, with eyes red and swollen, she was filled with compassion and wanted to tell him he was forgiven, but equally she was afraid to even admit that there was anything that required forgiveness.

Tessa and Tom were in the kitchen. Tom choked on breakfast and tears whilst his mother stroked his head. "Whatever takes you so long, Madeleine?" she asked in a histrionic tone. "We could all be saved this every morning if only you'd hurry up in there."

In an attempt at control she set her alarm for six-thirty and then six o'clock, meaning to be done by the time her parents were getting up, but until the first fist on the door she couldn't stop. It acted like the automatic cut-off in the school showers. The second thump cut short the drying, which made her pull on her dressing gown and go to the bedroom to dress.

It was under her grandmother's care, in this house, this very bathroom, that the counting in the shower had begun, over thirty years ago now, with the suggestion, *Why don't you set yourself a time limit?*

Back in the present she concentrated on the warmth of the water and her breathing to banish the memory.

Radio Four accompanied her through breakfast, after which she washed and rinsed her bowl, put it in the dishwasher then cleaned the sink with anti-bacterial spray. Next, she wiped down the surfaces then swept, hoovered and washed the floor.

Now it was nine-thirty and there was still no sign of Shibu. Madeleine went halfway up the stairs and looked at the closed door, wanting to know whether or not the occupant of the room was behind it, but all was so still and silent that the only way to be sure was to knock. Yet she needed to start the cleaning, and rock music was her aid. Wanting to warn Shibu, so that the music didn't disturb him, she hovered a while outside his door but finally decided against knocking.

She dusted the living room with the door closed and silenced the music while she vacuumed, but for the bathroom there was no choice, so she cranked up the volume. Invigorated hands danced beneath the scrubbing. Washbasin and windowsill had to be completed by the end of 'Long Road to Ruin', then there were five tracks left for the bath, tiles and toilet, allowing her to listen and sing along to 'Statues' while she cleaned the cabinet, then she could wash the floor before the end of the album. Madeleine had replaced the counting with this method of timing several years ago now, because as well as the necessary boundary, the music provided energy and enthusiasm too.

The contents of the cabinet were on the floor in ordered piles, one for each shelf, and she was singing away the memory behind the tears that the lyrics evoked. Suddenly she was aware of a presence behind her and jumped in response, as if it was a ghost rather than Shibu. She halted the song and the cleaning, but they both hung in the air like a paused breath.

"Oh! Sorry. You'll be wanting to move out if you have to listen to me singing." She giggled, then bit her thumb and cast an anxious glance over the items on the floor. "D'you want to use the bathroom?"

"Is okay. I can wait."

"You sure?"

"Of course." He went back to his room, leaving the door ajar.

Now the music was in the wrong place, the timing was all out and Madeleine had failed to sing uninterrupted. She felt her throat and solar plexus tense and clenched her teeth together in response. She hurried the final part, but it didn't feel as if the cleaning was adequate.

Back in the living room Madeleine replaced the Foo Fighters with Beethoven, which calmed her. She wondered what Shibu had been doing so quietly in his room and hoped he didn't feel annoyed by the music, while at the same time feeling annoyed with him in case it did.

It was lunchtime. Madeleine placed the two pieces of toast side by side on the plate, the fried egg on one piece, beans on the other, and sat down to eat. She cut a small mouthful of egg on toast, lay down her knife and fork, chewed thirty times, cut a slice of beans on toast, lay down her knife and fork, chewed thirty times then repeated the process until her plate was clear. Afterwards she washed the plate and cutlery in soapy water before putting them in the dishwasher, smoked her second cigarette of the day, cleaned her teeth, went shopping. With all of that done she had just enough time to read for an hour.

When it was time to cook Madeleine chose another CD and turned on the kitchen speakers. She washed her hands, taking care to clean between the fingers, wiped the surfaces down and then washed her hands again. She chopped, fried, stirred and tasted as she added ingredients, feeling happy because she loved the whole process, especially when cooking for someone else. Madeleine only wondered for a second before she decided to invite Shibu for dinner; it seemed totally appropriate as a welcoming gesture.

Outside his door she hesitated for a second time, her knock arrested this time by the sound of his voice in conversation on the telephone. Speaking in Malayalam he sounded quite different: sonorous, confident and light. When the talking had stopped for several seconds Madeleine risked a gentle knock. She heard him get up from the bed and felt him pause on the other side of the door as if checking something.

"Sorry to disturb you, but I just wondered if you'd like to join my boyfriend, Julian, and me for dinner – it's curry. It's probably not as good or as spicy as you're used to but—"

"Thank you. Is very kind. I'm sure will be good. Shall I come now?"

"You're welcome in the kitchen any time, of course, but dinner will be about forty minutes." She paused before saying, "You don't have to spend all of your time in this room, Shibu, I want you to treat the house as your home." Even though she meant it Madeleine felt afraid of the words.

"Thank you."

"Right!" Madeleine twisted her hair around her forefinger and looked away for a second, then, becoming conscious she had done so, looked back at him. "Right! See you soon."

Shibu knew that Julian had arrived even before he heard him speak, not only because he heard the door close, but also because there was a pause, in which he sensed their embrace. He waited a respectful time before leaving his room and going downstairs.

The first thing Shibu noticed as he entered the kitchen was the tense atmosphere. The next thing he noticed was how big the man looked leaning in towards Madeleine, and how small she looked pulling back from him. She looked no bigger than a child. And, standing with one hand on her hip and her chin in the air she presented as a defiant one. The words, spoken by the man, were almost whispered, but Shibu was fairly sure of what he'd heard: "…very considerate of you. We only get those evenings to ourselves."

Madeleine acknowledged Shibu with a glance, which made the man turn in his direction. He had a large face and nose, long square chin, and sandy brown hair, which hung into his eyes and over his ears. His small, thin mouth changed expression from fixed to smiling in an instant when he noticed Shibu, who sidled in and placed himself close to Madeleine.

"Hi." Julian offered an extended hand. He dwarfed both Madeleine and Shibu with his near quarter of a metre height advantage. "Julian, pleased to meet you."

Shibu responded politely and with a smile. Madeleine noticed that there was very little difference in the size of the two men's hands.

"Please, Shibu, take a seat," Madeleine said, claiming hers by standing behind the chair. Julian sat as near to opposite her as the round table would allow, leaving Shibu with no choice but sit in the middle. They drank wine; he drank water.

Madeleine dished out the rice. "Enough?" she asked. "Please say if you want more."

"No, is fine, thank you."

"We'll help ourselves to curry – you first, Shibu. Oh, please, have more than that."

He took another spoonful to be polite, although he no longer had much appetite for it.

He noticed but tried not to pay attention to the way Madeleine organised the food on her plate in separate sections, how she took small, precise quantities from each without mixing them and how she put the cutlery down between each mouthful.

The effort Julian, and especially Madeleine, put into including Shibu in the conversation stilted it.

"The other day I was telling Shibu how much I'd like to go to Kerala," she said to Julian.

"Mm." Julian finished his mouthful. "At least I'd get a decent curry there."

It sounded to Shibu as if he was joking, but Madeleine's curt reply made him wonder.

"I've never claimed to be any good in that department." *I never mentioned your coming with me, either,* she thought.

"I don't suppose you've tried many English curries, Shibu?" Julian asked.

"This is first, and is very nice, thank you."

"Nice, but different, yeah? So, how're finding England?"

"Excuse me?"

"How do you like England? Is it very different to India?"

"Some ways is very different, some ways not so much."

"Which d'you prefer? And you can be honest."

"Same, same like I said. Some ways better in India, some ways better in England."

"Have you seen much of England?" Madeleine interjected.

"Not so much."

"We'll have to change that for you," she offered cheerily. "I could be your personal tour guide, I'd enjoy that."

"Oh – thank you. I look forward to it."

Julian grunted and took a large gulp of wine. "So, you've come to England to study?"

"Yes."

"And then?"

"Get work, I hope. Job situation in India very poor."

"Job situation in England is poor too."

Shibu nodded.

"I thought employment levels were high in Kerala?" Julian continued.

"Compared with rest of India, yes, but pay no good and I have many bills."

"Ah! We have those too."

Shibu lowered his gaze.

"Well, that's why our arrangement is of mutual benefit," Madeleine interrupted, directing her words at Julian in a clipped tone. "I make a few extra pounds and Shibu saves some."

"Indeed. A happy situation all round. Shame I can't think of a way to achieve the same."

"Meaning?"

"Exactly what I said."

Turning his attention back to Shibu, Julian said, "I can't help but notice from the mail I deliver that there has been a marked rise in ethnic minorities in this town recently."

"And?" Madeleine quickly interposed.

"And nothing! Just making the observation."

Madeleine shot Julian a disapproving glance. "Do you think that is an entirely appropriate observation to make under the circumstances?"

"What're accusing me of?"

Shibu shifted his gaze to the floor and his weight from side to side feeling like he used to in response to his parents' whispered discussions about what sanctions to impose.

"Nothing, but... nothing." She turned to Shibu. "I'm sorry about that, Shibu. It was rude of me. Excuse me for a moment please. I'm going for a fag." Her chair made a scraping noise as she pushed it away from the table and flounced out of the kitchen, tossing her hair and her hips like a five-year-old.

Shibu didn't know how to respond to the expectancy that filled the space left by her. He felt like an intruder hiding in the shadows, waiting to find a way to leave without being detected. He sat very straight with his hands in his lap and his eyes fixed on his plate.

Julian tapped the side of his glass, rapped his nails on the table, pouted and pursed his lips, then almost jumped up and went outside, shutting the adjoining door. Shibu understood the actions and the atmosphere, neither of which could be closed out by a door. He wanted to go to his room but didn't want to appear rude.

Julian and Madeleine returned together. Madeleine went to clean her teeth; Julian sat back down and as he did so he asked, "Would you like some wine, Shibu?"

"No. Thank you."

"Something else? Beer?"

"No, is okay."

"Don't you drink?"

Empty vodka bottles rattled in Shibu's memory, like they had from the bin liner last Christmas, and with it the recollection of violent vomiting and self-loathing, which had led to his abstinence vow. "Sometimes too much, but not now."

Julian took a sip of his drink. "I'm… um… I wasn't suggesting that there are too many ethnic minorities in England, Shibu, sorry if it sounded that way." He took another swig of his drink. "I like to talk politics, though, how about you?"

"In Kerala I like, but here no. I think my English is not enough good to explain my meaning."

"It's a lot better than my Malayalam."

Madeleine returned and Shibu waited long enough for politeness then said, "I going bed now. Thank you for meal Goodnight."

Back in his room he thought over the conversation and recalled his arrival in England.

Light of body and mind from nine hours in the air without sleeping, he floated between states: sleep and wakefulness, euphoria and homesickness. So, when the woman customs officer asked in an African English accent, "Where is your placement letter?", he hadn't quite understood and just produced the documents he had ready, which included his nursing certificate from home.

"Why do you want to study an NVQ in care if you are a nurse?"

"Because nurse qualification no good here."

"And an NVQ is in India?"

"Excuse me?"

She sighed. "Can you use an NVQ in India?"

"I need for work here."

"So, you want to work here?"

He was puzzled by her question. "Maybe in future."

"Where is your placement letter?"

"I don't have yet. I don't need for six months."

"I think you do. Wait." She called her colleague over and explained the situation.

"Do you have your English test results?" he asked.

"Excuse me?"

"Your English test results." He was shouting as if Shibu was deaf. "Do you have them?"

"I came on points system."

Another colleague was called over. "I'm not happy about this one. The paperwork needs more investigation; take him to the Immigration Office, will you?"

Then Shibu began to feel afraid. He feared the

consequences of having to deal with unknown customs and laws. He feared no less the known consequences of a return to India, which would leave him unable to pay back his four-lach loan.

Although the room in which they put him was quite large and light, because along one wall there was a glass panel, Shibu felt as if he was suffocating. And eight hours later, when released into the bitter January night, the freezing air caused him to gasp for breath as surely as if he had been.

He responded to the memory by taking the Home Office-issued documentation from his case and staring at it. It bore his name, date of birth and the address to which he was confined for the first five days of his stay with instructions which read: "*I hereby authorise your (further) temporary admission to the United Kingdom subject to the following restrictions; you must reside at the address shown as X above. You may not enter employment, Paid or Unpaid, or engage in any business or profession. You must report to an Immigration Officer (for further examination for the purpose of deciding whether you may be granted leave to enter) at:*" then the Immigration Office address and telephone number and the date and time on which he should attend. And the line which read: "*The person named above was placed in your custody on,*" and the date.

Language that labelled him with criminal status and lodgings which reinforced the identity; those were his first experiences of England.

Chapter Three

As Shibu entered the empty house for the first time he felt how he affected it. It was as if the draught that entered the door with him stirred the air, and his weight altered the molecular structure. Madeleine's presence, which was evident everywhere, had an ethereal quality, to which his own brought substance. He rejoiced in the lightness of Madeleine's energy because it relaxed and excited him, but was glad too of himself, otherwise it might carry him away.

He put his perishables in the fridge, placing his value margarine, bacon and sliced cheese on the shelf above Madeleine's organic butter, strong cheddar and natural yogurt. He put his value onions and carrots in the vegetable rack, which was already packed with a large and varied selection of goods. The rest he stored in the cupboard Madeleine had cleared and cleaned for him. Then he went to his room and fell instantly asleep, waking late the next day to the sound of the vacuum cleaner.

When the booming music reached him he was praying. Like an automaton he mouthed the words, asking for protection for his family and strength to complete what he had come to do. But despite the airy ambience, which even felt ecclesiastical at times, direct contact with God remained elusive. There was something else in the house that demanded his attention more vigorously, so, although when the music arrived it shook him, it didn't surprise him. This was Madeleine struggling for substance, grounding herself in bass guitar and earthy lyrics. The very first note was portentous. It vibrated through his soul and stole away the little connection he'd achieved. Shibu abandoned his quest for God and gave in to the demands of his bladder.

Perhaps it was the need to pee that was distracting him most, he decided. He always tried hard to place God before his needs and urges, but so rarely achieved that aim. Nearby the church clock was just audible as it chimed the hour, reminding him not only of God but also of the distance between his family and himself. He opened the door on music that made them both feel more remote.

Madeleine's presence in the bathroom surprised him, not just the fact of her but the immediacy with which she brought him back to the now.

He was captured first by the physical qualities of her voice, which was strong, melodic and perfectly in tune, and then by the form of her body. She was stretching upwards, washing the top of the cupboard. The action tightened her torso and legs, creating the impression of a sculptured body beneath the clothes, and offering the occasional glimpse of flesh between her jeans and blouse.

In her voice there was pathos, which lifted it above the ordinary and planted an impression in Shibu's consciousness of something he could neither understand nor ignore. That there was a sad story behind her actions was confirmed in the ordered manner in which the contents of the bathroom cabinet lay on the floor, but most of all Madeleine betrayed herself in the way she suspended action when she realised he was there. Like a musical pause, it lent drama to the rest of the scene. And Shibu felt he had intruded upon an intimate moment.

Later, as he lay in bed after the shared meal, Shibu reflected on his new surroundings and tried to place himself correctly. Alone with Madeleine he felt at home, but Julian's presence had created more than a little tension.

The occasional lovers' sounds penetrated his thoughts, impressing on his imagination images which he had only ever experienced there. And the desire it aroused in him filled him with shame. He prayed it away, feeling satisfied with overcoming himself and relaxed enough to sleep.

Early-morning dreams were punctuated by sounds from the bathroom. Water running hard and fast, then the shower, finally the whine of an electric razor or toothbrush. At the first sound Shibu checked his watch and was surprised to see that it was past eight, because the room, protected from the sun by the heavy curtains, was still quite dark. He drifted in and out of sleep with the sounds seeming part of his dream. When he heard the click of the bathroom door and the pad of footsteps across the landing then down the stairs, Shibu checked his watch a second time, and was surprised once more when he realised that almost an hour had passed. He got up immediately, collecting his toiletries bag and towel and opened his bedroom door, but got no further because Julian, wearing only his boxer shorts, was headed towards the bathroom. He grunted a sorry to Shibu as he squeezed past him, seemingly unabashed in his near-naked state. Shibu returned to his room and waited again.

Madeleine was by the back door smoking and Julian in the lounge at the computer when he reached the kitchen. "Morning, Madeleine."

"Morning, a fine one, isn't it?"

"Yes. Later I want go to church; is near?"

"Church? Catholic? Pretty close. D'you know the town hall? Turn right into the road opposite and it's on your right. D'you know the times? We could look on line." She followed him back into the house.

"No, is not necessary, I take walk and look."

Shibu made himself coffee, cornflakes and toast. Madeleine watched as he washed the dishes afterwards, squeezing washing-up liquid directly onto the article he was washing and then rinsing it under copious amounts of hot water. Her automatic reaction to take over was arrested so close to the point of action that she felt as if her mind and body had separated.

"That needs to go in the dishwasher now, please." She giggled, shifting her weight from foot to foot; she rubbed her hands together, then interlocked them and tapped her bottom lip with her thumbs.

"I always clean the suds away too and wash around with a drop of this." She produced the spray cleaner. "Shall I do it?"

"Is not necessary, I can do." Shibu took the spray and cleaned the sink. He was acutely aware of Madeleine watching him and knew by her body language that he wasn't doing it to her liking.

She chewed the corner of her full, large mouth and twisted one ringlet of her hair. Becoming aware of her effect on Shibu, Madeleine left the room. There was a knot in her stomach; she concentrated on slowing her breathing until it untied. How she wished she wouldn't need to go back to the kitchen and clean up after him, but she knew she would. Sometimes it all got so tiring.

She had just about completed the task when Julian came up behind her and placed his hands on her shoulders, rubbing and squeezing gently. "Getting to you already?"

"What?"

"Sharing your living space with someone else."

"I'll get used to it."

"Hmm! I forgot he was here this morning and went off to the bathroom in my boxers. Hope you're dressing up more than usual for that visit."

"Of course I am."

"Sorreey! No need to snap. You hormonal or something?"

"Or something – and I didn't snap."

"Okay, whatever you say."

Madeleine tutted. "Haven't you got to fetch Jack from football?"

"I'm going now. Soon be outta your hair."

"Don't be silly."

Julian grunted. "See you later, then."

They embraced and kissed each other.

When he'd gone Madeleine let go of her breath. She unplugged the telephone and began her yoga session. Shutting out her thoughts was still the hardest part. Her inner-critic was never far away with her blaming and accusing. She had been a part of Madeleine's psyche for so long that Madeleine feared her absence would be tantamount to annihilation. Yet latterly, she was often quietened for several hours and Madeleine was afforded some peace.

When she'd finished the yoga, she plugged the phone back in and checked for messages. There was one from Sean saying he would be visiting at three, unless he received a request from her to the contrary. Picking up her mobile Madeleine noticed he had sent the same via text. The warm, round wholeness she felt in response to the yoga session was reinforced by the promise of a visit from Sean. To make sure there could be no mistake she sent a text to him to say she was looking forward to seeing him; then she made herself a lunch of salad, hummus and ciabatta. She ate in the garden, wanting to take full advantage of what was left of the warm weather before autumn took hold and all too soon gave way to winter.

The lawn needed cutting, she decided, and the jungle area needed weeding. She could certainly do the former before Sean's arrival and the rest she could do during the week after work. As she took the tarpaulin cover from the mower and headed towards the kitchen with the extension lead a childhood memory stirred:

"Ready or not, here I come." Although Madeleine stuck to the agreement and counted all the way to one

hundred, she sped through rather than pacing it, as she knew Tom did, but he always found the best hiding places and she always tried to catch him out. She knew he was in the garden because she felt the swish of energy as he scuttled past, and anyway, she'd opened one eye and turned her head to make sure. She was pretty sure she'd heard the shed door swing open too, so headed there first, expecting to find her brother squatting between the two tool cupboards, but he wasn't there. Neither was he under the dust cover with the lawn mower. Next Madeleine checked the jungle area – always a favourite, with the bushes and brambles to hide in and the opportunity to move around unseen – but she couldn't find him there either. He wasn't in the outside toilet, neither was he behind the compost bin. Now, she decided he must have sneaked back into the house. She ran around checking inside wardrobes, under beds, behind various pieces of furniture, until eventually she gave up. Finally, first from the hallway, then the kitchen, then the back door she called, "Okay, give up." And Tom dropped triumphantly from the branches of the beech tree.

The memory hurt only a little; it was warm and happy too. Some memories were voluntary and sought out, but it was always the spontaneous ones, like this, that had the most substance. So much so that for a second, he was real again.

She plugged the extension lead into the socket and her MP3 player into her ears to drown out the engine sound and relieve the monotony of the task. Her partial sensory deprivation shut out awareness of the watcher in the house.

Shibu didn't intend to watch. He was drawn to the window by the very fact of it and the garden view, but Madeleine's frenetic mowing wasn't something that could easily be ignored. She seemed at once to be dancing and fighting with the lawn mower. One minute she glided across the lawn, her hips responding with fluidity. The next she seemed to push it with great effort, shoulders arched forwards, hair falling across her face. Always the pace was high and always she appeared annoyed with having to stop and empty the cuttings. As he watched, Shibu's mind drifted home to his father patiently and methodically leading the oxen with the plough. A yearning for home stirred him to action, away from the window and towards the church.

He enjoyed the walk. The day was fine and the traffic sparse. The buildings were old, though not ancient, and well kept. He walked through the park, in which there were several floral landscapes and a pond with a fountain. Two white swans glided gracefully towards a parent and child, who threw them bread. Everything about this town spoke of its affluence.

Entering the church he felt nervous. A host of new people to encounter. But here at last, spurred on by the mutual seeking of the congregation, he was able to hear God in his heart.

When he returned the garden was full of people. Julian, Madeleine and another man, about their age, with wavy, greying hair and thin-rimmed glasses, all sat in canvas chairs, drinking beer. On the newly mown grass two boys lay, kicking each other in a manner that denoted both boredom and kinship. As Shibu stood in the doorway between the kitchen and garden, he heard Julian say, "Can't you two find something to occupy yourselves with for five minutes?" This was said in a tone so clearly parental that it drew to a close his assumption that the children and the new man were together.

Shibu waved at the company and was about to go upstairs when Madeleine said, "Oh, Shibu. Come and say hello." She beckoned him over. "This is my friend, Sean."

Sean stood up and took Shibu's hand between both of his, then shook it vigorously. "Pleased to meet you, Shibu."

"And these are Julian's sons, Jack and Harry. Come and say hi, boys." They shouted it from the grass without ceasing in their fight.

Sean patted Shibu's shoulder. "You gonna join us and have a beer?"

"He doesn't drink," Julian interrupted as Shibu was in the process of refusing.

"Well, you can join us anyway."

"No, thank you, I have some study to do."

"What about for dinner later?" Madeleine offered.

"No, I can cook something. I need cook rice for rest of week."

"Okay, see you later." *I'm not surprised after last night's carry-on*, she thought, hoping she would have the opportunity to apologise properly.

"Seems like a nice young man," Sean observed.

"Yes, doesn't he?"

"What's he studying?"

"I'm not sure, to be honest. Haven't asked him." Throughout the conversation Jack and Harry had been chasing each other around the garden, their actions interrupted periodically by their father's reprimands. Now they fell into the middle of the adults and Harry landed directly in Sean's lap, who caught hold of him and wrestled him to the ground, roaring playfully. Harry squealed with delight. Jack ran off, inviting a chase.

"Right, I think it's time I took you two home," Julian announced. Then, with a little annoyance as Sean began to charge around the garden with them, "Come on, then, your mother will be waiting." They obeyed and left, poking their tongues out at each other.

Sean flopped into the chair beside Madeleine. "Never a dull moment with those two around."

"No, they get bored here, though, nothing much for them to do."

"They'd be bored anywhere, they're at that age. They probably get frustrated with all the coming and going too. How're things now?"

"Okay. It's been three whole months since the last time he went back to her."

"Is that the longest ever?"

"Nope, he went nearly five months once. To tell you the truth, it doesn't bother me much anymore – if he goes back to her, he goes back to her."

"Time to end it?"

"Sometimes I think I should, but… it's easier carrying on as normal. There isn't actually any reason to end it."

"Doesn't sound as if there's much reason for not doing so, either."

"It'll probably come to it sometime. Don't want to hurt him, though."

"Course not, but hey, how'd you feel if that was the reason he stayed with you?"

"I think you know the answer to that."

"I rest my case. How're you finding it with a lodger?"

"He only arrived Friday. He's quiet and unassuming, he won't be a problem. The problem, as ever, is me and my hang-ups."

"Coping mechanisms."

"Well, whatever you like to call them, they're the problem, not Shibu."

Sean slapped his thighs: "Let's dance."

"Later, I need to get cooking."

"We can dance and cook, can't we?"

"Sure thing."

Billie Holiday joined them in the kitchen. Their voices blended with hers, their hips swayed, feet shuffled and hands rhythmically peeled and chopped.

Shibu paused in his studies, intrigued and entertained by the singing. He knew when Julian returned because the singing stopped and, though the music continued, it was on a much lower volume.

"So, you staying tonight, Sean?" Julian asked during dinner.

"Think I'll have to; I've drunk too much to drive already."

"There's no spare room now that Maddie has taken up your suggestion and got herself a lodger."

"I'll be fine on the sofa."

"What about Philip's bed, Mad?"

"You know I can't."

"He'll never know and it's about time you defied him a bit. Don't you agree, Sean?"

"Absolutely, but it's what Madeleine thinks that counts."

"It's ridiculous, the way he asserts control even when absent," Julian continued.

"I know, but it's just easier for me this way. I'll sleep on the sofa; I need the living room for yoga in the morning."

"I'll be away by eight."

"I expect you think I can hardly criticise on absent people being controlling when my ex-wife is doing such a good job with me," Julian said, distractedly.

"The boys are a big issue," Madeleine observed, feeling suddenly protective of him.

"Yeah! But I'd find it hard to forgive myself if she actually did what she threatens."

"Unlikely that she would," Sean stated categorically.

"I know but… and I know you think I mess Maddie about… no, you do – and you're right, but… well. Anyway, she's been fine for three months now, we can live in hope."

When he'd gone Madeleine said, "Poor Julian, he's a good man. It's a shame he's so uptight. I'd love it if he let go once in a while."

"On the subject," Sean said brightly, "let's dance. What do we want?"

"How about some Ramones?"

Together they hopped, jumped, shook hips, arms, tossed back their heads and pushed their bodies in and out of each other's personal space, squealing all the while with delight.

In the kitchen, Shibu ate rice and spiced chicken with yogurt. He smiled at the images the noises from the living room evoked in his imagination.

Chapter Four

When the alarm went off Madeleine silenced it then arose quickly, hoping to beat Shibu to the bathroom. She pulled on leggings and a T-shirt, running her hands over her breasts as she did so with a feeling of satisfaction that they remained firm and round. She dragged a brush and comb through her hair, then immediately shook her head to recreate the bouncy look.

The closed door and the rush of water made it clear that the bathroom was already occupied. Seven-ten, usually she was beginning her routine by now and the interruption to it caused her some anxiety, but she could wait another five minutes without the fear of it making her late. Yet, as the clock in the hall chimed the quarter hour, Madeleine's anxiety grew. She felt it as an ache in her belly. This was the first day that both she and Shibu were preparing for work and already it appeared there was a clash of routines. Now she decided to use the outside toilet and risk an encounter with the spider that had been in there the last time she used it, which was unlikely given that it was several days ago. And yet, when she couldn't see it anywhere, she felt barely less comfortable, imagining it emerging any second to make physical contact with her.

Shibu was preparing his breakfast when she came back through; he looked up from his task and smiled, revealing his perfect teeth. They greeted each other and then Madeleine shut herself in the lounge to do yoga. Sean would be getting up soon, she knew, and even though he understood and respected her routine to the letter she felt harassed by his presence too.

When she reached the kitchen Sean was there and Shibu was just leaving. She said, "Morning, hon," to one and, "See you later," to the other, before hurrying on to the bathroom.

Now, almost ten minutes behind schedule, Madeleine felt the need to hurry, but whenever she tried it seemed to make the whole thing take longer. *More haste less speed.* She heard her grandmother's words echo back from the past and was instantly reminded of the first time she got stuck in the shower.

Thanks to Sean her breakfast was ready and waiting on the table, but the man himself had already left. Beneath Madeleine's cereal bowl there was a note which read: *"Bye, babe – see you soon. S x".*

Before she left the house Madeleine checked all the downstairs windows were closed, and every appliance was switched off. As she buckled the bar on her favourite shoes she wondered how much longer it would be warm enough to wear them. If indeed, she might feel a little chilly today with her legs bare between the ankle and shin, but she no longer had time to swap the leggings for jeans. She had, at least, had the good sense to put a long-sleeved top underneath the floral dress. Just in case, though, she shoved her grey cardigan into the cloth bag that was going with her and slipped on a light waterproof jacket.

The heat that remained in the sun was sufficient to necessitate removal of the jacket after only a few hundred yards of walking, but the sharpness of summer sun was already absent and Madeleine could taste the autumn in the air. She slowed her pace in response, feeling, not for the first time, a sense of time running away and the autumn years of her life advancing. Fleetingly she experienced regret and questioned the usefulness of her life. She arrested the thought immediately, because it was a question with no satisfactory answer. Yet, like a theme running through a novel, it was always in the back of her mind and underlined her experience of life.

It was with her even as she served customers, offered them advice on the best product, bagged up purchases and accepted payment, and it was no less present in her personal life; although sometimes she lost herself in painting or in yoga for a while, and almost always when dancing.

Madeleine watched Emily serving a regular customer and instinctively knew that Emily never questioned her existence or the validity of her life. For this she felt both envy and contempt.

Between customers Madeleine weighed and packaged cereals and grains, restocked shelves with vitamins and various natural beauty products, checked stock in and out. She and Emily took it in turns to make each other tea and chatted about the things they had done over the weekend.

Twelve o'clock was Madeleine's lunchtime, so she took her bowl of bean salad and her book and went to the park, but there was no chance to read because Julian was already waiting with two cardboard cups of coffee. They talked little and parted after twenty minutes with a quick kiss. Madeleine strolled around the park smoking, before returning to the shop in time to clean her teeth and take over from Emily. In the absence of any other necessary chore she dusted and tidied shelves between customers. At five-thirty she and Emily closed the shop together.

Shibu checked in with his key fob at five minutes to eight. He signed the fire-log book and checked the noticeboard before ascending in the lift to the third floor. Edith's bell was already ringing. He responded to her request for breakfast with tea, juice, cereal and toast – then moved on to answer the next bell. His two co-workers had paired up and begun getting residents out of bed. When he had served breakfast to those who needed no assistance, Shibu started on the round of feeders. As soon as everyone was fed he began the singles' toileting routine. He helped residents from bed, washing or showering and then dressing them, putting on pads, changing beds and documenting it all in the care plans. At eleven-thirty he had his fifteen-minute break.

His return to the floor was met with the ringing of bells and requests for commodes. Then it was lunchtime and the round of serving food and feeding began again, followed by another round of toileting. Afternoon tea and cake soon arrived and then it was time to catch up with care plans. At three-thirty Shibu had his half-hour lunch break, a sandwich, a chocolate biscuit and an apple. He followed it with coffee, which he hurried down even though it was too hot, because he had to get back on the floor in time to allow his colleagues their break.

Shibu liked to be busy because the spaces were full of longing. Longing for the company of his parents, to whom he spoke every day, and longing for a life with more meaning. His mother's reassurances of love and his father's talk of pride reinforced homesickness, and in their words were memories of familiar customs and shared experiences and expectations, which emphasised his alien status.

At seven forty-five he emptied the bins and at seven fifty-five the laundry basket, but he didn't clock out until spot on eight.

The measure for Shibu's work performance was his own parents, on whose imagined future needs he matched his care delivery. Although, he knew that neither of them would end up in such a place as this because his wife of the future would provide care in the family home.

Sometimes he tried to imagine his future wife. Her character was easy. She would be kind, clever and family-orientated, and she would share his opinions on the vital aspects of life – like politics, religion, management of finances and discipline of children. Yet her physical appearance was almost impossible to envisage. He thought she'd be small and voluptuous, but he had no idea about her facial features. There were two girls he'd admired at school and one at college, but they had never known that. If he didn't meet someone soon, he knew his parents would be looking on his behalf and this worried him a little. It wasn't that he didn't trust their judgement; it was just that he was terrified by the whole idea of sex, and much more so with someone he hardly knew.

He remembered the films he'd watched with his college friends and how the sexual acts he witnessed had embarrassed as much as they had excited him. Even when alone he felt slightly ashamed of an erection; he could neither imagine sharing it with someone else nor making a woman moan with pleasure like the women in those films. Yet, sometimes his desire was such that it was impossible to concentrate on anything else. At those times it was hard to fathom why God had cursed humankind with sexual desire, only to forbid its expression in all but marriage. Yet, he also understood it to be the biggest test of all.

Shibu was tired when he reached Madeleine's house and grateful that he had had the presence of mind to prepare his meal the day before. His senses were bombarded as he entered the house. The hall was full of the smell of ground coffee and the sound of piano music, the combination of which had a profound effect on his emotions. The coffee had a homely smell, which left him feeling safe, yet also with a feeling of longing. And the music, to which he stood and listened for a while, touched him like a prayer. As he passed the living room, he took a furtive glance in and saw Madeleine reclined on the blue velvet sofa with a book, it and her hands rested on her belly. Although he couldn't see her face Shibu sensed that she was crying.

Madeleine felt the energy change as he passed; she would acknowledge him in a moment, but for now she needed to stay in the place Schubert had taken her. Her hands tightened on her abdomen, as if she wanted to grasp the notes which poured into her. The feeling was agony and ecstasy, like the second before an orgasm. The tears, which flowed gently and quietly, were the inevitable response. She wiped her eyes before getting up and going into the kitchen.

"Hi, Shibu. Good day?"

"Not too bad."

Madeleine knew he'd noticed her tears and felt more than a little embarrassed.

"It's a very long day for you," she said.

"I like keep busy."

"Hard work too, I think. My mum worked in a care home for a while when we were kids, children," she corrected. "She used to come home exhausted."

Madeleine remembered how she and Tom were hit by the silence of their absent mother and disappointment at the ready meals. Not to mention Philip's own particular brand of dessert. She remembered too the arguments against Tessa's need to work with Philip's solicitor's wage being, in his opinion, more than adequate for their need. But worst of all was the memory of how the raised voices, when silenced, were replaced by the sound of the bed rocking, for which she despised them both.

"Was Carol in today?"

"I think, no – I didn't see her, but sometimes she work different floor to me. She is good, kind lady."

"Yes. She is. D'you have many friends around here, Shibu?"

"No."

"Did you come to England without knowing anyone?"

"I had agent and he brought four of us together. Also I have cousin in Reading."

"Well, that's somewhere you could easily visit in a day by train."

"Maybe I go for Christmas."

"Good idea."

Madeleine went to the back door for a smoke; while she was there she listened to the flow of water down the drain and tried not to be annoyed by it. When she returned to the kitchen Shibu was wiping the sink around with cleaner, but he was using the wrong cloth.

"Thanks for doing that, Shibu. Actually, I normally use this one," she said, passing him the correct one.

"Oh, I'm sorry."

"There's no need to be, you didn't know."

There was a tension in the silence. "I think I shower now," Shibu said. "I think morning is too busy."

"It's up to you, we both had plenty of time this morning."

"Just I think this way work better." He stood for a moment, looking unsure of himself, then suddenly said, "Okay, goodnight," and was gone.

Chapter Five

Madeleine woke engulfed in the black cloud. She wanted to return to the oblivion of sleep, but the blackness kept nudging her to consciousness, like a cat prodding her tired hand every time she stopped stroking. Although Madeleine currently lacked the conviction, she knew from past experience that this was a temporary state, and it was only this which offered sufficient motivation for getting up. She pushed the duvet off and sat up, feeling the loss of its weight like the loss of maternal arms, so she crawled underneath it again, pulling it over her head. The tick of the alarm clock was gentle yet still reminded her that time was passing and she must get up.

She pushed the duvet off for a second time, shivering in response even though the room was far from cold. Then she pulled on her leggings and T-shirt and avoided the mirror as she dragged the brush through her hair, not wishing to be reminded of her resemblance to her father. Hair which hung in natural ringlets, a long straight nose, and hands and feet that were a little too large, were all inherited from the paternal line, but worst of all, from her own eyes shone the reflection of hereditary character. In them she glimpsed a soul that was doomed by its ancestry to belong to the devil.

The burden permeated every level of her life. Her body felt heavy and cold as she forced herself through the morning routine. Her limbs moved clumsily through the yoga poses as she pushed them through solid air. The shower water stung skin that felt raw, yet at least it warmed her on the outside. Madeleine was forced into eye contact with herself as she brushed her teeth. *I look fucking hideous*, she thought. *Old, ugly*. She rinsed and spat, then squeezed more toothpaste onto her brush for a second clean. On leaving the bathroom she met Shibu, with whom she exchanged morning greetings, and for whom she enacted a smile. His expression made it clear he wasn't fooled.

Madeleine took the smile to work, where she continued to feign cheerfulness, for which she only felt increased self-loathing.

In her youth Madeleine had often given in to the blackness, but the loss of several jobs and impaired mental health had taught a hard lesson.

She didn't go out for lunch; the brightness of the day only emphasised the darkness of her existence. Instead she sat in the staff room, eating mechanically and feeling chilled by walls that absorbed the damp but never the heat. Then she sat and stared, as the seconds and minutes ticked away on the clock, feeling an overwhelming desire to curl into a foetal posture and remain like that until the universe reabsorbed her.

She half expected Julian to arrive in the shop in the afternoon to check on her well-being. *Shows how much he really cares,* she thought, knowing even as she did that her disappointment wasn't genuine.

At home she sat wrapped in a blanket and silence, sipping at a cup of tea. When her mobile rang, she ignored it. "You can't be bothered to visit at lunchtime, so I can't be bothered to speak to you now," she told him. But then, feeling guilty and not wanting him to come to see her, she rang him back.

"Sorry, I was busy. No, didn't go out this lunchtime. Yeah, maybe see you tomorrow. Night, then."

When she was sure of being alone in the kitchen, she cooked herself dinner. Ate it, cleaned up, went to bed.

As a child the predominant emotion in her life had been fear. A useful emotion for responding to real external danger, because it sharpened her senses, but when there was no longer need of it, she found that same feeling had become a part of her psyche. So much so that she was dulled to the outside world by inward watchfulness, and it was this that allowed the dark cloud to descend unheeded.

In her youth she'd lain in bed all day – like a vampire, waiting for the light of day to pass – because in the shadows nothing was as stark and there was comfort in the knowledge that another day would soon be over. But it had cost her good A level grades, several jobs and more than one relationship.

Today she crawled gratefully into bed and hoped that the morning would bring a brighter day.

But it didn't. And because it was her day off there was less incentive to get out of bed, so she lay there for most of the morning, drifting in and out of a sleep which was maintained almost by force and punctuated by accusations of laziness. Contempt for idleness was a lesson hard learnt. There had been countless accusations against her mother: a hand run across pieces of furniture pointing out dust, criticisms of creases in freshly ironed clothes, and, worst of all, marks left by coffee cups, which were not only sins in themselves but evidence of a bigger crime, that of a visit from a friend.

"I don't pay you to sit around all day chatting," Philip's voice echoed in Madeleine's memory, *"I pay you to look after my children and my home, but you don't seem to be able to do either properly."*

And Tessa screaming back, *"You'd best find someone who can, then."* The memory provoked another.

"Tom, I've just looked at that room you've so-called cleaned and I suggest you get up off your lazy backside and go do it again, properly this time." Philip addressed his son *from the sitting-room doorway, but Tom was so engrossed in* Doctor Who *that he didn't hear. Madeleine felt her stomach tighten and lurch in response to the deliberate way their father crossed the room towards her brother and stood now, hands on hips, leaning forward. "I said, you had better go and clean your bedroom properly, and I mean, now!" Tom stood up and moved towards the door, keeping his eyes fixed on the television screen.*

"You lazy little…!" Philip lunged at his son, dragged him back to the television and pushed his face hard against it. "Better have a really close look if it's that important to you." Then he pushed Tom back onto the sofa and ripped

the plug out of the socket, causing it to spark. Tom laughed. It was an act of hysteria.

"So, you think it's funny, do you?"

"No! No, I didn't mean to laugh." But it was too late. Tom covered his head with both arms, but Philip pulled them away and slapped him around the face, leaving a handprint in evidence.

Then Philip turned on Madeleine. "And don't you dare think of helping him." He stormed out of the house.

"Bastard!" Madeleine screamed at the door as he slammed it behind him, then at Tessa. "Why don't you stop him? What sort of fucking mother are you?"

"Don't swear at me," Tessa hissed through tears.

"Oh, does it offend you? Fuck! Fuck! Fuck off, useless mother." Madeleine stopped, startled by the slap her mother issued. Then she and Tessa huddled into each other and sobbed.

Although she now understood the complexities and reasons, Madeleine still felt some resentment towards her mother. Why didn't Tessa stop him? A mother should protect her children. But then, why didn't she herself stop him? Things might have been very different if Madeleine hadn't been such a coward herself. Now, as she headed towards the bathroom, another memory stirred her. She recalled how later that same day the three of them had sat huddled together in front of the television, Philip in the middle, a child under each arm.

"I've got such a bad temper." He squeezed them both, ruffled Tom's hair and stroked Madeleine's upper arm. "I just hope you both know how much I love you. Do you, eh?" And the children responded appropriately, in the way

expected of them. But Madeleine hated herself for her lie and understood this was collusion.

Now, as then, Madeleine needed exorcism. In the bathroom she took the razor from its wrapper and laid it carefully on the washbasin, then opened the gauze without removing it from the packet and put the micro pore on top. She slid off her leggings and underwear and climbed into the empty bath. Picking up the razor, careful not to cut her hands, Madeleine sliced across her right thigh. Then she did the same to the left. The pain brought with it a gasp. The flow of blood was like the release of an orgasm, ecstasy and agony. Crimson blood poured from her thighs and ran over her knees; she turned on the tap and washed the razor and her hands, watching her blood turn scarlet on its journey down the plug hole. She put a temporary dressing on the wounds then she stood, removed her top clothes and turned on the shower.

Madeleine's tears were heavy and loud. The shampoo drips seemed to fix them to her face like glue. She rinsed the tears away and hoped the sound of water flowing would prevent Shibu from hearing her crying. She followed her washing routine, and then eased the dressings from her wounds, patted them dry with a clean flannel and dressed them again quickly before the bleeding started again. Then she wrapped the razor blade in several layers of toilet roll before throwing it in the bin and washed out the bloodied flannel, ready to hang it on the radiator in her room. As she left the bathroom Madeleine heard Shibu stir and called out a cheery good morning to him.

Shibu had quickly become accustomed to the half-hour hour wait for the bathroom and had adjusted his rest-day routine accordingly, but today's extended wait was becoming uncomfortable. The sounds and silences were different, the gaps between them longer. And in them there was tension.

Madeleine hadn't been the same for the past few days. There was a darkness about her that had pervaded the entire house, replacing the ethereal with gravity. She had remained polite and kind, but there was no music, no singing; instead a brooding silence hung heavily in the air. Shibu felt disquieted by it and even wondered if he should leave.

But now the air was light once more. Her 'good morning' genuine once again. The relief Shibu experienced as a result felt fresh, like the end of the monsoon.

As if they were linked, the blood flow from the wounds all but coincided with the flow of menstrual blood, and with it Madeleine came back to the light. She dressed in her calf-length orange dress, partly to avoid clothing that had contact with her wounds, but also because it suited her mood. She was not only grateful for the period because of the release from tension, but also because of the protection it offered from Julian. This weekend there would be neither need for explaining her wounds nor struggling to enjoy the sex.

Despite several lovers, there were only two who had witnessed fresh wounds. Paul, with whom Madeleine had her first sexual relationship, reacted so strongly that it was over twenty years before she again allowed any man, other than Sean, to see her legs bare when wounded. She knew that Julian would feel disappointed that she had failed in her resolve to him not to do it again, and she would feel she had let him down.

Having learnt from previous experience Madeleine had tried a different approach with Julian.

"Wait!" She stopped him in his sexual advances. "I have to tell you something first. I've cut myself. Deliberately, I mean."

He ran his hand up one of her legs and felt the dressing. "Let me see." And when he did his reaction was as she had feared: at first shocked, then almost angry, as if she had done it to spite him. Julian shook his head in disbelief. "You told me those scars were from a one-off."

"Because I knew you'd react like this."

"Well, who wouldn't?"

Sean, *she thought. "I'm sorry," she said.*

"You promised you wouldn't do it again. You've really let me down."

"I know." She turned her face away from him.

"Not only that, you've let yourself down. I don't understand how cutting yourself makes you feel better. No, I don't get it."

"I know you don't," she said into the pillow.

"I don't feel like making love now."

"Okay."

"You've ruined it for me."

"Sorry."

Julian coaxed her face back around and kissed her deeply. He touched her breasts. "You could probably still

50

persuade me, as long as you promise not to cut yourself again."

"I'll try."

"Good girl. Now, where were we?"

Madeleine reluctantly acquiesced to his advances.

Like every vow to herself to quit smoking, she'd intended to keep her promise to Julian. But, like the more acceptable habit, as soon as there was a perceived need its pangs became impossible to ignore.

The first few times Julian returned to his wife the black cloud had descended with intensity, and Madeleine's inner voice spoke of blame in accusatory tones that only the razor could silence. Reconciliation with him was always accompanied by the reiteration of promises, and assurances on both sides that this time would be the last. Julian, at least, seemed to be adhering to his side of the bargain this time; whilst she had broken hers again.

She would definitely have to keep it from him.

You are truly pathetic, she told herself. *You can't stop cutting, neither can you stop being afraid of his reaction.*

Now she found herself wishing that Julian would return to his wife; both of them would have broken their promises then. Not only that, it would be the perfect excuse to end the affair. She was fond of Julian, but increasingly not fond enough.

She thought over a conversation she'd had with Sean on the subject. He'd accused her of colluding with Julian by keep having him back, then said, *"I understand when you love someone you'll do anything to keep them, but..."*

And she had replied, *"You know I don't love him. I don't think I know how to love, not in that way, anyway."*

"Then why?"

"Interesting conversation, similar politics to me, the sex is okay. He makes me laugh – at least, he did – and he doesn't push me to live with him."

But Madeleine also had to acknowledge that now only one of those remained strictly true.

She thought over conversations with various girlfriends over the years and observations of their behaviours when jilted. Many hours she'd spent offering comforting arms and a listening ear to woeful tales, which always stirred compassion in her, and sometimes jealousy and contempt as well. The contempt was born from their lack of pride, which was great enough to allow for behaviour that led them to humiliation. Jealousy because she had never and believed she would never experience that kind of love. Whenever a relationship ended for Madeleine, she felt only an increased self-loathing at her inability to love and her need to prostitute herself.

Partly because this pattern of thinking could lead her back to depression, but also because it was what she often did on her day off, Madeleine headed for the spare room to do some painting. At the top of the stairs she met Shibu.

"Hello," he said, offering a broad smile. There was nothing unusual in the greeting and yet it was subtly different. He seemed confident and relaxed and Madeleine felt it indicative of his feeling more at home, which pleased her immensely. She watched him descend the stairs. At the bottom he turned, smiled and shrugged one shoulder in a playful manner. In an instant he seemed less a boy and more a man, and perhaps, neither quite as vulnerable nor as innocent as she had imagined.

It always took a little while to settle into painting. Time to sweep the cobwebs from her sub-conscious and the paintbrush and inspiration to flow fluidly, but this time Shibu inhibited her too. The impression of him clung like gossamer. Finally, Mozart carried Madeleine away to where she needed to be.

In the early days Madeleine's art had been abstract, but those works had only been intended for catharsis and not for others to see. The later ones were easier, both to the eye and to comprehension, and a print of her favourite one of Tom had even sold after her one and only exhibition. Although she still had the original, Madeleine felt some regret that she had even made a print, leave alone sold it to a complete stranger. The reason was because in it, Tom's face was exactly right, his expression the correct mix of joy and torture. For a stranger to look upon that seemed a violation, and she felt she had profited from the exposure of Tom's soul.

But Madeleine wasn't thinking about that now; she wasn't thinking anything because she was lost in the experience of painting. The brush stroked the canvas smoothly and gently, and the painting responded as if it were alive beneath a lover's touch. She felt in tune with Mozart's piano concerto number twenty-three, which responded in the same manner to the fingertips of Murray Perahia, and the music dictated the pace of their encounter.

The pangs of hunger eventually reunited Madeleine with herself. She rested the painting against the wall and reviewed it as critically as self-appraisal would allow. An androgynous face could just be distinguished in the twists and knots of bark that protruded from the tree trunk. The branches swept down like hair and the exposed roots created the appearance of feet. In the topmost branch a dove roosted. The painting was supposed to represent oneness with nature and the dawning of peace which resulted. Madeleine's reaction to her paintings was very much dependent on her mood, so today she rather liked it and considered it a good representation. On other occasions she would have to apply fervent resistance to the urge to destroy anything she had ever created.

She cleaned the brushes and herself, feeling for the first time in over two hours the need to fill her lungs with tobacco smoke. It was an urge she resisted for a further half an hour because otherwise she would have one before and after lunch, which she didn't allow herself to do.

As she stood by the back door, finishing her cigarette and inhaling the smell of autumn, Madeleine heard Shibu arrive in the kitchen; when she returned there herself she was greeted by his calm presence. He was as peaceful as an empty church. She was reminded of their first encounter, and how instantly all her fears about taking in a lodger were dispelled.

Madeleine had rarely been wrong in her instincts about a person and when she had it was never drastically so. She might, for example, with the benefit of time and knowing the person better, decide they were a little more or less likeable than she first thought, but never would she change from one extreme to the other. Based on this, she was mystified as to how it could be different for anyone else.

How, for example, could her mother have so misjudged Philip? Tessa had laid claim to a reversal of character as soon as the marriage took place, but Madeleine simply couldn't understand that. She didn't believe it possible for anyone to hide their true nature for any length of time. Yet, Philip had more than the average number of friends, many of whom she liked. Perhaps some people were completely different depending on who they were with, or abusers so adept that there was craft in portraying themselves as the opposite. After all, how many times had she heard expressions of disbelief and accounts of impeccable characters when someone was publicly exposed?

She tried to imagine Sean behaving as Philip had, but it was utterly impossible. And she had to admit to herself that if it were proven to her with catalogued evidence, she would still find it so, but equally she felt sure she'd remain friends with him.

Sometimes Madeleine wondered if her memory distorted the facts and exaggerated Philip's behaviour; there were, after all, plenty of good memories too: camping holidays, Christmas and birthday parties, theatre trips and days at the seaside. Yet, even as she remembered she felt the knot of fear, because inside every ice-cream cone and underneath every gift wrapper, there remained a threat if she did something wrong. And she never grasped the rules because they seemed to change without reason or warning.

Madeleine was distracted by these thoughts, which must have shown on her face because when she looked up, she noticed Shibu's expression was a little alarmed. She smiled to offer reassurance. He gazed at the floor, shying away from the direct eye contact but smiled back at her.

"I'm going shopping soon, Shibu, is there anything you need?"

"I don't think so there is." But he opened his cupboard and then the fridge to check, and Madeleine noticed again the cheap tins and packages.

"D'you ever eat European food?" she asked. "Have you ever tried lasagne, for example?"

"No."

"Would you like to?"

Shibu shrugged and pursed his lips, keeping his gaze downcast. "Maybe."

"Maybe?"

"Well, yes, okay, thank you."

"Great! We'll decide on a day next week."

A few minutes later she breezed out of the door and Shibu felt the essence of the house leave with her, emptiness occupying the place she'd been. It stirred a memory for him of the first time he'd returned from school to an empty house. He felt again the fear of uncertainty that accompanied the feeling of certain change, and heard his seven-year-old voice full of tears as he called for his mother.

Then his aunt arrived, her face smiling like his mother's but not warm, not happy to have him home.

"Mummy has gone to the hospital to get the baby. I'm here to look after you for a while."

But how long was a while? Shibu knew a little while was how long it took between the meal being prepared and his father coming home. And a long while was so long he no longer recognised the people who had come to visit, but which of these should he expect? By bedtime it seemed this while was a long one, and he cried. The first tears were met with comforting arms and reassurances that Mummy would be home soon. When soon wasn't soon enough he cried again, and this time he was told not to be so silly and to go to sleep, an order he tried to obey, but how can you make yourself sleep? His disobedience was met with a sharp slap to his leg that quieted the tears but wounded his heart.

He went three times more to school before his mother and sister came home. His joy was dampened with instructions from his aunt to 'let her rest' and 'be careful with your sister'. And the baby was always in the middle of the cuddles.

It was the first time he felt lonely.

Feeling that same emotion now reminded him that it was in this house he first stopped feeling homesick.

Into her shopping trolley Madeleine dropped some chickpeas and red lentils. Perhaps for now she'd cook something with which Shibu was more familiar.

Chapter Six

A stranger's voice reached Shibu's ears, and, as he entered the kitchen, he noticed the air felt charged with irritation. It was this that confirmed the relationship between the two women, even more than the physical resemblance, which was only slight. Each of the women had large mouths that curled upwards into natural smiles, each face was oval in shape, and both bodies spoke in large, theatrical language. Both were beautiful, Shibu decided, although in quite different ways: the older woman because her face remained soft and pretty, concealing her age well; while Madeleine's features were strong and sculptured, especially when, as now, they were viewed in profile. As Shibu came into the room she turned, smiled enthusiastically and beckoned him over.

"This is my mum, Tessa. Tessa, this is Shibu." The two shook hands and exchanged greetings. "We were just talking about you," Madeleine continued. "Were your ears burning?"

"Means?"

"It's an English expression. When your ears are hot it's supposed to mean someone is talking about you," Tessa explained.

"Oh!" Shibu raised a hand to one ear and said, "I think I have big burn then."

Madeleine studied him quizzically, wondering what he meant and whether she had caused offence, but then realised from his tone and expression that he mocked himself and the size of his ears. She would never have described them as big, but now that he'd pointed it out, they were a little on the large side. Viewing him objectively she decided he wasn't quite handsome: his nose was too wide, his skin not as clear as it might have been and his hair already beginning to recede. But the shape of his face was strong, his mouth soft and full, and his eyes shone with sincerity. Not handsome, no, but so very beautiful in his soul. There was nothing shallow about Shibu; he was like a novel with hardly a wasted word. And, because of this he was very attractive.

The smile slipped from Shibu's face and was replaced by a look of apprehension under Madeleine's scrutiny. She was about to apologise when she realised there was no need, because the cause of his alarm was not her looking, but recognition of a mutual feeling that had passed between them. And, although it evaporated instantly, it misted the air like light autumn rain.

"So, are you enjoying being in England?" Tessa asked.

"Mostly." Shibu felt a fleeting fear at the memory of last winter. Dull days darkened by the darkness in his soul and how he felt his energy sapped in response. "But it has taken some adjustment."

"I'm sure. I only moved counties and it was hard to adjust."

"My mum lives in Devon. It's a very beautiful part of the country; I would love to take you there sometime."

"And you would be most welcome, Shibu. My husband and I run a bed and breakfast. You wouldn't be the first of Maddie's friends to visit us."

"Oh! Thank you." Shibu felt surprised to be referred to as Madeleine's friend. He was struck by the contradictory nature of the conversation and the atmosphere, the one being light and friendly, the other quarrelsome. It reminded him a little of the tension between his own mother and his aunt. Whenever the two sisters were together irritability and competitiveness pervaded the air, but it was always half-hearted, and it was obvious that in fact the two women loved each other dearly.

Contradictions weren't limited to the relationship between Madeleine and her mother; there was also the paradoxical nature of Madeleine herself. A moment ago, he had seen right to the very core of her and found it far from her chaotic outward self. She was like a stormy ocean whose depths were calm, and in the second their souls touched he knew that, while it was the treacherous waves that would pull him in, it was the tranquillity of the still waters that would extinguish his life.

He had experienced a similar feeling once before, in Jobin's eyes, the instant the life left her body. Fully alive she had the look of a wild animal – wary, watchful and full of frenetic energy – but in death there was such peace in her eyes that it troubled him. For, although it might offer confirmation of God, suicide was, without question, the work of the Devil.

The memory stirred in him now. *There were shouts from the boys who were fishing. He and his father ran to the river, his fifteen-year-old self feeling like a man as they pulled Jobin from it. It was then he had seen how peace filled her soul, and at first he felt reassured, but when he realised the significance of the rocks tied around her ankles that same stillness repelled him. While his father pumped water and slime from her lungs and tried to reinstate her breath with his own, Shibu's childish hands fumbled with the untying of the stones, doing so because there was nothing else to be done.*

It was the first, in fact the only, time he witnessed his father cry, carrying Jobin, muddied, drenched, drowned, up the hill to her parents' house.

Then later he watched in confusion as all of the men young enough to fight, and old enough to understand, pummelled first on the door and then on the body of the person they blamed for the death.

That same man, Jobin's father, wailed with distress, pummelled his own chest, tore at his hair and wiped away tears that spilled from his bruised eyes, as he watched Jobin's remains given up to the same river that had claimed her life. The next morning, he and his family were gone.

Shibu didn't understand for many years to come. Not until he read about the kind of abuse that leaves scars in places other than the body, and manifests as silence rather than as screams.

He was brought back to the present by Tessa calling a cheery farewell to him and then a moment later Madeleine was back in the kitchen.

"Boy do I need a coffee!" She rubbed the temples on either side of her face. "D'you want one?"

"No, thank you, I have."

"I need some music too. Will it disturb you?"

"Is okay."

She breezed out and back in quickly. The music she had chosen was loud and aggressive but exciting too. Inhibited only slightly by Shibu's presence and needing to release the tension of Tessa's visit, Madeleine swayed her hips in time to the beat. Shibu, moved by the sensual rhythm of her body, turned away from her and continued cooking his meal.

"I find my parents such hard work. She's been visiting friends up here," Madeleine explained to the wall, then, turning around, said, "D'you have a good relationship with your parents, Shibu?"

"Yes."

"You probably miss them, then?"

"Yes."

Madeleine understood a response was required. "What're you cooking? Is it very spicy?"

"I don't think so – you want try?" He was already crossing the room and loading a spoon as he asked.

Madeleine took a tentative taste. "Not bad. Who taught you to cook?"

"No one, I learn since I came here."

"Well, very good in that case."

Their eye contact was a little longer than was either necessary or customary. Flustered, Madeleine turned and tossed the used spoon into the sink. She could hardly believe what she was seeing in his face. Now she watched him, in the corner of the kitchen that had quickly become established as his own, as he measured rice, then water, in a cup. She reflected on how easily they had fallen into roles and established routines, and pondered the significance of how well they worked around each other. She adjusted the volume of the music downwards.

"When're you working next, Shibu?"

"The day after tomorrow."

"Then that's the day I'll cook for you. If you'd like, of course."

"If you want means you can."

"I do want. It's good to have someone to cook for."

The very idea of a meal ready for him when he returned from work made Shibu nostalgic. He remembered being home, sitting in the kitchen, conversing with his own mother, as Madeleine had been with hers. Before he left for the UK they had chatted about everyday things in a totally natural way, but now, despite their daily telephone conversations, rapport was being lost to the lack of common experience. And gradually a distance was coming between them.

"Anyway, I feel responsible for you now you're in my home. I'm going to cook for you at least once a week, if you'll allow me. I'll be your English mother." Although Madeleine's words were said in jest, they perfectly punctuated his thoughts.

Madeleine wondered now what his mother was like. She had seen photographs of both of Shibu's parents, but what could a photograph reveal beyond inherited physical characteristics? There was surely more of a clue as to the woman in the behaviour of her son? For Shibu to be the lovely, easy-going man he was, his mother must surely be the same and she, by that very nature, would have raised him in an atmosphere of love and patience. Madeleine had often wondered, sometimes bitterly, how different she would be if the same had been true for her; surely even someone with bad genes would be the better for it? She wished she could be convinced that malevolence had been beaten rather than bred into her, because at least there was hope of a cure that way.

The house telephone and Madeleine's mobile rang simultaneously. She glanced at the mobile's handset, saw it was Julian and left it to ring while she answered the landline.

"Oh, Kumar, how good to hear from you… yes, of course, it would be lovely to see you." She replaced the telephone on its cradle. "Kumar is coming, I've been meaning to introduce the two of you; you're not busy, I hope?"

"No."

"Good. Kumar's wife was a very dear friend. She died four years ago – she was only forty-eight. Cancer. Left two young teenagers. It's been very hard for him. He's a dear man."

Motivated by bad memories of Christmas and the belief that it should be based around the Christian ideals of sharing and caring rather than the commercial event it had become, Madeleine spent her Christmases cooking and serving food at the local homeless project. It was there that she met Nitty doing the same. *"It doesn't seem proper to celebrate Christmas like a Christian when I'm not one,"* she told Madeleine, *"but it doesn't seem right to ignore the main festival of my adopted country. In my own country there are many people homeless and hungry; I always wanted to help them, but I never could. Now I have that chance."*

Afterwards Nitty invited Madeleine to her home, fed her, explained to her about Sikh and Hindu religion.

The ideas were not entirely new but Madeleine's knowledge was sketchy, so, to improve upon her knowledge, she read *Mahabharata* and *The Upanishads*, then *The Tibetan Book of the Dead*, and even large chunks of the Bible, all of which she later discussed with her new friends. Soon she was spending large portions of her weekends in the company of the Bhat family, taking the two-year-old Beldiv to the park when Nitty's pregnancy made her tired enough to need a day-time sleep, and gifts of food to add to their table when Madeleine joined them for meals. Then together she and Nitty joined a yoga class.

"It was Kumar's wife who got me started on the yoga," she explained to Shibu now.

And it would hardly be exaggerating to say it saved my life, or my sanity at least. Madeleine thought as she said it, fleetingly recalling panic attacks, fear of the dark and copious quantities of alcohol to compensate for both, followed by hangovers from which she felt bound to die.

"In my opinion yoga is the greatest gift India gave us, with tea a close second."

"Tea not from India, is from China."

"You're right, of course. It was grown in India after the opium wars, I believe. Anyway, it grows there now, and it and yoga are two of the things I love most. Thank you, India."

Shibu laughed.

"D'you speak Hindi, Shibu?"

"Little bit."

"Good, you can speak to Kumar in his native language; that will be so nice for him."

"Is rude to you and I only know little bit."

"Then only speak a little bit." Madeleine mockingly told him off as if she was a child playing at being a teacher. Then she picked up her mobile and returned Julian's call. They spoke for only a couple of minutes and ended the conversation with the automatic: "Love you," from him and, "Me too," from her. Increasingly Madeleine felt guilty for speaking words she didn't mean; it seemed like blasphemy, but to respond with anything less seemed cruel.

Kumar arrived through the back door; he tapped gently as he opened it.

"I did come to the front, but there was no answer."

Madeleine greeted him with a hug. "Sorry, music's probably a bit too loud. Kumar, this is Shibu, Shibu, Kumar."

They shook hands and had a brief conversation in Hindi, and then Kumar said, "I have music."

"Fab. The mix you been promising for ages?"

"Finally. I have been so busy at work."

"What's your job?" Shibu asked.

"Computer programmer."

"Oh!"

"It's very useful sometimes, Shibu, for technophobes like me," Madeleine said.

"Means?"

"Sorry. It's useful to have a friend like Kumar when you're scared of technology."

"Where you learn, here or India?" Shibu asked Kumar.

"Both. My qualifications got me a job here, then I studied some more."

"That what I want do, but I think now is very difficult. I study NVQ so I can be senior carer, but my friend say English government take it off list."

This was news to Madeleine, who paused in the act of putting on the CD so that she could hear more.

"When did they do that?" she asked.

"Not yet, I think they will do in April. I was going to apply for visa extension, but now I think I won't get."

"No harm in applying anyway," Madeleine continued.

"I don't want spend money on another course if I can't get."

"How much will it cost?" Madeleine asked.

"Maybe one and half or two thousand pound."

"Wow! Will you get it back if you don't get the visa?"

"No, that's why I don't want try. No course, no visa, but is too much money to lose."

"Indeed." The thought of Shibu leaving so soon was a shock to her, and so too was the extent of the disappointment she experienced at the idea.

Madeleine hadn't had a cigarette since dinner, so she donned her coat and headed outside.

"Just gotta have a puff." She kept the door ajar so that she could hear the music, and because she didn't like to cut herself off completely from her guests.

She came back in and went straight upstairs to clean her teeth. Upon her return she restarted the CD.

"I hope you don't mind, I really need to listen properly, been waiting ages for it."

"Why you not dance?" Shibu soon asked. "Don't you like this music?"

"I like very much, but I'm too inhibited with you both here."

"Means?"

"Means I feel shy. Unless you both dance too."

Kumar raised his hands and shook his head. "Uh huh!"

"Never," said Shibu.

"Then, I'll have to either stay still or get drunk."

"Shibu, pass me that wine."

Shibu passed the bottle to Kumar and laughed, obviously enjoying his part in the conspiracy.

"Can't be done, boys, gotta get up for work."

"Aw! Then you shouldn't promise," Shibu teased.

"Quite so!" Kumar agreed.

"Is anyone else drinking? Well, then neither am I," she said emphatically.

But when Kumar had left and Shibu gone to bed Madeleine sneaked a glass, needing the soporific effects of red wine to lure her to sleep.

Chapter Seven

Shibu drew back the curtains on a bright morning. The sun's rays glinted from the garden mirror, dazzling him slightly. The washing barely moved in the still air. As if it was a premonition, Shibu imagined the fresh smell that would permeate the kitchen later when Madeleine brought it in. The house was quiet, but not silent, because, as always, despite the lack of her physical presence the echoes of Madeleine hung like a phantom so that Shibu never felt fully alone. Although he knew her return from work wouldn't be until six o'clock he expected to find Madeleine in every room he entered. The bathroom smelt of her coconut smell, and in the hallway there was still a whisper amongst the coats that told of her recent departure. But it was in the kitchen she lingered most of all, in the tasks she had completed before leaving and especially in the preparations for those she would return to.

As Shibu ate his breakfast he turned on the radio, expecting to hear music but instead it was a news channel. The man, in his BBC voice, was announcing the latest immigration figures. Although he didn't recognise her voice, Shibu knew the name Theresa May, who now offered assurances that the statistics indicated the figures were in line with her former promises. He sighed and turned the radio off, because this talk added to his insecurity concerning his status.

Breakfast over, he strolled into the garden, feeling his senses enlivened by the cool air. He stood a while beneath the beech tree, resisting the boyish urge to climb into its branches. He remembered with more than a little shame a tree in India into which he and his friends had climbed as boys to steal eggs from the nesting birds, at the time feeling amused by the angry squawks of the parents. He recalled too, how they used the nests as target practice for their catapults, and how they hid in the tree's upper branches from their mothers when it was time for chores.

Shibu crossed to the wild part of the garden, squatted down in front of and then ran his palms over the stone Buddha. The face was calm, expressionless, in contrast to the face of Christ, who was so often depicted in crucified agony. Shibu wondered about the story behind this Buddha, and whether Madeleine subscribed to Buddhist philosophy.

Still feeling restless, he went into the living room, which he barely ever entered, although Madeleine had more than once invited him to. The invitation extended to use of the computer, over which he now hovered uncertainly, before making up his mind to check his emails. If any replies were necessary it was easier on the computer than on his mobile phone.

In the lounge there were further indications that Madeleine was interested in Asian culture. On the shelf above the fireplace there was another small Buddha, a prayer wheel and a statue of Ganesh. In the fireplace itself, which was iron and marble, there stood an elephant about a quarter of a metre in height.

The largest wall was devoted to her music collection, in the form of CDs, cassettes and vinyl. On the remaining walls there were several pictures; two were paintings, the others photographs. Although Shibu had never seen any of Madeleine's paintings he felt sure she was the artist; there was so much of her about them. The photographs were all of the same young man. Someone related to Madeleine he felt sure; not only because the very fact of them lent importance to the portraits, but also because he had hair like Madeleine's. A brother, he guessed, or cousin at the very least.

Now he looked out of the bay window onto the quiet street. For Shibu the lack of activity in English streets was one of the biggest contrasts to India. The street outside his home would be buzzing with life way before this time of day. He stood for a while just looking, then he sat at the computer and turned it on.

Madeleine kicked her shoes off as soon as she was through the door, then picked them up and put them on the shoe rack. She smoothed her jacket down as she hung it up, and did the same with her hair in response to the mirror image. On the table were three letters; Shibu had recently begun to put them there rather than leave them on the floor. Madeleine tasted the air; the quiet and stillness of the house belied her instinct that Shibu was in. Then, as she glanced into the lounge on passing, she realised why and was drawn into the room by the sight of the single naked foot dangling from the sofa. She baulked at the memory it provoked. His other foot was curled underneath him, where he lay sleeping, so soundly there was barely even a hint of his breathing. Again, the memory taunted her. Madeleine banished it by concentrating on Shibu; she stilled her own breath, for fear of waking him. Asleep he looked even more peaceful. She stood and observed him for a second or two. *Beautiful boy*, she thought, and imagined a hand stroking that tranquil look onto his brow, as she was sure his mother had done when he was a child. This thought filled her with the deepest regret that she would never experience maternal love. Above Shibu's head the photograph of Tom smiled without conviction. Suddenly Madeleine was overcome with grief and fled the room.

In the kitchen she cried, as quietly as she could. Tom. Tom. Every cell in her body longed for him. The yearning was for the most ordinary of things, even those over which they had sometimes quarrelled. She longed to hear his voice and see the ageing of his face, instead of the one in her memory and in the photographs, fixed in eternal youth. Even the memory of him was fading now; without those photographs she might not accurately recall his features. Yet the hurt was as sharp as ever. Tom.

Shibu came into the kitchen. Madeleine straightened her shoulders and patted her eyes dry.

"What happened?" he asked.

"Nothing."

"Then why you cry?"

"Memories."

"Memories?" For a second Madeleine thought Shibu was unfamiliar with the word, but then he said, "Sometimes is necessary to silence them."

The words stimulated more tears; she bit her bottom lip to prevent the flow. "Sometimes they insist on being heard."

Shibu's expression was so empathic, it pained her all the more. She grabbed the washing basket and hurried into the garden. Madeleine was startled by the ghost-like quality to the shadow cast by the beech tree in the fading light. The routine task of fetching in washing and hanging it on the indoor dryer focused her mind on the present once more. She considered apologising for her tears but decided in favour of pursuing another subject.

"So, how have you spent your day?"

"Shopping, cooking, internet."

"Then sleeping," Madeleine said in a teasing tone.

"Oh! Sorry about that."

"There's no need. I want you to feel at home."

Shibu giggled. "Then I give you all my clothes to wash. And when I in bad mood I shout at you."

"Okay. Then you can look after the garden."

"Then I think I find new address. Anyway, I have no experience of looking after garden. Yours is very fine."

"Well, thank you. I have made it easy to maintain because I'm not much of a gardener myself and I have things I would rather be doing."

"Why you have Buddha?"

"Don't you like it?"

"Yes, I like – just I ask."

"It used to belong to someone else." She checked the catch in her voice, which didn't go unnoticed. "I thought it was too big for the house."

"So, you not Buddhist?"

"I'm not anything."

"You don't believe there is God?"

"I don't not believe."

"Means?"

"I believe in a spiritual connection between people, but I don't subscribe to any religion and I no longer believe in a supreme being called God. I was brought up a Christian and when I was a child I believed in that sort of a god, but then I began to wonder certain things like – if God is love how come there is so much talk of punishment? And if He is so powerful why doesn't He stop bad things happening to innocent people?"

"We can't know reason, we just have to trust Him."

"Yeah, heard that argument before, but it seems to me innocent people suffer more than guilty ones. And my problem with a personal god is, if He really is all powerful and all loving how could He not interfere? How can He allow war? Starving children? And beautiful people like Nitty to die young while dictators stay alive?"

"Who Nitty?"

"Kumar's wife."

"Ah! Maybe God have another plan for them."

"Well, I sure can't make sense of His plan and that's why I lost my belief."

"Maybe these things sent to test our belief."

"So, God took Nitty as a test to Kumar and his children? Nah! Doesn't make sense to me."

"Peoples are like childrens and God like strict father."

"Strict? More like abusive. What would you think of a father who ordered you to kill your brother as proof that you loved him?"

The words were harsh and alarming to Shibu. "God sacrificed His own son too."

"That doesn't help me like this God any better, Shibu. A murdering god is no god at all in my opinion. Love has nothing to do with punishment and everything to do with nurturing, understanding and respect, which is exactly what Jesus taught."

"You believe in Jesus?"

"Yes, as a prophet, but not as the son of God."

"Means?"

"Jesus was a man – born of human parents, not a virgin and the Holy Spirit – but he was a very special man who tried to teach people another way to live."

Shibu had stopped listening properly. With Madeleine's denial of the virgin birth came anger. "I don't like when you speak against God, is like speak against my parents."

It quashed her passion. "Sorry, I didn't mean to offend you. Why should you care what I think anyway?"

"Just I ask."

"Yes, you asked if I believe in God and you got a lecture, sorry. It didn't need to be quite so brutally honest. Guess I have a problem when it comes to punishment."

"Peoples need rules to live by."

"Maybe, but maybe not. I believe deep inside we are sincere and know the right way to behave, but punishment confuses people. Takes away their self-belief. If God is anywhere to be found He's in the depths of our hearts."

Shibu acknowledged that his rare encounters with God had been reached through looking into the silence and stillness inside himself. "Of course, the soul is always with God."

"So, we agree then." Madeleine rubbed Shibu's shoulder in a conciliatory manner. "I could cook for you tonight."

Madeleine's touch lingered on Shibu after her hand had left. "Is not necessary."

"It may not be *necessary*, but wouldn't it be nice?"

"Maybe." He shrugged then relaxed a little. "But I already have food for today."

"Okay. Some other time then."

"I could cook you instead."

Madeleine smiled to herself at the image generated by the lack of one word, but she didn't correct him. "Thank you, that would be nice."

And yet, it was what she always did at this time of the day. She made a clicking noise, as if she were imitating the clock she now took a glance at.

"Should I help?"

"I don't think so there is much you can do."

She bit her bottom lip and rocked from one foot to the other as she imagined the disarray. Would she be able to ignore it until after they had eaten? She wondered.

"I could clean up as you cook."

"I can do."

"Yes, of course. Right. I'll leave you to it, then."

She turned to go then paused to say, "I know you were joking about the washing, but actually it's more economical to share it. So, why don't we do that?"

"If you want means we can."

"Right. I'll leave you to it, then. Um. You'll give me a shout when it's ready?"

"Of course."

There were only a few junk emails, nothing to which Madeleine needed to respond. The sound and the smell of frying put her on alert.

This isn't leaving him to it, she thought. *I can clean up afterwards. I could go and do some more work on that painting.*

It would be a constructive use of her time as well as a distraction from what was happening in the kitchen. Despite this it was difficult to resist looking in as she passed. It was only a glance, but it didn't look too bad.

The attic room was quite chilly and already growing dark; neither of these was conducive to creativity, but neither of them was the real cause of her lack of concentration. The conversation with Shibu trundled around her head. Perhaps she would have done better to keep silent, but the words had left her lips the instant the thoughts reached her mind. It was a character trait which Madeleine was often irritated by, and for which she just as frequently berated herself.

Why can't I learn to keep my big mouth shut? she asked herself, remembering several occasions on which she had launched into a lecture with other people. And the two on which it had become so heated she'd almost fallen out with both Julian and her own mother. Even as she thought this, she felt the venom rise. In her there lurked a bully imprinted by virtue of paternal genes. She always worried that one day he would overcome her, despite her efforts to subdue him. Now she worried that Shibu's gentle nature might make him an easy target.

But then he did ask, she said to herself. *And it can be good to have your beliefs challenged. I didn't need to be so damn brutal, though, did I? It was like I was telling him not to be a Catholic.*

Downstairs the same conversation plagued Shibu's mind as he diced and sliced the vegetables for the meal. He thought back to his school days, and, just for a second or two, he was again in touch with the feelings of fear and resentment that accompanied the physical lashings with which his disobedience had sometimes been met. And in his memory he heard his mother's warning voice: "*You'd better pray God can forgive you because it's going to be difficult for me.*" Or his father's: "*You can lie to me, son, but not to God. He's always watching and He knows what's in your heart.*"

Now he remembered his first confession: *the theft of a toy car from a neighbouring boy, whose family had been visited by a friend now living in Europe. Shibu had to have that car, not only because it was new and shiny, but especially because it was from a foreign country. He would tell his parents it was a gift from his friend, he decided, but then realised the danger of them offering the family thanks so decided instead to pretend he'd found it. Soon, in his imagination, he was visited by the boy's father and asked if he had seen the missing car, so he hid it in an inside pocket of his school bag, which he then kept with him wherever he went, even placing it under his pillow at night.*

It wasn't long before Shibu realised this prize was no prize at all, when it was locked away from him so effectively his eyes barely ever looked upon it. And even before the priest instructed him to Shibu knew what he had to do. Returning the car unnoticed to its rightful owner felt more terrifying than removing it had, but it was also an immense relief.

Was it fear of his parents and God's retribution that had taught him it was wrong to steal? It seemed now, to his adult mind, that there was also natural shame to which he had responded. Perhaps that was God in his heart.

His memory stirred again, back to the dying face of Jobin. How many years of abuse went unheeded by a whole community? His heart told him now, had told him even then, that she deserved salvation in death after such a pitiable life. But the priest and the community were clear: no one who had committed suicide could go to heaven. Just for a second, he dared to understand Madeleine's point of view.

And if she's right about that, then…

He recoiled from the thought, appalled and afraid, and heard the warning voice reminding him of Hell.

"Smells good." Madeleine had come to the kitchen in response to Shibu's call, but for much longer she had hovered around the house, busying herself with pointless chores to keep hunger and impatience at bay.

In furtive glances she took note of the cloth still heavy with water and the traces of food on the work surface. Yet she realised Shibu had made a good attempt.

"D'you want some wine?" she asked.

"If you want means we can."

"Do you want?"

He shrugged. "I drink if you do."

"D'you like red?" She poured it without giving him the chance to answer.

"I only try one, maybe two times, is okay, I think." He took a large slurp. "Yes, I like, is good."

"You're supposed to sip it slowly, though, like this. Savour the taste."

"Means?"

"Really enjoy every mouthful."

"I think this European way. Asian way is drink fast; like this." He downed the remainder of the glass. "Get drunks fast."

"You're not supposed to aim to get drunk. The wine improves the taste of the food."

Shibu dished up a generous portion of food.

She took a tentative mouthful. "That is really nice."

"Thank you. I like get drunks sometimes, don't you?"

"I like to feel the effect, yes, but not get drunk. I have had too many hangovers and there is too much behaviour I regret."

"Oh! What behaviour?" Shibu raised both eyebrows and spoke with a giggle as he helped himself to more wine.

"I can't be telling you the secrets of my past now, can I? I don't want to give you a bad impression of me."

"Never!"

They ate in silence for a minute or two, Madeleine deliberately keeping her eyes on her meal. When the silence was becoming uncomfortable, she looked up and asked, "So, what d'you think you'll do about your visa?"

"I don't know. I wait see what my friends do. Some of them say they expect rules will change in year or two and may be easier to get job as senior carer, I wait to see what happen in April."

There was barely a pause before Madeleine said, "If I can do anything to help just ask."

"Thank you."

After Madeleine had poured herself a second glass of wine, she realised there was hardly more than half a glass left in the bottle. She held it up and gasped in mock annoyance.

"Sorry about that."

"It's a good job I don't want anymore."

"If you want means I can buy some more."

"I have more." Madeleine got up and took another bottle from rack in the cupboard. "You sure you want some?"

He shrugged.

Madeleine put the bottle on the table, poured what was remaining in the other into Shibu's glass and a small one for herself from the new bottle. Shibu drained his glass and poured himself another.

"You're going to have a hangover."

"Never. Once I drink whole bottle of vodka and don't have."

"Okay, but let me warn you, a hangover from red wine is bad. The last one I had I felt like I was dying and I wished it would hurry up and happen."

Madeleine's mobile rang. "That'll be Julian – excuse me, please, won't be long."

She took the phone into the lounge. "Hi, how's your day been?"

"The usual," Julian replied. "Gotta be quick, sorry, gotta call Carrie back, she's phoned several times but I keep missing her. Jack called, said he's worried about her, she has started sitting around in her night clothes and drinking in the day. I'll see you Saturday, all being well."

"Okay – night then."

"Night, night. Love you."

"Good luck with Carrie. Night."

Here we go again, she thought, and sighed. But only because it was so tiresome.

She was more transparent than she realised because Shibu asked, "What happened?"

"Nothing."

"I don't think so is nothing, your face say something happen."

"It's a long story."

"Is only" – Shibu checked his watch – "eight-forty."

Madeleine took a long, slow sigh. "Julian has a wife; they aren't together, as such, but he keeps going back. She has a mental health problem – you understand? Yes, that's right, she is a bit crazy, and when she's crazy Julian goes back to her because he's scared she'll kill herself. His son has phoned him to say he's worried about her."

"So, tomorrow he go back to her?"

"If not tomorrow, then soon."

"Why you stay with him?"

"That's rather a bold question."

"Just I ask. Sean make you dance and laugh, Julian make you serious."

"He has children to consider." Madeleine's tone was defensive.

It was Shibu's turn to wonder if he had caused offence and he lowered his tone and eyes as he said, "Of course. Just I ask."

"It's okay. You're not the only one."

"Why you don't have childrens?"

"Another bold question. You've had too much to drink."

"Maybe," he said with a giggle, as he poured another glass. "But you like childrens?"

"Yes, too much to have them."

"Means?"

"I don't think I'd make much of a mother."

"Oh." Despite the wine Shibu knew he'd gone too far.

"Well, any other bold questions?" Madeleine asked, light-heartedly.

"Maybe." He shrugged his shoulders, lowered his head and gaze slightly then looked up and into her eyes; his were twinkling with suggestion. A coy smile teased the corner of his mouth. There was no ambiguity; the invitation was clear.

Madeleine laughed nervously. She licked her lips and swallowed hard, but both her throat and stomach continued to tingle and Shibu continued to hold her gaze, the request resonating in his eyes. Madeleine looked away. "Right, better get those dishes washed." She almost jumped from her seat.

"I help," Shibu offered.

"It's okay – you cooked, I'll wash up."

Shibu reached for more wine, then changed his mind; his heart was full of shame.

"I think I go bed now, goodnight," he said, in as matter-of-fact a tone as he could manage.

"Goodnight – thank you for the meal, it was very nice." Madeleine didn't turn away from her chore because she didn't want him to see that she would be incapable of refusing him a second time. The air remained full of him for several minutes, so much so that it took as long for Madeleine to turn around to check he'd really gone.

Now, in his absence she was less sure that she had read him accurately; it just seemed so unlikely and yet she had enough experience to know when she was being flirted with. Flirting was surely all it was, induced by the wine, not a serious invitation into bed. Now she felt stupid and a little ashamed to think she could have believed he was in earnest.

Why would he be interested in me? she asked herself. *He must be all of twenty-five. I'm old enough to be his mother.* She carried on tidying the kitchen, unnecessarily. *Happens, though. He's a man, not a boy. Stop it! How could you even entertain the idea? That really would make me my father's daughter.* She poured herself another drink.

And what about Julian? Yet even as she thought it Madeleine knew he was becoming less of an issue every day. The likelihood that he would soon be reunited with

Carrie left her feeling neither sad nor angry, and she knew there would be no need for slicing her legs this time.

Shibu has a point about that. Why am I still with him?

Shibu's thoughts were disordered, but one kept returning: *I have offended her, and now she will kick me out.* He kept changing his mind about whether to apologise or ignore it; finally he decided the morning would be a better time to make up his mind on that.

Now he knelt beside his bed and prayed for forgiveness for his sinful intentions and for the strength to resist the desire that seemed bigger every day. *No more alcohol*, he promised himself, as he climbed into bed, but as he closed his eyes to seek sleep he found behind them a portrait of Madeleine.

Chapter Eight

Next morning they met on the stairs. Shibu bowed his head and gaze upon seeing Madeleine, who said, "Morning, got a headache?"

Her tone was cheery and so reassured Shibu.

"No, fine, just I little bit late." He hurried down the stairs and out of the door. In fact, he had woken with a fuzzy head, if not with any pain, but experienced it with some gratitude because dull senses blunted his embarrassment.

It was Madeleine's day off and there were many chores to do. Music rocked her dusting, polishing, scrubbing hands and competed with the sound of the vacuum cleaner, but she silenced it in favour of the radio as she ironed. However, this was no longer fit for purpose; the quiz programme bored her and the news depressed her. Over the years only the details of the news stories had changed – the number of deaths, the name of the country – otherwise the abuses remained the same. She tuned to Radio 6 instead, but soon turned off altogether, this time irritated by the DJ's banter, which seemed a repudiation of the reports that had made her retune in the first place.

Silence and stillness were dangerous because into them crept Shibu. She remembered, *"Any other bold questions?" "Maybe."*

Supposing he hadn't left it unspoken?

But he did. Yes, it was the result of too much wine, she felt sure.

She ate her lunch and went for a walk, taking great gulps of air as she did so, as if she'd been locked inside for years. The freshness of the air stung her face and tingled in her lips. She imagined them tingling in response to Shibu's kiss.

No, stop it, she told herself. Then, *I can do what I like in my imagination.*

Back home she made herself a coffee and sat down to read *The White Hotel*. It wasn't a straight-forward read and the sexual language disturbed her – not the fact of it, but the effect of it, because she found it arousing. Now the tingling was in her loins and solar plexus. And her mind was full of Shibu's face as he said, *"Maybe."*

Oh, for fuck's sake. She put the book down and picked up her cigarettes. There were three left in the packet and it was only four-thirty-five. *I could just smoke half*, she told herself.

She went to the back door and lit it. Madeleine looked up at Shibu's window, but it was obscured by light. The same light, through the branches of the beech tree, cast a ghostly aura.

I wish I didn't have such a high sex drive, Madeleine thought. She'd often wondered if it were normal, for how would she know what that was?

She remembered a conversation on the subject with Carol. *"Nothing like marriage for killing your libido,"* Carol had laughingly said.

"P'raps I should get married then," Madeleine had replied in the same manner.

It would certainly be more peaceful without a libido, she thought now. *And one less reason to hate myself. What is it with Shibu? He's not like anyone I ever met before.* Madeleine put the cigarette out, having smoked it all.

Back in the lounge she picked her book up again, but concentration was once again interrupted by the memory of Shibu saying, *"Maybe."*

Madeleine put the book down and gave way to her thoughts. What was it about Shibu? What was it about her, more like? Who wouldn't want him? He was so gentle and polite. And so young, she reminded herself.

Not to mention she was in a relationship. Julian was a good man by society's standards; he took care of the needs of his children, he worked hard and cared about Carrie. And Madeleine cared for him, or at least she had once.

But Shibu. How could she believe that he was in earnest? He was drunk; that was all. And, even if he were in earnest, she could never allow herself a sexual encounter with him. He was too young, too vulnerable; her inability to love would be bound to hurt him. And yet. *Just stop it. You shouldn't even think like this when you're with someone else. Never mind all those other things.*

Madeleine thought of the story of Adam and Eve and the forbidden fruit. The temptation of Adam, the woman at fault. Why was it always the woman's fault?

She wished above all else to conduct herself correctly yet acknowledged that sometimes it was difficult to decide exactly what that was. It was this dilemma that made it easy to understand the attraction of deferring to an organisation like the Church. Shame she was personally unable to subscribe to any such establishment, because sometimes, like now, the demands of her body were so great they endangered her ability to remain true to her conscience. Even as she thought this Madeleine was teased by the hint of Shibu's sensual mouth and the allusion of his touch. And the mere idea of him was more exciting than the actual experience of her current lover.

She headed for the music collection but once in front of it couldn't decide on which genre would improve the mood: rock to fuel it and burn it out, or classical to calm it down. Eventually she chose Kumar's mix, which sent her to the kitchen with dancing hips and bouncing feet. They were interrupted by a call from Julian, by the end of which Madeleine's mood was entirely sobered, more by her disappointment at hearing his reassurances not to return to his wife, than to the knowledge that he would.

She was eating dinner when Shibu walked through the door and she saw immediately his confusion was as great as her own. In Madeleine it elicited a feeling of responsibility; she then, must behave as an adult. Alongside this emotion there was another: resignation; it was like unwrapping the gift and finding exactly what was expected inside.

"Hi. Good day at work?"

"Not too bad."

Madeleine watched him as he left the room, feeling his energy linger in the roots of her hair.

In the shower Shibu closed his eyes against the shampoo and found Madeleine behind them, again. If he had been a Hindu he would have believed himself bewitched, but the Christian boy knew only too well that the temptation was born of his own flesh, and it was entirely up to him to control it. True, she was beautiful and sensual too, but he had seen other women who were that and never felt such a keen longing for them. Maybe it was because she was foreign and this made her seem exotic. Or because she expressed herself more freely than the women he had previously encountered, or perhaps it was simply their close proximity to each other. In that case he should find another address. Yet maybe God was testing him, and if his lust forced him to leave, he would have failed. Besides, he liked living here.

He dried himself, feeling angry with the erection that had happened in response to his thoughts, and for a second, he considered the possibility that the temptation was not of God's making after all but of the Devil's. And she, with her condemnation of the Church, was his handmaid. His heart and mind were full of contradictions. The only things of which he felt sure were the fact of God and his own longing for Madeleine.

Before he went downstairs Shibu knelt and prayed for guidance and felt strengthened by it. It lasted exactly as long as it took him to descend to the kitchen and set his eyes upon Madeleine, who was loading the dishwasher. She stood up and closed the door then turned to face him. The red dress she was wearing hung just below her knees; he noticed how shapely her calves were and how tightly the dress clung around her breasts, which weren't large but looked firm. He forced closed the door which began to open in his imagination to allow glimpses of the body beneath the clothes.

"There you are," she said, smiling warmly, "I thought you'd been washed down the plug hole."

"Excuse me?"

"Never mind, daft joke. How was your day? No hangover, you say."

"Maybe little bit sleepy but otherwise I'm okay."

"That's good. Was Carol at work today? And she's okay, is she? I don't see much of her since she started that job."

"I think she very busy, she tell to me like this. She say when she go home she have to cook and clean and everything because her husband and childrens don't do."

"Sounds about right. Her husband lost his job last year and most of his confidence with it, poor man. Carol understands, but sometimes I think she is cross with him anyway."

"Yes, I think that correct. Carol is very good woman with big heart."

"Yes, she is. She has been my friend since school. I should go and see her a bit more often, really."

"In Kerala is like this. Kerala peoples like to spend time talking with their friends."

"D'you think English people don't then?"

"I think *you* do, but peoples in work with me talk much about television and Facebook."

Madeleine thought back to her school days, remembering dumping her bag and shoes, hurriedly changing her clothes and rushing over to Carol's house. Then of her late teens and early adulthood, during which she spent copious amounts of time in heated conversation with her peers, soul-searching and philosophising on life aided by large quantities of cannabis and alcohol. She thought fondly of herself and Sean, sitting crossed-legged on his bed, setting the world to rights. His bed was their soap-box, from which they countered the arguments of their friends who were sprawled on the bedroom floor. She wondered if it was really the case that virtual relationships were replacing face-to-face ones.

"Personally, I'm not a big fan of either of those," she said. "I guess Facebook is another way of connecting with people, but I'm a bit suspicious of it. You never know who might be watching when you're online. And it all seems a bit odd to me. Telling the whole of the virtual world every detail of your day. I'd rather phone someone, or better still visit them. So, am I more like a Kerala person?"

"I think, yes."

Madeleine put the kettle on. "Tea? Sorry, coffee?" she offered.

"No, thank you, just I eat in a minute." He began to prepare his meal.

"There is one good thing could come from computer relationships, of course."

"What?"

"It could solve the population problem."

"Means?"

"There won't be many babies born by virtual sex."

Shibu laughed. "This good idea for India."

"Exactly, just remember it was mine if you're thinking of selling it."

The air was light with their laughter. Madeleine made her tea then went to the sink with the spoon. Shibu's arrival at the sink, though coincidental, seemed synchronised with Madeleine's turning away from it. Their faces were no more than inches apart; each inhaled the other's out breath. In the second it took for Madeleine to sidestep, the future was revealed with all the clarity of the mystic's crystal ball.

"Oh! Sorry."

Her words scorched Shibu's nostrils. He swallowed hard as if in danger of suffocation.

"Is okay."

"I'm going to have a cigarette."

Standing in the doorway, looking out into the garden, Madeleine shivered in response to the chill of the air and the expectation in her body. The future consummation of their mutual desire was totally known to her body now, but her mind still refused to believe it.

Shibu's meal preparation was noisy and induced the impression of an ordinary domestic scene, but there was nothing mundane in the match between them and there was an inevitability of disappointment in the end.

Shibu still experienced the taste of Madeleine's breath, which continued to tease the back of his throat, and her smell lingered in his nostrils. Never before had he enjoyed such close proximity to the object of his desire; he had only ever been taunted by distant flirtation. Although Madeleine acted with propriety Shibu knew from her face that she felt the same as him.

When he heard her come in and go to the bathroom, he turned his cooking down to a simmer.

Madeleine returned to the kitchen to find Shibu standing with his back against the sink; his arms were extended as he gripped the work surface either side so that the sinews in his biceps were exaggerated.

She smiled and said, "Meal not ready yet?"

"Yes, is ready. Just I wait."

"What for."

"I think maybe you will like some?"

"That's kind, but not today, thank you."

He didn't move.

"Is there something else?"

"Just I wonder, do you have wine?"

"You want more wine?"

Shibu shrugged. "If is okay."

There were only two bottles left in the rack. Normally she liked to replace the stock before it got this low, but things weren't normal at the moment. She uncorked it and poured them both a glass, giving Shibu a larger one.

"So, you've noticed it improves the taste of food?"

"Uh huh."

"I'll leave you to it. Don't drink it all, I'll be back for more in a minute."

The only reason for leaving the kitchen was not knowing what to do. *Don't have any more wine, for a start,* she told herself.

She stood gazing out of the living room window onto the empty street. She was drawn to the aura of light from one of the street lamps, imagining a mackintoshed, cigarette-smoking detective standing beneath it.

What could possibly be gained from a liaison with Shibu? How many times had she discussed this with herself and come to the same conclusion? And yet. The way her body felt just thinking of him. No one else had ever provoked such a feeling.

And Julian? She had never cheated on anyone. *You could finish it with him*, she thought. *But I can't do that. Finish with him for another man?* She'd never done that either.

Into her mind crept the thought, *It's over with Julian anyway.*

She took a deep sigh, returned to the kitchen.

Shibu was sitting eating. He'd drunk most of the wine she'd poured him, but the remainder was as she'd left it. She sipped hers, keeping her back to Shibu. Neither of them spoke. Unable to bear the expectant air Madeleine went for a cigarette, hoping and fearing that Shibu would have left the kitchen by the time she returned.

He hadn't. He was cleaning up, increasingly to her standard. When he'd done he turned and looked at Madeleine. They held each other's gaze without talking.

Madeleine giggled like a teenager. "You seem like you're waiting for something."

"I am."

"Oh. What's that, then?"

"I think you know."

She took a long, slow breath in and exhaled even more slowly. "Yes, I think I do."

"Then?"

She repeated the breath. "Then – I'm not sure yet. Are you?"

Shibu shrugged.

"There's Julian."

Now he nodded, and looked so much like a disappointed child that Madeleine wanted to rush to him immediately.

"And there's the difference in our ages."

"I don't think so this matters."

"And the fact that one day, maybe even soon, you'll be leaving."

Shibu nodded again.

"So, for now it's…" She hesitated, waiting to be talked into it.

Shibu continued to look intently at her, but said nothing.

"I mean, I'd need to be sure it's what you really want."

Still he voiced nothing, but his eyes said much.

So, it was up to her now. One step closer and she would take a great leap. Her breathing was hard and fast, and no amount of effort could calm it.

They were staring into each other's souls.

And then her phone rang. She knew it would be Julian, and she knew she could return it later, but somehow it seemed like an alarm, waking her to her senses.

She spoke to him in the living room and when she returned to the kitchen it was empty.

Alone Madeleine drifted on thoughts which were barely that; like impressionist paintings they only made sense from certain angles. Besides, they were old and over-evaluated: Madeleine not only knew what she wanted; she knew she would do it.

Never mind an act of infidelity; even thinking and feeling as she did was such. She'd have to end it with Julian imminently. She feared Julian's distress, but it had to be done.

Perhaps she'd be spared the need and Julian would come on Friday simply to tell her it was over because Carrie needed him more. That was what she hoped for as she began her getting ready for bed routine, all the while keeping part of her consciousness on Shibu's whereabouts.

The animal part of her longed for satisfaction at that very moment; the spiritual part of her still felt inclined to refuse altogether. All of the old arguments were underlined by the fact that from the start she would know this could never be more than a temporary liaison. At the outset of every other relationship Madeleine had the intention of it being a long-term commitment, and at the end of every one her conscience berated her lack of the same and echoed with the labels of her past: 'user' and 'whore'.

That night a sound sleep was prohibited by both men, who played on Madeleine's mind for very different reasons.

Desire burned Shibu's body. Self-contempt weighted his soul. On his knees he prayed, forcing his mind away from lustful thoughts and images to those of the divine and suffering Christ. Rarely was he granted direct experience of God, and, in his mind, there was not the slightest doubt that this was proof of how weak was his own faith, but worse than this today, the other image kept creeping in. His body responded with a desire that rose and steadfastly remained to taunt him. He remained on his knees as he opened his eyes and slowly, quietly, relieved himself, all the while keeping an ear on Madeleine's whereabouts for fear of her hearing. He was grateful to her for refusing him but knew she would soon acquiesce.

Afterwards he returned to the prayer and, with redoubled guilt, once more sought communion with God, but once more discovered her impression was the stronger and his desire for her had hardly lessened. In bed Shibu cried from the shame of it all.

Chapter Nine

In shame Shibu had fallen asleep; in shame he awoke. He crept quietly to the bathroom, performed his ablutions then, in the same manner returned to his room and waited until Madeleine went into the bathroom. The rush of the shower heralded a safe exit, of which he took full advantage, so that he didn't stop to eat breakfast but poured dry cereal into a plastic container, grabbed his things and left the house fifteen minutes ahead of time.

His journey to work was always accompanied by a telephone call to his parents. This morning the sound of their voices made him feel all the more remorseful; it took no more than the mere sound of them to act as a reprimand and reinstate the child in him. There was no doubt as to their advice should he have sought it, or even had he not, if they had known the situation. Shibu decided he would ask the Filipino boy if there was still a room to spare in his shared house. Yet, although there were several opportunities throughout the day, the question was never asked. As he made his way home – for it very much felt that way now – Shibu told himself another story; it was that Carol might have overheard his conversation with the Filipino boy, and he wasn't yet ready with a suitable excuse as to why he wanted to leave his current lodgings.

The empty kitchen confirmed what Madeleine already knew from the atmosphere. Her initial disappointment was accompanied by relief that the sexual boundary remained intact; how much greater would her insecurity be if this moment had arrived post-coitus? The thought reminded her of the first time and the agonising three days' wait until they met again. Not only because at the she time erroneously considered herself in love, but also because she feared the loss of Paul's respect and that there was truth behind her father's oft-spoken words: "*Sex is for marriage – men don't respect easy women.*" Words that were reinforced by the overheard accusations regarding her mother's fidelity. The word 'whore', muffled only slightly by the closed door, echoed through the chambers of her ears and heart.

Even though Madeleine now knew herself incapable of love, and believed in sexual freedom as long as all parties agreed to the terms, in the very core of her being she lacked self-respect to such an extent that only a lifelong union stood any chance of eradicating it. But fate, it seemed, had other plans for her, and any such relationship remained elusive.

With Paul she had almost consented to marriage yet soon realised it wasn't love she felt so much as the desire for it. And the sensible part of her knew he'd already become too accustomed to maintaining control with his fists for that to ever change. Yet, she had no trust in herself that, should she be the one in control, she wouldn't use it to her own advantage. Control, or be controlled; neither was right.

So, the scene was set: through all her relationships thereafter she remained just distant enough to protect them both, hoping every time that this was the person who was happy with exactly that. Julian, wounded by his marriage and still dependent upon it in so many ways, had seemed at first to be that person, but latterly he was giving himself up more and more to Madeleine.

The thought of Julian disturbed her, knowing, as she did, that the next time they met would be the last. Another end, another failure.

The house became an awkward place in the next few days as both Madeleine and Shibu struggled to mark and maintain boundaries. They moved around each other as if they were dancing. Meeting in doorways and the hallway they'd brush lightly past, almost touching, the air between them vibrating with expectancy and ringing with their apologies, which were spoken softly under lowered sideways glances. In the kitchen turn-taking was cautiously observed, pots and pans, plates and crockery piled and washed separately, individual mealtimes strictly adhered to.

Madeleine hid in the lounge, camouflaged by music, while Shibu took to his room and made lengthy and pointless calls to his friends. Yet, whilst at work, each found the other in the spaces between chores, and the lunchtime tastes were tinged by the name that lingered on each of their lips.

Their midweek day off coincided. Madeleine began hers with a session of yoga. Into the oil burner she dropped three drops of lavender, into the CD player she loaded reiki healing and into her mind she coaxed calm. But it gave in all too easily to even the tiniest noise from above her head, so at every moment Madeleine knew where Shibu was and her imagination responded to the clues that kept her guessing at what he was doing. She knew exactly how long he was in the bathroom and guessed at the prayers he performed in the near silence that followed, the only sound a groan from the elderly floorboards on which she pictured him kneeling.

The day was crisp and bright but not yet cold. After the yoga session Madeleine decided to go for a walk, partly to enjoy the crisp autumn day, but mostly to avoid Julian, who often stopped mid-delivery for coffee when she was home on a weekday. She took a route through the park to town then back along the river to home.

Enlivened now, and sure she'd missed Julian because the letters were on the table, she pulled her hair onto her head and clipped it there, then, donning dungarees, armed herself with cleaning equipment.

Outside the nursing home Shibu hovered uncomfortably; if someone saw him, he would have no choice but to carry through his plan and ask the Filipino boy about the room. But he still wasn't totally committed to it. His journey there was born of fear, because he was almost tripping over the sexual tension in the house. If this was a test from God it was too much for him. If he didn't move out, he was going to give in. A face appeared at the window and he flinched away as if he were a criminal; when he realised it was that of a resident, who would neither be able to see this far nor remember his face even if she could, he felt immense relief. He turned quickly and walked away.

He slowed his pace as he approached the house, subdued both by heavy bags and by disappointment in himself. The gate was closed, which puzzled him because he knew he'd left it open in order not to have to put down bags on his return, and he knew Julian had been before he left because he'd put the letters on the table himself. As he opened the gate it produced its usual creak and at the same time Madeleine appeared at the window shaking her duster from it. She smiled and signalled something to him; he didn't understand until the door opened a second before he arrived at it.

"Oh, thank you," he said.

"You looked rather loaded up."

There was a slight hesitation before she moved sideways to allow him entry. With her hair piled on her head she looked even wilder, even more desirable.

"Shall I help you put the shopping away?" she asked.

"I think you too busy."

"Never too busy for you." Madeleine's tone was playful and her eyes were ablaze with exactly the thing he wanted.

"Oh!"

Madeleine took two of the bags from him and as she did so their hands briefly touched. Shibu jumped slightly in response then tried to recover the situation by saying, "I think those the heaviest."

"Don't worry, I'm stronger than I look."

Madeleine first emptied the bags onto the table and then she opened the cupboard in which the tinned and dried goods would go. Immediately a knot of anxiety tightened in her stomach and throat at the sight of the chaos therein. Madeleine used few tins, but those that she did were stacked according to type and, as far as possible, in alphabetical order. Now, putting Shibu's tins away, she found herself creating order.

"Oh, thank you for do this," he said.

"This way you can see what you have without having to move things around."

"Yes, it make sense, just I too lazy."

"Maybe I'm too obsessive."

They stood and looked at each other intently for several seconds. It was Madeleine who looked away first, but when she returned her gaze she again met his eyes. He took a step closer. Madeleine moved neither her body nor her eyes; she knew they were full of the same intent as his and that his mouth tingled with the same desire as hers, but from it came something unexpected. "Excuse me – just I need to get to cupboard."

"Oh! Oh, sorry. Right! I… I guess I'll leave you to it then."

Now she cleaned frantically. She sensed Shibu standing behind her on the landing and knew he watched for a while, but she couldn't bear to look at him again so soon.

Shibu knew that she knew he was there; he almost reached out to touch her, almost called her name. He was moved by what he'd seen in her eyes in the second that followed his defensive, untruthful words, "*just I need to get to the cupboard*"; it was the flicker of self-contempt. An emotion to which he was himself no stranger.

Consequently, he took another step back and only cautiously pushed at the barriers, while Madeleine played a defensive game in return, batting back just enough to save herself from further embarrassment and buy her time to work out what the new rules were. The game excited yet disquieted her and in the back of her mind Julian remained, like a third competitor.

When he arrived on Saturday evening it was with flowers and heavy mood. Madeleine felt annoyed with the flowers because they softened her towards him; she felt sympathy for his disposition. She put the flowers in a vase.

"Thank you; they're lovely."

"You deserve them with all you put up with from me."

She didn't answer.

"With the boys and… well… well, you know with… I won't go back to her this time, though, I promise."

There was an opening here, but somehow it seemed so cruel when Julian was down in spirits and trying so hard to please her. She'd have to have a drink first, just one to calm her nerves without turning her into someone who would get it all wrong.

"Beer or wine? Meal's almost ready." She poured one of each and sampled the food. "In fact, I'd say it's ready." Now she began dishing up.

Julian pushed the food around his plate and took child-sized bites.

"Not hungry?"

"No. Sorry. I've been at home before I came here. Things aren't good."

The word 'home' grated on Madeleine. "If you feel you need—"

"I can't, can I? Can't help feeling I've abandoned the boys, though."

"You've hardly done that, you're there every day."

"That's not how she sees it; unless I live there, I've abandoned them in her eyes, and she's always telling the boys so."

This was awful. She must hurry up and say what she needed to. She felt the words form in the back of her throat – *Sorry, Julian, I know the timing's bad, but it's over* – and took a sip of wine to help them slide out, but instead the wine washed them back down.

She reached for more.

If the second drink had been avoided then the third could not have followed. She took it in the lounge and then snuggled back on the sofa. She inhaled a large gulp of air, as if it would help consolidate the decision, then she breathed out long and slow as she said, "Julian, I—"

"God, you look beautiful tonight."

"Huh! I think you drank too much beer."

"Don't say that. I know I don't tell you enough, but you know that I find you beautiful."

"Oh, Julian! I'm afraid I'm going to hurt you." She put her hand on his shoulder and rubbed it gently.

"You never could." He grabbed hold of her hand and kissed it as he pulled her towards him.

"No, wait!"

"Why? What's the matter?"

"I need a minute, I—"

Now he gently kissed her mouth. At that moment Madeleine was more acutely aware of her need to end this relationship than she had ever been. She pulled away.

"Something the matter?" Julian didn't wait for an answer; he began kissing her again. "I want you; I need you," he whispered into her neck as he ran his tongue along it.

I don't want to be needed, Madeleine thought, but she said, "You mustn't rely on me."

"Oh, but I do, and I love you."

Madeleine closed her eyes, looking desperately for her resolve, but instead she found obligation, and it was underlined by the overpowering desire in her body. She tried once more pulling away as she said, "Julian, I—"

He pulled her back and kissed her more urgently.

"Not here," she whispered. "Anyway, I don't have my cap in."

"Okay, I'll go up and wait for you then."

The haze of red wine made her clumsy as she put the cap in and clouded her reason, although she knew whatever she did now, she would hate herself in the morning. How could she refuse Julian what she had just promised him? How could she refuse her own body what it needed? How could she allow Julian to satisfy a craving that wasn't for him? How could she finish with him if she did this? How could she fail to finish with him? She went to the bedroom, feeling the deepest self-contempt and still unsure of what she would do. But her body knew what it needed. Like a starving animal it devoured Julian, leaving not a crumb behind.

"Wow!" he said when it was over. "I should bring you flowers more often." Now he cradled her from behind, his hands upon her breasts, and in seconds was breathing low in sleep.

Madeleine lay still and stiff, her desire hardly abated and her self-disgust immense. Despite the wine and her best efforts sleep remained elusive, and every near miss was punctuated by the accusation, '*whore!*' It echoed in her memory, but the reality of it was current and she had just proven again that it was part of her fundamental way of being. She eased away from Julian and climbed out of the bed, feeling the evidence of his love and her prostitution run from her. She headed for the bathroom.

Fearing to wake either of the men with running water she allowed it only to trickle into the bath. She opened and closed the cupboard door as quietly as possible as she gathered together the necessary materials and climbed into the tepid bath, keeping the temperature deliberately cool because this was not a reward.

First, she washed then she cut. Each slash was accompanied by the whispery voice in her memory, "*Little whore, look what you made me do,*" and this time the door began to open to allow a glimpse of what she worked so hard at forgetting. She tried to force it closed, but the push from the other side was stronger and the images too insistent to ignore as they leapt from unconscious to conscious, forcing every detail of the replay on her. She responded angrily, slicing again and again, until eventually the memories subsided, overcome by the sharpness of the razor. They drained away through the plug hole, watered down with the blood flow, and the resultant weakness in her body felt relaxing. She dressed the wounds and then herself in loose T-shirt, took a sheet and blanket from the airing cupboard, and spent the rest of the night on the sofa.

"Why're you here?" Julian woke her with a cup of tea and a kiss on the forehead. "Did I snore?"

"No. I couldn't sleep and didn't want to disturb you."

"You wouldn't have disturbed me last night, I had an exceedingly good sleep thanks to you. I'll go and get the boys straight after breakfast. Okay?"

"Okay."

"Something wrong? Still sleepy, I guess."

Madeleine considered asking him not to come back and not to bring the boys, but she wanted to see them one last time and she wanted to end it as kindly as possible. The words were so small – *It's over* – but the impact so big.

"Yes, I'm still sleepy. We'll talk later, eh?"

"Sure thing."

Madeleine was grateful for the short absence before Julian returned with his sons, because the last thing she needed was time to think.

"Let's go out," she suggested. "Lunch and then the cinema, my treat."

"Yeah, great!" Harry said.

"Can I choose the film?" Jack asked.

Julian ruffled his son's hair. "We have to choose something together, preferably something we'll all like."

"Oh, Dad!"

"He's right," Madeleine said. "That will be an impossible task, but if we can find a film that one of you likes and the other finds acceptable that'll do. Julian, you and I will just have to put up with it."

The more cheerful Julian seemed the more guilty Madeleine felt. As they walked the streets together looking like a real family, her guilt extended to include the two boys. The family problems were neither her fault nor responsibility, she knew, and yet she also knew that they would experience some sense of loss when she left their lives. And she'd miss them.

"It's been a great day, Maddie, thanks for suggesting that; they really needed something with all that's going on at home."

Julian's appreciation made Madeleine feel like an unexposed liar.

"Please hurry back," she said, "I need to talk to you."

The last remark was intended to banish any idea that she was urgent for his company, but it appeared to go unnoticed and he walked away from the house in a jaunty manner, teasing the boys with light, playful punches. Madeleine watched, feeling like the wicked stepmother whose plan was about to come to fruition.

Julian didn't hurry back. "I'm sorry, it was hard to get away. I hope you have eaten because I ate with them. I should've phoned, I know."

"I'm not hungry. Anyway, I can eat later when you've gone."

"I thought I might stay again tonight."

"No, Julian, you can't."

The slight sting of her injured legs martyred Madeleine just enough to get her through the next sentence.

"You can't stay anymore. It's over."

"What?"

"I'm sorry to just blurt it out like this, but… I… there's no easy way to… I tried to tell you last night, but—"

"Last night? Last night was the best in ages."

"I know. I'm sorry. It was… I'm sorry."

"Don't spoil it with sorry. I don't understand. Is there someone else?"

"No." It was said a little too quickly.

"Then why?"

"It's just not right for me anymore."

"Then last night?"

Throughout the conversation they had sat at the table and looked directly at each other; now Madeleine cast her gaze downwards.

"Was very emotional for us both and now we have a good memory to end it on."

"What?" Julian stood up and wandered the room, his hands in his pockets, his head hung low. "You were pretending?"

"No."

He turned to look at her again, his face stern. "How could your heart be in it if you knew it was over?"

Now he lent forwards in a manner sufficiently aggressive as to excite a little fear in Madeleine. "Sure had me fooled, lady. A nice memory? Are there no more?"

"Of course, there are, but… I didn't mean. Let's not do this, please."

"*I'm* not doing anything."

"I don't want to get into blaming and stuff."

"No, you wouldn't want to take any responsibility." He sighed hard and then sat down. "I know I have put my family first too many times—"

"That's how it should be. And yes, sometimes it has felt like you weren't sure what you wanted; but like I said I don't want to get into who did what. Please, just accept it's over."

"Two weeks ago, one week ago, even, it wouldn't have been such a shock, but today, after... after last night." The last few words were spoken in a soft, almost pleading tone.

"I understand that confused you; I shouldn't have done it."

"No. It has made me think we still have something really strong and worth working on."

Madeleine looked at her feet. She dared not look at him for fear of losing herself in his distress. "Sorry!"

Julian thumped the table; Madeleine jumped in response.

"Right. Goodbye then," he said. "Have a nice life."

Then he stormed out of the room. Madeleine heard the door open and felt the draught of chill air, but a second later he was back.

"Just realised, I owe you something." Onto the table Julian threw a fist full of coins. "That's for last night." Then he slammed both doors as he left.

For a second or two Madeleine sat in shocked silence. The echo of the coins still trembled through her psyche and was quickly joined by the voice of blame relentless in its condemnation. Slowly her bottom lip began to quiver, in time with the rhythm, and the tears to flow. *Snivelling bitch!* the voice denounced. *No good feeling sorry for yourself, it's me you should feel sorry for, making me do this.* Madeleine bit her hand hard and slapped herself around the face several times, attempting to silence the tears, but they just kept flowing.

When she heard Shibu's key in the lock Madeleine panicked; she had no desire for him to see her this way, so she went quickly into the garden and lit a cigarette. She heard him enter the kitchen and felt him looking for her. She sensed him leave again, but just to be sure she checked there was a light in his room. Then she went to the bathroom, where she cleaned her teeth and washed the tearstains from her face.

Feeling much calmer now Madeleine composed a text to Julian: "*I am truly sorry for hurting you. I hope you will soon recover and, like me, remember the good times. Madeleine.*"

Twice she added and erased a line which referred to the night before, but everything she wrote sounded like a lie. She saved the text in drafts, deciding to check it again the following morning before sending it. Feeling much more composed now, but more than a little sad, she went to the lounge and sought out some music.

Into the space left by Julian she poured memories. Good ones to remind her of why she had planned her arrival on the doorstep to coincide with his letter delivery – now it would be necessary to do the opposite, of course – and bad ones to reinforce her decision. The loss of him felt like the death of a very sick relative, whose inevitable passing, though sad, was also a relief.

Worse was the solidification of her feelings towards herself, strengthened so much by Julian's last act of defence. She understood, of course, and forgave him. She just hoped she was soon able to forgive herself. The crescendo of *The Tempest*, towards its climax, brought with it the other sadness; the greatest loss of her life now crept in between the notes and erupted from her heart in violent sobs.

The music warned Shibu of a tragedy and to be quick with his chores, but he wasn't quick enough. He had only just begun to wash the dishes when Madeleine entered to the kitchen. He turned around to acknowledge her; her distress remained evident.

"What happened?" he asked.

"It's over with Julian."

"Ah!" Shibu felt the slight blush rise in his cheeks and excitement tinged with fear in his loins. "I'm sorry for that. I think you little bit sad." Despite himself he meant what he said.

"A little, yes, but it had to end."

Embarrassed now, Shibu turned back to the washing-up.

Madeleine went outside for her final cigarette; upon her return the kitchen was empty, so she stood for a while feeling acutely aware of the silence and the space, then turned off the lights and went to bed.

Chapter Ten

In the days that immediately followed self-hatred coloured Madeleine's world in grey. Outside it was bright, but the trees wore fewer and fewer leaves, the air began to feel chilly and the sun to retreat a little earlier every day; all of these darkened Madeleine's world and induced in her the sense that time was running out. In a few weeks it would be Christmas and the end of another year. *What*, she asked herself, *have I achieved in my life?* She had done nothing that was of any worth. She was a worthless individual with a worthless life, not even capable of achieving the most ordinary of things and totally incapable of maintaining a relationship. Julian had been right to treat her like a whore, because that was how she behaved.

I don't have to do this anymore, she told herself. *I can do without sex.* Even as she thought it, she knew it wasn't true. The desire was sometimes so strong it was a distraction to her normal everyday activities, and masturbation made her feel no less ashamed.

Shame drove her to the comfort of the razor. The first cuts had only just scabbed over and so tingled and itched by turns. The new ones were blissfully sharp, sharp enough to dull the word 'whore'.

Humiliation trickled away with the blood and cleansing tears soon followed. Awareness of Shibu crept between the sobs, his humble nature making it clear to Madeleine that this time the desire was less about sex and more about him.

But I can't, I mustn't. No, no, no. She sobbed and rocked herself. *He's too young, too gentle. I can't.* She dressed her wounds, then herself and carried on with the day as near to normally as she ever did.

Avoiding Julian was easy. The post never arrived before she left for work or after she returned, and on her days off she was careful to either be out of the house for the morning, or so lost in housework no awareness could break through. Yet, there was still some sense of sorrow and nostalgia at the site of the letters he left. For a while she anticipated a personal note from him, and felt a mixture of relief and disappointment when there wasn't.

Avoiding Shibu was harder. A cat and mouse game became necessary. She set her alarm early and hurried her routine to be out of the bathroom before his alarm went off, all the while keeping an ear out for it. The time between its ringing and his leaving his room seemed an eternity. The click of the bathroom door was the call for breakfast, feet on the landing a call to retreat from the house, or to her room. Twice she sensed him taking his time on the landing. She held her breath. And held still. The anticipation felt like waiting to be found in a game of hide and seek. Except she mustn't be found. She feared his ardour and its cooling in equal measure. The one because it would test her resolve, the other because it would disappoint her.

Shibu was puzzled by Madeleine's behaviour and more than a little ashamed of himself. Both because he supposed he might have offended her with his advances, but also because he found her current behaviour made her all the more beguiling.

When she was alive Nitty had been Madeleine's main confidant at the end of her affairs. Daily Madeleine had sought her counsel in telephone calls that could last as long as an hour. But the end of the affair with Julian resulted in no more than two fifteen-minute calls; the first to Sean, the second to Kumar. The latter of whom arrived the same evening with wine and sympathy.

"So how d'you feel now?" Kumar asked.

"I'm okay. It was me who ended it. It had to happen; it wasn't right."

"So, no regrets?"

"Some, but not for the reasons you might expect."

Immersed in wine and a calm ambience and with no intention of doing so, Madeleine vented her feelings of self-disgust.

Kumar listened without comment until her tirade ended then said, "These are such harsh words, you are none of these things and it hurts me to hear you say them."

"Well, sorry, but that's how I really feel."

"I had no idea."

"Why would you?"

"We've known each other a long time."

"But never that well."

"Obviously not."

Kumar sighed deeply and looked hurt. Madeleine regretted her words, realising now they could be misconstrued. They were sitting on the sofa, she in a half-lotus, he almost reclined. She reached out for Kumar's hand; he took hold of hers and pulled it to his chest.

"Sorry!" Madeleine said. "You've been a wonderful friend to me, never think otherwise, it's just that – that isn't the kind of stuff you tell many people. It all sounds so self-pitying."

"Not so, just very sad. I can't imagine what makes you feel that way. You're a beautiful and popular person."

"Thank you."

She pursed her lips and lowered her head, feeling exposed and vulnerable. Then she launched herself from sitting to standing. "What d'you fancy listening to now?"

"More of you."

"Nah, that's boring. You choose some music or I will – don't say you haven't been warned."

Kumar's laugh was unconvincing.

Shibu came in through the front door. His intention was to go straight to his room, but Kumar called out to him.

He kept his eyes on the floor until he was certain that the only gaze they would meet would be Kumar's. They shook hands vigorously.

"Won't you join us for a drink?" Kumar invited.

Shibu shrugged. "I haven't eaten yet."

"One won't hurt."

Shibu could feel the magnetic pull of Madeleine's presence. He was powerless to resist a glance in her direction.

"Okay, just one then."

"Good man." Kumar handed him a large glass of wine. "How's your day been?"

"Same like any day."

"Busy?"

"Always."

"That good?"

"Makes time pass quick."

"And is that good?"

Shibu shrugged.

"Funny how we like to fill our time up. Shouldn't we really be savouring it instead?"

"Ideally we could fill it up doing the things we enjoy, then we can savour it and be busy," Madeleine offered.

Shibu drained his glass; he needed to escape.

"Guess I'd better go," Kumar said a few minutes later. "You can call me anytime, Madeleine, you know that, don't you?"

"Yes, thank you."

The doorstep hug was a little more intense than usual. It made Madeleine feel uncomfortable; she assumed it to be born of pity.

Now she felt the need to check in with Shibu. She stood for a moment in the doorway just watching him.

There was no fat on him, that much was obvious, despite the unflattering cut of the tracksuit bottoms he wore. She wanted to go up to him and test the theory by placing both arms around his girth and touching his stomach. She wanted to run her hands the length of his arms and then interlock the fingers of his hands with hers. Yet, along with these desires came the sense of herself as a predatory animal, admiring the thing upon which she was about to pounce and deprive of its life. For an instant she understood the transference of energy which occurs when prey becomes lost to its captor, each defeated by the other, each made victim by hunger, such, it now seemed, was the promise of their sexual union.

She entered the kitchen fully, saying, "Hi, it seems ages since I saw you properly, how're you doing?"

"Same like always. How you?"

"Fine."

Shibu kept his eyes on his food, feeling unnerved by the air of expectancy in the room, but then he remembered there was something he could talk about and said, "Today morning I saw Julian."

"You did? Did he speak? Did he seem okay?"

"Yes, he speak. He look same like he always do."

"Good. That's good."

The atmosphere became tense again.

"I'll have a quick ciggy."

She took long, deep draws, responding to warm tingles on the inside and the chill air on the outside. The heat in the kitchen was welcoming.

"It's getting cold out there."

Shibu didn't reply.

"Be back in a minute. Just give my teeth a quick clean."

The dishes were washed. The kitchen was tidy, the way Madeleine liked it; Shibu knew he should go to his room now. He got up and strolled over to the window and closed the blind; he remained there, quite still, with his back to the door. He heard Madeleine return. The feel of her behind him sent his heart pumping at a pace that made him dizzy. Taking deep breaths to calm it, he turned around.

Madeleine smiled at him, holding his gaze a little too long.

"Can I have more, please?" Shibu nodded his head at the open bottle of wine.

"Sure."

He poured two glasses, offered her one and took a large gulp from his own.

Madeleine took a sip from hers. "You're supposed to drink it slowly."

"You tell to me before, but I drink like this." He took another gulp, almost draining the glass.

"You'll be pissed at this rate."

Shibu didn't reply. He stood perfectly still. And perfectly quiet.

"You look like you're waiting for something," Madeleine said.

"I waiting for you."

"For me?"

"Yes."

Madeleine took a step towards him and looked him directly in the eye. "What d'you want from me?"

He shrugged.

"You don't know what you want?"

Shibu shrugged again. "Maybe."

He took a step towards her; simultaneously Madeleine took another step forward; a second later they were in each other's arms. The room stilled under their embrace as their mouths softly explored each other's. The rustle of clothes beneath their hands was deafening.

"Is this what you wanted?" Madeleine whispered between kisses.

"Yes."

Their kisses were deep and soft, but they explored each other cautiously. They pulled away from each other and each drank a little more wine. This time it was Shibu who pulled Madeleine into an embrace and resumed kissing. And this time with more urgency. Madeleine was aware that he was shaking.

"You're scared?"

"I have no experience."

"Oh! You mean you're…?"

"Yes, I am virgin."

The news was like a fist in the stomach. Madeleine kissed him very gently. "You are sure, though?"

"Yes, I sure."

"I don't want you to regret it."

"Then I won't."

Madeleine stalled for time with a sip of wine. It had hardly passed her lips when Shibu pulled her into another deep kiss.

"Shall we go to my room?" she whispered.

"I bring wine."

Leading the way Madeleine felt a little like she was a mother leading her child astray; all of her objections regarding his age and status seemed redoubled in light of this latest revelation. It didn't feel right to continue, yet, having gone this far, it didn't feel right not to.

She closed the heavy curtains and sat down on the bed. Shibu did the same, then gently pushed her onto her back in the midst of kissing. Madeleine calculated in the back of her mind whether she needed to stop him long enough to put in her cap, but he was urging her on so fast that stopping, even for a few minutes, felt inappropriate. *It'll be okay*, she told herself. Soon the sensations in her body were so insistent she paid no attention to this or any other thought.

"I want you to be my teacher," Shibu whispered into her ear. And the feel of his breath on her neck was electric. And the taste of his mouth was full of promise.

The promise was fulfilled. He needed no teaching. Although sometimes she led, she as often followed. As they kissed and coaxed and stroked, Shibu spoke softly to her, checking that what he did pleased her, asking how she felt, informing her of how his own body was responding. And Madeleine stopped feeling like this was an adult-child relationship.

The moment he pulled her leggings off Madeleine braced herself for the questions and prepared herself for his accusations, but he said nothing. She flinched as his hands made contact with the scars, felt him hesitate and knew his eyes strayed there. The next minute he was kissing the wounds. Now she relaxed fully and their bodies worked as one. They stopped and started under each other's direction, until first Madeleine and then, a few minutes later, Shibu reached a climax.

They lay in silence for several minutes, holding hands. Both were a little shocked, Shibu by the ease with which he entered manhood and Madeleine by the whole experience.

It was she who broke the silence. "Are you okay?"

"I'm very okay."

"Good. So, I haven't put you off for ever? You will want to do it again?"

"Maybe I can wait." He paused. "Twenty minute."

They both laughed. There was another pause and then Shibu said, "What happen to your legs?"

Madeleine braced herself for a second time. "I cut them with a razor."

"I think that – why you do?"

Now she took a deep breath and swallowed the lump in her throat. "It's hard to explain. Sometimes I hate myself."

Shibu put his arms around her and pulled her close. "How you can hate yourself?"

"Many reasons – this time because of Julian."

"You say you don't love to him?"

"I don't, but I didn't want to hurt him."

For several minutes they lay quietly then Madeleine said, "I've never… no one ever…" She was too embarrassed to use any sexual words. "It's the only time I was satisfied the first time. D'you understand?"

"I think, but I not sure."

"It was very special."

"For me too." Shibu brushed the hair from her face and kissed her forehead. "You tired now?"

"No. Why?"

"Just I ask," he said playfully, running his hands over her breasts.

"You want to do it again?"

"If you want means we can."

"I'd like very much. Let me go to the bathroom first, though." Madeleine took the cap from the dressing table drawer. Stupid to risk it twice in one night, unlikely as it was at her age, especially so near the end of this month's cycle.

Back with Shibu she asked, "Shibu, what do you feel about contraception? You being a Catholic and all?"

"I don't understand."

"Catholics aren't supposed to use birth control, are they?"

"No one tell this to me."

"Really?"

"We have to use. We can't have baby. You take pills to stop?"

"I use a cap, you know what that is?"

"Yes. You use now? I was stupid, I should have ask before."

"Well, you've asked now. Anyway, I'm too old for having babies."

"I don't think so you are."

They made love for a second time. Afterwards Shibu lay so still and quiet Madeleine thought he had fallen immediately asleep, but then he said, "Why you think Catholics can't use contraception?"

"I thought it came directly from the Pope."

"Kerala peoples never heard of this."

So much for the Pope having a direct line to God, then, she thought, but said, "Guess I've made a mistake."

They cradled each other. Shibu felt so at peace that it didn't occur to him to ask for God's forgiveness. He lay listening to the sounds in the room and those emanating from his body. Both were quiet and rhythmic, so eased him gently into sleep.

Madeleine lay awake thinking for an hour or more. Shibu's soft snoring was comforting, so too was the warmth of his breath on her back, but the weight of his arm across her was uncomfortable. No less so was the feeling in her heart. She felt no guilt or shame; the whole experience had felt so natural and inevitable. And yet, there was a tingling in her solar plexus that felt like a warning. It was as if a seed had been planted that was as beautiful and deadly as aconite. A part of her hoped that this would be their one and only liaison, so that it could never be spoiled, but equally she hoped for many more.

Chapter Eleven

Madeleine slept fitfully and woke to the sound of flowing water. It was her bathroom time; the butterflies in her tummy weren't entirely down to this. She climbed out of bed and into her dressing gown, brushed her hair, and waited for Shibu. The click of the bathroom door put her on alert. Like an animal warily sniffing the air she tilted her head towards the door, sensing him pause on the other side, but then heard him go downstairs. She quickly followed, entering the kitchen nervously.

"Morning," Shibu said, smiling softly and lowering his eyes.

"Morning, how're you?"

"Fine." He spoke quietly. "Very fine. How about you?"

"I'm very fine too."

Madeleine made herself a cup of tea and sat down opposite him. He reached out and touched her hand, continuing to do so as he ate the last few mouthfuls of his breakfast. For Madeleine there was reassurance in the action.

"I go now." Shibu picked up his backpack. Madeleine stood up and they exchanged a quick but full kiss and then she knew for sure that the first time was not to be the last.

As soon as the front door closed, she tidied the kitchen to her standard and then went to the bathroom, hardly caring that she was running late. Because of this her hair had only a nominal dry with the dryer, so she felt cold when she stepped outside.

The start of a relationship was always exciting, although often it was tempered with a little apprehension, as the lessons of the past were never neglectful in their reminders of what could go wrong. This time, however, despite knowing from the start that she and Shibu would never be able to be together, Madeleine felt only elation. And it was such that she no longer entered into discussion with herself as to its prudence.

"Sorry I'm late." Madeleine knew her tone sounded anything but.

"Only a bit, but so unlike you," Emily replied.

"Shibu, my lodger, held me up. He was in the bathroom when I needed to be." Shibu, Madeleine loved the sound of his name and loved to be talking about him.

Lunchtime she wrote a text to Carol. "*Thanks for introducing me to Shibu. What a lovely man.*" She read it, reread it and then deleted it.

Checking herself in the mirror before ending her break Madeleine had two thoughts: the first, she looked younger and more relaxed; the second, despite this she was definitely too old for Shibu. But then, what did it matter? He knew her age. And they both knew the arrangement was temporary.

As usual Shibu telephoned his family on the way to work. His parents' voices usually resurrected the child in him and, had he thought about it, he would have imagined the events of the night before would make him feel guilty in response. However, that sentiment was entirely lacking. Instead the sound of his parents' voices instilled in him a sense of his life as separate from theirs and subject only to the demands of his own making. Shibu felt himself fully a man at last.

He arrived home to the sound of Madeleine singing and the smell of cooking. He lingered a while in the hallway, out of sight of Madeleine, savouring the stimulation to his senses. As soon as he entered the kitchen they rushed into each other's embrace.

"I've cooked us dinner," Madeleine said. "You hungry?"

"Yes, for you."

Their kisses were deep. Their hands strayed over each other and under clothes.

"I'll lock the door," Madeleine said.

"I need take shower."

"Be quick then. I'll wait for you in the bedroom."

"Bring wine."

Madeleine obeyed. Taking an uncorked bottle and two glasses with her, she felt some alarm; perhaps he was ashamed of what they were doing. She put her cap in. While she was putting it in, she considered whether or not she needed to get the morning-after pill; the chances of getting pregnant at her age were remote, but maybe best not to take any. She sat on the bed, feeling like she was waiting for her client.

I don't have to do this, she told herself.

But one look at Shibu, dressed only in a towel, changed her mind.

He sat down beside her, kissed her, stroked her naked legs, then gently pulled away to pour wine.

"Why d'you need this?" Madeleine asked.

"I still a little bit scared and I don't want it be too fast." He gulped the drink down in one mouthful then poured another.

She sipped at hers, not wanting to dull her senses.

Soon they were lost in the moment. Their experience of each other was no less intense than the first time. Afterwards they lay cuddling and saying nothing.

It was Madeleine who broke the silence. "I'll be back, just need the bathroom."

While she was gone Shibu took proper notice of the room. This time he was fully aware of the brass-framed bed and of the long, lined curtains that shut the light out so fully. He even took some time to notice the three paintings that hung on the wall, two of which he was sure were Madeleine's, but the third was different: a dark, screaming face that was so expertly painted it scared him. Returning to the room Madeleine noticed him looking at it.

"Good, isn't it?"

"Who do these pictures?"

"I did those two, but the one you were admiring was done by Tom."

"Who Tom?"

"My brother."

"You have brother?"

"Had." She swallowed, putting her left hand to her throat. "I had a brother. He's no longer around."

"Where he?"

"Dead!"

"Oh! Oh! I sorry."

An uncomfortable silence followed.

"It was a long time ago," Madeleine suddenly said.

Shibu pulled her in close and rubbed her back. Madeleine felt the tears stinging her eyes; she didn't want them to flow. Her throat was tight with the effort of holding them in. She sought out Shibu's mouth to help. He kissed her softly. Grateful for his comfort she gave him her body once more.

The next day was Madeleine's monthly Saturday off; there was much to do, but if she was going to get the morning-after pill she should really do it today, although the internet had told her five days, so there was no rush. The local chemist closed at one, but there was yoga to do and there were chores. She decided to use the supermarket pharmacy instead.

She went there before starting the chores.

"I need some ellaOne." Her voice was almost a whisper.

"Ah, we don't keep anything like that. I'll phone the emergency chemists and see if they have any."

Waiting Madeleine felt on the one hand like a naughty schoolgirl, and on the other like a stupid old woman who was refusing to accept her advancing years.

"They only have Levonelle, as long as it's been no more than seventy-two hours you'll be okay. Here's the address."

It was on the other side of town, a minimum of an hour's walk away.

What a pain, she thought. *I've got so much to do.*

She started out in the direction of the chemist, chores piling up in her imagination. *Is it even necessary?* she asked herself.

She was weaving her way along, eyes on the path. *Twenty-five fucking quid. And over an hour's walk.*

She stepped into the road because there was no other way to avoid walking on cracked paving stones. *I'm halfway there from work. Should have thought of that before. I know. I'll go Monday.*

She took a side street home to save herself from a second walk in the road.

At home she quickly ate her lunch and selected the necessary music. But by the end of the first track she felt irritated and turned it off. On her way up the stairs she spilt water. *Stupid fucking bitch.* She squeezed the cloth out and gritted her teeth as she mopped up the spillage.

The bathroom cabinet looked particularly dirty; she took everything from it, resenting it and herself for the need of it. She responded to the face in the mirror by slapping it. As if it brought her to her senses Shibu appeared in her mind. *Beautiful, gentle Shibu, whatever do you see in me?*

"What d'you think?" she said out loud to her reflection. "You're available. He was a virgin and you,

you, were around and behaving like a tart. What did you expect? Stupid, old tart, that's what you are."

I shouldn't have let it happen. "I'm going to have to make sure it doesn't anymore," she told the now sparkling-clean mirror. *Really? Who are you trying to kid?* It was almost as if her reflection talked back to her.

It had been her intention to cook for them both, but Madeleine knew she was going to have to avoid him for a day or two. She ate early and went to bed with a book.

When he came in Shibu called out to her, "You okay, Madeleine?"

"Just a bit tired. I'll see you tomorrow."

Shibu knew it was a lie. It worried and puzzled him. It wasn't the first time; it had been like this before, but before they hadn't been intimate. Shibu was scared that he was to blame. He wanted to pray but was afraid of what God would tell him. Instead he went on YouTube and stayed on until bedtime.

Madeleine's morning visit to the bathroom confirmed what she already knew. No pills were necessary and everything was back to normal.

Shibu was woken by the sound of her singing mingling with that on the radio. He sighed with relief and went down for breakfast.

"How you feeling?" he asked.

"Just fine." She punctuated it with a kiss.

They lived through November like a couple, sharing meals, the washing, the ironing, their beds. Sometimes they bathed or showered together; many times they lay on the sofa listening to music and exchanging life stories, although Madeleine was careful to leave out the ones that would shock him. There was the outside world in which they acted out their everyday lives, and then there was their secret world in which they hid in the comfort of each other.

This time when Kumar visited it was his gaze Shibu was wary of.

When Madeleine called out to him that it was Kumar at the door, he understood his presence was required.

He moved quickly out of the kitchen doorway as she passed through it, flowers in hand.

"Just going to put these in a vase. I'll meet you both in the lounge in a moment."

"There you are, my man." Kumar stood up as Shibu entered the room; he shook Shibu's hand enthusiastically then, sitting down again, he asked, "How you doing?"

"I fine, thank you. How you?"

"The same."

Shibu went to sit down on the sofa, but then remembered he should wait to be invited.

"So, what you been up to?" Kumar asked in Hindi.

"Same like always." Shibu answered in English, looking up from the floor only briefly.

"Nothing new then?"

Madeleine entered the room.

"I've just been finding out about Shibu's week," Kumar told her.

"Oh?"

"I tell to him nothing to tell. Only work and sleep, same like always."

"Indeed." *Good job he's not in front of a judge*, Madeleine thought, then said, "You *can* sit down, Shibu."

"Thank you." He perched on the opposite end of the sofa.

"What will you do for Christmas?"

"I think I be working."

"Is that okay?"

"I don't have choice."

"You could probably argue it on religious grounds."

He shrugged.

"She's right. They have to allow people to practise their religion in this country."

"Maybe then." *If God can remember who I am*, he thought.

"Could I have a cup of coffee, please, Madeleine?" Kumar asked.

"Oh my God, I'm so sorry. How rude of me not to offer." She almost ran out of the room.

For a minute or more there was silence.

"I really think Madeleine has a point. If you don't want to work Christmas it's worth checking that out. Oh! Excuse me a minute, will you? I forgot to tell her something."

Now he had the chance Shibu strolled out of the room, although he felt like running. Madeleine and Kumar were on their way back. Shibu stood aside to let them pass. He was almost on his tiptoes and pushed right against the wall.

"Nice to see you, Kumar," he said. "I go to my room now."

As soon as they were alone Kumar said, "So, now you can tell me. Are you really okay?"

"Yes, really. I've not even given Julian much thought."

"Do you mind being on your own?"

"At the moment I'm enjoying it."

"Oh, good. That is good." He shook his head up and down in time with the words.

When Sean came a few days later Shibu did no more than acknowledge him before excusing himself. But in his room, listening to them laughing, he felt something stirring in him. A restless, untamed feeling that took him to the top of the stairs, and then to halfway down so that he could hear them properly.

"I have to say, Madeleine, you don't exactly look like you're in mourning – no, I'd go as far as to say you're positively glowing."

"Actually, I'm happy."

"I never wanted to tell you, but I always thought you'd be better without him. It's not so bad being alone, is it?"

"I'm not alone. I have my lovely friends to support me."

Shibu needed to hear no more. He crept back to his room, feeling a little ashamed. He watched clips of renegade elephants on YouTube, but the beast in his belly didn't settle completely until he heard Sean leave.

A few minutes later Madeleine knocked on his door.

The first days of December were particularly dark and damp; a wet mist hung over everything like a weeping phantom. It enveloped Madeleine and sapped her energy and enthusiasm; her only light was Shibu. The anticipation of being with him warmed her as surely as lying in a bath, sipping mulled wine.

Tired from a late night with Madeleine, followed by an early start, Shibu felt himself assaulted by the artificial light rendered necessary by the dull day. His thoughts were hardly more than dreams. He struggled through his working day. As he was washing his hands at the start of his lunch break, Shibu reviewed himself in the mirror and was shocked by what he saw. His face had thinned, his eyes looked bright, yet wild, and Shibu felt both were indicative of a deeper and more significant change. It seemed to him now that he wore the look of a primitive man. One to whom God had not yet spoken. He closed his eyes against the image and found Madeleine behind them, wearing an expression that was full of him.

He remembered the few occasions upon which it had pleased him to find the way to his inner world paved by images of the divine; finding them usurped by Madeleine sought only to assure him of his damnation. Now that he finally remembered Him, he feared God's judgement, both for the fact of being Madeleine's lover and for the pain she must surely suffer on behalf of his leaving. He resolved to end the affair.

His resolve lasted exactly as long as his absence from Madeleine. The greeting kiss dissolved his determination and Shibu vanished in their coupling.

They were lying in the afterglow. Madeleine was stroking his chest and in her fingertips he felt such tenderness it scared him. Resolve returned.

"I think we must stop have sex soon," he said into the top of her head.

Madeleine flinched against the words as if she'd been slapped. "Why?"

"We can't be together."

Now she pulled away from him and pushed herself up to sitting. "I know. I've always known that."

"When I leave is going to hurt you."

"I'll survive."

"I see in your eyes you will miss me."

"Of course. But I'll be okay."

"I don't think so you will."

"D'you think it'll be easier living with you and not doing this anymore?"

"Won't be easy, but we can do."

Inside Madeleine screamed a protest. "I thought it would end when you went back to India."

"Maybe I don't go for two years. How you going feel after two years?"

She didn't reply. She wanted to hold him so tight she'd crush him. She wanted to push him away so hard he'd fall over.

"Anyway, I not sure now, maybe God be angry and punish me."

"You haven't done anything wrong."

"Maybe He test me and I fail. God say sex for marriage only, and only one person your whole life."

"Then you're going to have to marry me, aren't you?" She tossed her head back and stuck her chin in the air.

"How I can marry you?" Shibu got out of bed.

"It was a joke, for fuck's sake."

"Don't swear at me." He was pulling his clothes on.

Madeleine got onto her knees and pulled the duvet around her. "Don't go. I'm sorry. If what we're doing is a problem for you, we'll stop."

"If you want stop means we can."

"I don't want. It's not a problem for me. I'm sorry that it is for you."

"Sometime is, sometime not, but one day we must stop."

"I know. I just want to enjoy what we have as long as I can."

The sincerity of the look that accompanied Madeleine's words penetrated Shibu's soul, and her eyes were ablaze with the very thing that had led him into this situation in the first place.

Madeleine reached out and touched him. "Just come and lie with me for a minute longer, please."

She stroked his chest; soothing energy began to circulate with his blood. He climbed back in beside her and they cuddled into each other. There was so much comfort in the warmth of her body.

"It's not even the sex that's important; it's this – the cuddling, the human contact," Madeleine said, underlining all that he was feeling. "Why would God want to deny anyone this?"

"Because this lead to sex." Shibu snuggled in close, smelling her hair as he pulled it lightly through his open fingers.

"The only time sex is wrong is if it's used to hurt someone deliberately and I know you'd never do that."

Even less than she could bear the thought of being without him, could she bear the thought of Shibu's guilt damaging him.

"My father will be here soon and we won't be able do this then."

In truth she had been looking forward to etching out secret liaisons with Shibu to help her through the yearly visit from Philip.

"When he come?"

"The weekend after next."

"Then that when we stop."

In the back of his mind Shibu heard the accusing voice that named him with many shaming labels: faithless, hypocrite, womaniser, and behind it there was a vague warning of a consequence unspecified but unquestioningly grave.

That she couldn't bear the thought of his leaving was hard for Madeleine to admit even to herself. She wanted to make him prisoner in the same way that she was. To capture his heart so that it ached as much as hers when they were separated.

Logic dictated that she enjoy every moment with him to the full and accept the inevitable end, but her heart was not as rational as her mind, and her body seemed to have developed a will entirely of its own, becoming rapacious in its desire for him. That she not miss a second of him as lover became the paramount driving force behind everything Madeleine did, or did not do, in those last two weeks. The bathroom had no more than a quick spray of cleaner; excess soap suds left stains behind them; routines were hurried; emails and telephones left unanswered; the ironing pile grew high.

Madeleine was determined to make the most of their last shared day off and so planned a sightseeing trip, to which Shibu agreed. Knowing he liked to stay in bed until ten or later she rose early and carefully subscribed to every last detail of her routine, as if to reassure herself that everything was as it should be in her life. As she worked through her yoga postures her thoughts drifted back to the end of her affair with Paul, with Julian and all of the others in between, and she remembered the feelings of self-loathing that accompanied her sense of failure. At least there wouldn't be that this time because far from having failed, this relationship continued to be a success. The cruel irony of that struck her now. For the first time there were no power struggles, no quarrels or endless discussions on who should take the blame; she and Shibu got on so well.

Now Madeleine lay herself down for the relaxation, but partway through she heard Shibu stir, heard his feet pound the floor towards the bathroom and then her concentration became focused on him.

Chapter Twelve

Gentle music floated into the dream, stirring it up like a summer breeze scattering dry dust, so that, as he drifted towards consciousness, Shibu knew he had been dreaming of Madeleine. The music told him she would now be in the reverse postures, so about halfway through her routine. He lay, waking up still. He could neither keep his mind from remembering nor his imagination from seeing and, as he felt desire burgeoning in his body, he wondered how he would ever forget sufficiently to separate himself from her.

The feelings stirred in him by these thoughts were, as ever, contradictory, so that along with the surge of warmth, which accompanied the thought of Madeleine came the fear of retribution, and excitement was matched by guilt. Their chastity might be assured more easily by the presence of Madeleine's father, but Shibu sensed that more than this would be required to subjugate his craving. It had been only two days since their last sexual encounter and already his body yearned for her. The only hope was to end the affair he knew, not only for himself but for Madeleine, in whose face he had seen the need for him growing.

These thoughts drove him from bed. He'd promised to spend the day with Madeleine, but now he needed to avoid her.

He was in the kitchen preparing breakfast. He heard Madeleine come in and deliberately kept his back turned.

"Morning," she said, accompanying it with a hug from behind and a kiss on the neck, which sent a shiver through his spine. "Will you be ready soon?"

"I need go to supermarket."

"We can do that when we come back."

"I have no food left."

"I'm going to buy us lunch. I'll drive you to do your shopping when we get home."

Shibu didn't answer. "*When we get home.*" She made it sound so cosy and natural; right now he regretted that that was also how it felt.

"What's wrong?"

He shrugged.

"Don't you want to go?"

He shrugged again.

"I've been looking forward to it. I borrowed Kumar's car."

Shibu now felt ashamed on Madeleine's account, because he didn't want to let her down.

"Why you want to take me out?"

The question took her aback. "Because I love to be in your company. Because you haven't seen how pretty England is. Because up until now all we've done together is go to bed."

"So, you don't want do sex anymore?"

The relief in his voice was distressing.

"I didn't say that. Anyway, my father arrives tomorrow."

Shibu wore a pouty expression.

"Are you saying *you* don't want to?"

He didn't answer, but he lowered his gaze and bowed his head. It was a look of shame. The feeling was one with which Madeleine was well acquainted, and she responded now with the same emotion.

"I hoped we'd make love one last time of course, but if you don't—"

"It's not make love, it's sex."

The words were like a slap around the face. They brought tears to prickle the backs of her eyes. She swallowed, left the room, stood in the hallway biting her lip. She picked up her shoes, put them back down, wandered back to the kitchen.

She and Shibu brushed past each other in the doorway.

Madeleine put the kettle on and slumped into a chair.

In his room. Shibu got ready to go out. As he did so he looked at his reflection in the mirror and saw humiliation in his eyes. The voice in his head was parental. *That was really unkind*, it said. He returned to the kitchen a few minutes later, but Madeleine wasn't there.

She was in the lounge. She sat upright and still, breathing so low her diaphragm hardly moved. The words were like a stone in her throat and heart. If she were to go out with him now it would be as if she were a parent forcing the birthday party on her child. And yet her disappointment left her feeling like a child whose birthday has passed unheeded. The clock marked time.

Can't sit here all day, she thought. *I'd better find something to do.*

Shibu sat at the kitchen table. The silence was deafening. When he heard Madeleine leave the lounge he braced himself for her entrance, but she didn't come in. He sat for a few minutes more, until the apprehension became unbearable, then he went to the bottom of the stairs and called out to her.

The contents of the underwear drawer were on the bed and she was sorting knickers into piles according to their colour. She jumped to attention and was on the landing in the same moment in response to her name.

"Yes? What?"

"Just I ready to go."

"Oh! I thought we weren't going. I'll be there in a sec." She kept her tone light. She hurried to finish the task.

There was portent in the stiffness with which Shibu now sat in the passenger seat of Kumar's car. It wasn't with the nervousness that would accompany the premonition of an accident, rather with the apprehension of the hitchhiker who was uncomfortable with his host.

They drove out of the town on a road Shibu had never encountered before. The street was full of three-storey white houses, some with iron balconies and most with intruder alarms. "What period these houses?" he asked to break the silence.

"Georgian. Eighteenth to early nineteenth century."

"They same like yours. Are they traditional?"

"I think you mean Tudor. I'll show you some of those later."

They returned to silence. "D'you want music?"

"If you want means we can."

"There are plenty in there." She indicated the glove box.

Shibu riffled through the CDs; finding nothing he recognised he chose one he knew had come from Kumar.

"Ah! Good choice." Madeleine wiggled her shoulders about and after a few minutes began to feel genuinely more cheerful.

As she relaxed so did Shibu; he laughed at her mock dancing. Feeling safe again, Madeleine reached out and touched his leg; after a moment's thought, a moment that was a little too long for Madeleine, Shibu responded in the same manner and touched hers.

The Asian music took his thoughts in the direction of home. He began to imagine that he was driving across India in the company of his future wife. But when he looked out of the window there were no brightly coloured trucks piled high with animals, no buses with people hanging from the doorways, no one selling wares by the side of the road. Most significantly of all, the figure of an imaginary future wife was supplanted by the very real present lover sitting in the driver's seat.

"That's where we're going." She interrupted his thoughts and pointed towards a tower on a hill that seemed to rise from nowhere. The hill, as well as the monument, seemed incongruous.

Cast in profile, without the depth of her eyes or the sensuality of her mouth in view, Madeleine's beauty, though just as evident, seemed more superficial and Shibu was able to convince himself of a lack of attraction. "What it for?" he asked.

"It has no purpose; it's called a folly. I don't know about this one, but often they are built as a demonstration of great love."

"Oh! Like Taj Mahal?"

"That's one grand folly."

A few minutes later they turned off the main road and onto a track that climbed towards their destination. Sheep grazed either side of the road; they had to pull in to allow a Land Rover to pass. At the top of the hill they pulled into a small car park and purchased a ticket.

"Why you bother?" Shibu asked. "Who going to check up here?"

Although the day was bright it was crisp and made chilly by a strong wind. Shibu pulled his collar up against it and a woollen hat onto his head. Madeleine wrapped a shawl around herself, wishing as she did so that she could follow her instinct to take hold of Shibu's arm.

"There's a lovely church this way." She had to raise her voice to be heard over the wind, which was loud enough to obscure the delighted squeals of two young children, who, aided by an adult, wrestled with a kite.

Madeleine felt harassed by the wind; it buffeted her skin and constantly blew her hair into her face, promising tangles that later the comb must battle. Shibu felt enlivened by it.

They walked the short distance towards the village without conversation. Silence hit them as they stepped over the hill and out of the wind, into the shelter of a small valley. Fewer than a dozen houses made up the entire village, but at its centre, looming authoritatively, there stood the church. The sun hung so low in the sky that it seemed to be penetrated by the spire, which cast its shadow in their direction. At the sight of it Shibu straightened his pose.

Inside both he and Madeleine were touched by the calm and stillness. For a few minutes they held hands, as if being in the church made them more conscious of their deeper link.

But then that same connection provoked a different emotion in Shibu and he let go of Madeleine's hand. He walked away from her towards the pulpit. Madeleine's hand felt heavy as it fell away from his, her heart the same as she watched him step up to the altar and cross himself. His whole manner portrayed obedience. In that moment Madeleine understood that in her abandonment of him lay Shibu's salvation. And that to gracefully accept this was the best she could offer him. She rested a hand on the wall, as if seeking solace from the solidity and endurance of antiquity. As she did so she noticed the remains of a fresco, the details of which it was impossible to determine, and was reminded instead that everything fades with time.

Madeleine closed her eyes, seeking out the serenity of the building and smelling the musty smell. Here was the manifestation of humankind's quest for permanence, but though it was ancient the church was not unchanged. It was that same desire for something enduring, Madeleine now realised, which kept people in relationships no matter how bad, for the alternative was to have to admit that even love is temporary. No wonder people wanted to believe in God and His enduring love.

Even she had wanted that when Tom died. Now, she realised that it had been a day or more since she'd thought about Tom. This had never happened before and it filled her with unease, because once the memory of a person was lost it was as if they had never existed at all. When he'd passed away the days had been endless, and sleep either evasive or full of nightmares. The only way for Madeleine to reach any kind of acceptance was to keep him alive in her memory. Yet sometimes in the very effort of doing so some authenticity was lost, like with the touching-up of a classic painting. If Tom could fade from memory, then the same was true for Shibu. And yet, to accept that one day Shibu would be no more than a memory was almost impossible.

They left the church silently; for Shibu this was generated by the deepening of humility. For Madeleine it was born of a fear deep in the pit of her stomach.

They drove over the hill in the opposite direction to which they'd come, all the time sinking deeper into the countryside, several times pulling over to take a photograph and admire the landscape. Here it was quiet enough to hear the bleating sheep who were now a mile or two behind them, and Shibu was reminded of the bellow of the water buffalo that used to be his wake-up call.

The pub to which they went for lunch was traditional, with both ale and fire that were real. He tasted a local beer, and felt warmed enough by the effects of it to snuggle into Madeleine for a photograph of the two of them together.

"We'll take the scenic route home," Madeleine said. "I'll show you some of those traditional houses as promised."

Although the villages through which they drove were undeniably beautiful, with their thatched roofed houses and squares with monuments or ponds, Shibu was growing bored after the third. Well aware of the fact, but reluctant for the day to end, Madeleine encouraged him to take walks and more photographs to extend their time together. Finally, the fast-encroaching darkness forced them in the direction of home.

It had been the contrast between the summer and winter light that had surprised Shibu more than the cold weather, for which he was well prepared. He'd enjoyed his first experience of snow, watching in fascination as it fell in sheets of silence, transforming grey to white, and it had seemed to him as if God was re-announcing the virgin birth and purifying the world.

"I need to go shop," Shibu said as soon as they pulled up outside the house.

"I'll give you a lift."

Walking around the supermarket together it felt to Madeleine as if they were a proper couple. Shibu felt exposed, and hurried, fearful that they would bump into a work colleague.

"I should take the car back. Think I need a cuppa, though," Madeleine said as they drew up outside the house.

As he followed her into the house Shibu was again full of contradictory feelings. He went straight to his room and immediately telephoned his cousin.

In the kitchen, drinking tea, Madeleine could hear the murmurs of his conversation and was annoyed by it because it seemed to her that Shibu was trying to avoid her.

When he came into the room it was with an attitude of defiance, like a teenager who was determined to have his way.

"Okay?" Madeleine asked.

"I speak to my cousin brother I go to his house for Christmas."

Disappointment sank into Madeleine like water into sand.

"That's good – it'll be nice to share it with someone who's not a complete misery about it, like me."

Disappointment, Shibu decided, didn't suit her: it aged her considerably; it emphasised the lines that were beginning to appear around her eyes and took the sparkle from them. He felt ashamed again, knowing he was the source of her discontent.

In the shower, with the warm water coursing his body and the hot smell from the kitchen teasing his tastebuds, Shibu began to feel cosy; there was something about the long winter nights that made him desire domesticity. The scene in the kitchen reinforced it ten-fold. He wouldn't ask her, he decided, but neither would he refuse her; it was, after all, their last chance before her father arrived and so the last time they would ever do it.

Madeleine put two glasses on the table. "I didn't know if you wanted, but it's rude not to offer."

"Yes, please, I have."

Madeleine took a sip of wine. Shibu took a gulp of his. Both acknowledged, from the look in each other's eyes, what was soon to come.

Chapter Thirteen

They lay in the afterglow, wrapped in each other and in silence. Body satiated, heart calm, Shibu had never felt so content.

Madeleine felt as if all the holes in her being had been filled. In her mind she whispered the words she dared not utter.

Into Shibu's psyche there came an aeroplane carrying him away. For the first time since his arrival he wished to never be on board. He imagined their parting, saw in his mind's eye Madeleine sobbing as he walked towards the terminal. He felt the wrench in his solar plexus, as if it were already happening. The fear upon arrival was nothing in comparison. The thoughts exited his body as a sigh. He kissed Madeleine on the forehead, then gently moved her away from him. "I get up now."

"Must you?"

"I have to ironing."

"Stay a while, I'll do it for you."

"I can do."

"I know." She was afraid to ask too insistently.

Shibu lingered, not wanting to hurt Madeleine by refusing her request, yet neither did he want to hurt her by granting it. He was saved by the arrival of a visitor.

"Whoever is that?" Madeleine grabbed her dressing-gown and headed for the door.

Feeling like the adulterer almost caught in the act Shibu hurried to his room.

"Sean!" Madeleine was annoyed by the presence of the one person she was always happy to see. "This is a surprise. I was going to have an early night," she added, aware of her attire.

"Something you want to tell me?"

"Huh?"

"Going to bed, you said; was he going with you?"

"What? Who?" Madeleine was still trying to work out what she had done to give herself away and decide how she, and especially how Shibu, would feel about Sean knowing, when he said, "Kumar. Don't look so surprised, his car's outside."

She breathed a sigh of relief. "Oh! I borrowed it for the day to take Shibu sightseeing. Should've taken it back, really, but Kumar said tomorrow would do."

"How disappointing! I thought I'd come across some scandal. No, seriously, I'd love to see the two of you together."

"Me? Kumar?"

"Why not? He's the obvious choice; after me of course," he laughed, "but with a bit of luck I'll be spoken for soon."

"Now you've got me interested. Come and tell all."

Sean's words were inaudible, but the excitement in his voice drifted into Shibu's room, where he loitered, avoiding contact for fear of giving himself away. It was impossible to believe that, without a forensic cleansing, such an intense experience would not leave behind some observable trace. A hint of her smell, perhaps, a stray hair, an echo of her in his eyes – any of which would ensure man, as well as God, would be his witness. Potentially Sean's judgement was equal to that of the Almighty who, though severe in His retribution, would at least save it for the afterlife. But if Sean spoke a word of the liaison then Shibu's life in this world was assuredly condemned.

Feeling the need to destroy the evidence Shibu took another shower. This time the water cleansed and warmed him in a different way, so that by its conclusion he felt as if he'd been baptised and, back in his room, he prayed.

As always behind his eyes was the face he could never quite see, and in front of that, the one he could never fully escape, but this time there was a difference. It wasn't that he hadn't recognised Madeleine's vulnerability before, it was just that this time, in the context of his own, it became clearer.

The very same characteristics that made him desire her so eagerly were those that left her open to being hurt. If he stood to lose reputation and community, she was at risk of losing something no less significant. To continue to love her physically was to abuse her emotionally. As if that weren't enough, now he needed to take account of his own feelings. He now feared not only God's wrath but also his own love. This was going to have to stop.

He didn't want to face Sean, but he hadn't been lying about the ironing.

He just popped in for the sake of civility. The atmosphere in the room was intense, as was the conversation; his heart dropped to his stomach, fearing himself the subject. In the most casual manner he could muster, Shibu greeted Sean. There was an air of something in the way Sean returned his greeting. A hesitation, as if he were observing something, and a glance that fleeted from him to Madeleine. He left the room feeling anxious and hovered outside within earshot. It was then that he caught a snippet of conversation.

"She has a couple of kids."

"And? You love kids."

"But I worry about how they'll get on with me, and about maintaining a relationship with the father always around."

"Those aren't unreasonable worries, but if two people love each other…"

"Love conquers everything?"

"Well, yes."

Shibu lowered his head and covered his ears with his hands. Then almost ran to the kitchen.

"Though what do I know?" Madeleine continued. "I'm hardly the expert on love. I always get involved with the wrong person, so how can I advise you?"

Sean felt a little sprinkle of sadness, as if someone had placed a hand under a tap that was turned on too fast and he'd been caught in the spray. And now he realised that when Shibu had been in the room he'd noticed something: a tiny change in the atmosphere, the way Madeleine overplayed her casual role and how she stared questioningly for a second at the space left after Shibu quit the room. Though, surely not? But then, why not?

"Madeleine, I... I." No, he'd better not ask. "I'm not looking for advice, I just want to use you as a sounding board. Anyway, I don't even know if she's interested in me in that way, maybe she wants a friend."

"You haven't asked her? Why not?"

"Too scared of the answer."

"Would it be so bad if she just wanted a friend?"

"I think it would."

"Oh dear!"

"Oh dear indeed!"

Sean sighed then clapped his hands together, "Well, that's enough of that. I'll keep you posted."

"Please do."

"Kick me out if you still want an early night."

"Nah, I'm not tired now. I'll stay in bed attire if you don't mind, though."

"Don't be so daft. Tell me about your day. Where'd you go?"

Driving home Sean reflected on the evening. For whatever reason, perhaps the lateness of the hour, or because he'd arrived unannounced, Madeleine hadn't been quite her usual attentive self.

Although she acknowledged the same and she did feel a little guilty, all that really mattered to Madeleine was that she should see her lover one more time before the morning. She hurried upstairs, knocked on his door and called his name.

Shibu lay wide awake in the dark, hardly daring to breathe in case she heard him.

Madeleine, knowing he'd deceived her, went woefully to bed, feeling as insecure as the child whose night-time cries go unheeded.

She awoke in a panic with the feeling that something was dreadfully wrong. The soundless house soon reminded her of what that was. She listened for Shibu then checked the clock. It confirmed the hour was too early for him to have left already, and yet it was too late for the silence of him still sleeping.

The sight of his bedroom door ajar panicked her because from it issued a message of escape. She peered cautiously around it and observed the signs indicative of hurry: open wardrobe door with clothes draped over it, crumpled duvet, un-plumped pillows, one flip-flop upside down upon the other. She slumped down on the edge of his bed and picked it up. It looked too small for him. If this was the glass slipper, he would surely fail the test. In the bottom of the wardrobe Madeleine noticed the suitcase, which had never been completely unpacked, and she imagined a not-too-distant future in which he hauled it, fully laden, from her house – from her life.

She lost count in the shower and had to start again. In yoga she had no interest so forced the routine upon herself, but by its conclusion she felt slouched rather than upright and restless rather than energised.

The only time yoga had ever failed her before was when Tom died and she abandoned it to grief. For a month or more her stiff body dragged itself through the days and fell gratefully into night, as if she herself were a corpse. She refused the refuge and recovery offered by yoga, feeling disloyal for even being alive. Dead, Tom was in her mind and heart with greater intensity than he had been in life.

In the staff room Shibu ate his breakfast and occupied his mind with games on his mobile phone. His call home had been short and full of smiles and lies. Because a Chinese girl now occupied the room he had previously considered, he scanned the week-old paper for vacant accommodation, but in every case the prices were far too high.

Restlessness informed Madeleine's day and prevented full engagement in anything she did. Her heart was filled with a lament that played on quarter volume throughout the day but rose to deafening levels in every under occupied moment. And on top of it was Philip's imminent arrival.

Shibu was in his room. She could hear him deep in conversation through the closed door, the sight of which made her feel desperate and as lost as a child coming home to an empty house. Strange how the status of a door could so affect her mood.

Madeleine prepared a meal for herself and Philip, leaving the radio off in order to hear every clue as to Shibu's whereabouts, and she sensed him doing the same. She felt as if she was the chess piece and he the grandmaster.

When he finally arrived, it was deep in conversation on his mobile phone. He spoke in Malayalam and listened through earphones; it hurt like a best friend's scorn. She watched every detail of his meal preparation with a burgeoning rage, so intense she was convinced Shibu could feel it in his spine. Anger locked her into him as surely as his exclusion repelled her, and his determination to leave her unacknowledged was matched by her resolve to have his attention. Yet he entered into one conversation after another, without as much as a glance in Madeleine's direction.

Eventually she walked up behind him and touched him on the shoulder; there was something in the way he turned around that was suggestive of compliance, but then he froze, held up his hand in a commanding manner and looked at her disapprovingly.

"I'm busy with call." He unhooked one earphone.

"I want to speak to you."

"What? What you want?"

"How long will you be? My father will be here any minute. I want to talk to you before he comes."

Shibu looked angry. Madeleine felt humiliated.

He hung up the call. "I need to be quick and phone my cousin brother back. What you want?"

"Is everything okay?"

"Fine."

"Last night was – well, you know how it was."

"Last night was last time."

"I know. And it was amazing, but I get the feeling you're avoiding me now."

"Your father is coming."

"Yes. But we don't need to act like strangers."

"How else we can be?"

"Like friends. At least polite to each other."

"Am I being rude?"

"No. Well, sort of."

"I'm just talking to my friends and family. I have to make plan for next week."

"I know, but—"

"I have to call back now." He reconnected the earphones.

Madeleine felt tears in her eyes and throat.

And then her father arrived.

Chapter Fourteen

"Darling." Philip dropped his bags and threw his arms around his daughter.

Madeleine tensed, experiencing the hug more as an assault than an act of affection. "Welcome home, Dad." Her tone failed to hide her true emotion. "Good journey?"

"Had worse. How're things? Good. Julian?"

"We split up."

"Not improved at relationships then."

Madeleine felt her blood solidify and her muscles clench, preventing the anger from flowing and ensuring its expression would be turned on herself, as usual.

Now she watched Philip shaking the weather from his coat and turning off lights, bringing winter into the house.

"I've cooked stew, made some dumplings," she said.

"That's good of you." He walked into the kitchen, still wearing his outdoor shoes, then made himself coffee, which he took to the lounge without mopping up the spilt milk. As Madeleine cleaned up and rinsed the sticky spoon, she was greeted by the sound of Frank Sinatra's voice through the speakers she'd forgotten to turn off.

She was in the process of doing so when Philip returned to the kitchen.

"When's dinner?"

"Whenever you'd like – it'll be ready with ten minutes' warning."

"I'm ready now, if you are." He turned the speakers back on, then immediately left the room again.

The turning on of the speakers reignited Madeleine's anger. Sometimes, as the rage boiled away inside her, she wished she had the courage to tell Philip what she really wanted to. Now she recalled one of the rare occasions on which she had stood up to her father:

Tom stood wringing his hands behind his back and casting his eyes around the room, as if waiting for clues. The unopened letter lay on the table where it had been all day. It was addressed to Tom but was really for Philip's attention and he seemed in no hurry, with the Financial Times *spread out in front of him and his second cup of coffee only halfway through.*

"Can I open this now?" Tom finally asked meekly, waving the letter in the air.

"Be with you in a minute." Philip didn't even raise his eyes from the paper.

The air was heavy. It was like holding your breath in slimy water.

Because she wanted to scream Madeleine dropped the saucepan she was washing, splashing water on the floor. "Ump!" she muttered, as she squatted to wipe it up.

"Use the floor cloth," Philip ordered. "And wipe the grumpies off yourself while you're at it." He sighed. "Might as well take a look at these results, then."

In his hurry Tom fumbled.

"Well?"

"Two As and a B." He handed the letter to his father.

"Not bad – three As would've been better, but…" Philip shrugged.

"This is good enough, it's what they asked for."

"Won't go far with that attitude."

Tom kept his eyes on his father whilst flinching away from his sister's congratulatory hugs. When Philip returned to reading the paper without further comment, Tom sidled out of the room and Madeleine followed.

"Well done, Tom."

"Cheers." His tone was sulky.

Madeleine sat down next to him on his bed. "He's dead proud, he just can't show it."

"I don't even care. I don't want to go to university. I don't want to study law, and I don't want to be a fucking lawyer. That's what he wants. He wants me to be like him. Fuck knows why anyone would want that." Tom's bottom lip quivered with the effort of controlling his tears.

For her own sake the last thing Madeleine wanted was to talk Tom out of university, because his leaving home would finally grant her the same opportunity, but she couldn't bear to see him hurting.

"Don't do it then. Don't be who you don't want to be."

"Oh, yeah, like I have any choice." He shoved her arm away when she touched him. "One consolation is I'll be getting away from him."

Tom's distress manifested in tears, which sent Madeleine into a rage that blinded her to the consequences and sent her stomping down the stairs.

Seeing that Philip had moved neither physically nor in attitude Madeleine's anger erupted and she snatched the paper from her father's grasp.

"You should see the state Tom's in. Why couldn't you be proud of him? Just for once. No conditions. Just proud."

"How dare you!"

Even when her father stood up and pushed the chair that was between them out of his way Madeleine felt no fear, nor when he grabbed hold of her so hard it pinched, not even as he pulled her dress up and slapped her hard on the thigh.

"Tom's so upset he's crying," she screeched.

This time she did flinch away from the expected second slap, but it didn't come.

"Crying?" Philip sneered. "Like some snivelling girl." And he thundered up the stairs.

Afraid for Tom now Madeleine chased after him and so was witness to the way her father dragged Tom to his feet and bellowed, "Come on, hit me," almost nose to nose with his son. "Stop your snivelling – if you have a problem with me let's deal with it, man to man." Philip shoved his son in the chest.

Tom shuffled backwards, but Philip persisted, dancing around and punching tauntingly at the air either side of Tom's face. "Come on, come on." The words produced spittle that splashed onto Tom's face.

Suddenly Tom threw a punch. A single resounding punch to Philip's left cheek that sounded like a ball thudding against a hollow wall. It was followed by silence.

No one moved. In their unfamiliar roles they were like actors without a script. But then Philip sighed and nodded his head. "Well, that's better." He jiggled his head from side to side and pouted his lips. "Couple of years and you might even be able to hurt your old man."

Then he pulled Tom into an embrace. "Course I'm proud of you. You're my son." He patted Tom on the back and left the room, looking as if he might cry himself.

"Why d'you go and tell him?" Tom yelled at his sister the moment they were alone.

"I was angry, he hurt you."

"Well, I'm hurt worse now. I didn't wanna hit him."

"What?"

"It makes me as bad as him."

Madeleine went to hug Tom.

"No. Just leave me."

The rejection was too much to bear. "I was angry. I can't stand how he hurts you."

"Just leave me."

A red mark remained in evidence of the slap, and her pride was wounded by the humiliation of her twenty-year-old thigh being bared to her father; but neither of these hurt when compared to the pain of rejection from Tom.

Rejection – it felt like walking alone towards the dim and distant light at the end of an echoing corridor.

The key in the latch had sent Shibu to his room, but now he cautiously entered the kitchen. It was the tension in the air and the fear of giving their relationship away that made him cautious, but avoiding her father for days was impossible so might as well get it over with.

Philip arrived in the kitchen a second or two before him. Shibu's entrance both imprisoned Madeleine's emotions and rescued her from them. The mystique of the shared past between her and Shibu seemed like a secret passage in the house, which reclaimed it a little from its master.

"Oh, forgot to tell you I have a lodger," Madeleine said, enjoying the seconds of misunderstanding as Philip drew his own conclusions. "This is Shibu – my father, Philip."

"Very pleased to meet you," Shibu greeted in his usual polite manner.

"Likewise," Philip replied.

Madeleine was dishing up the dinner. She didn't offer for Shibu to join them. Things were awkward enough as it was.

"I come back later," Shibu said. "When you have finish."

As soon as he had left the room Philip said, "Surely you don't need a lodger?"

"Actually, I do."

"Not making any money out of the jewellery? Nor the painting? D'you want me to lend—"

"No! …No, thank you."

"If you'd listened to me and finished your education… no point going on about it, you know my feelings."

A few minutes later Shibu was back. "Just I go in the shower. Then I have dinner."

"Okay." Madeleine smiled softly, noting how, with her father in the room, their conversation was easier.

"He seems polite enough," Philip said.

"Why wouldn't he be?"

"Christ! I was just making an observation. I wonder what he makes of the Christmas fuss?"

"Actually, he's a Christian himself, but they don't do all this present stuff in Kerala. They just go to church and have a special family meal."

"Quite right too. I notice you haven't asked after Hils."

"Sorry, she okay?"

"Fine. She sends her regards."

"Return mine."

"I hope you're not offended by her absence. It's only the inconvenience of finding someone else to run the place if we're both away."

"I know."

"Your mother okay?"

"Fine."

"You're very conversational."

What would you have me say? Madeleine thought. *Since the only subject we should discuss is off-limits.* "Sorry," she said, "just a bit tired."

"Tired? A young woman like you."

Madeleine wanted refuge, but there was no ally in the house, and she was unable to evaluate which of her two companions she currently felt most awkward with.

A few minutes later Shibu sidled back in. His reverence towards her father, who now fired questions at him, felt to Madeleine like a betrayal. And Madeleine sensed that Philip felt relieved to have him in the room.

She pushed her chair back noisily from the table and in the same manner began clearing up.

"Something wrong?" Philip's tone was condescending.

The conspiratorial glance that he shot in Shibu's direction didn't go unnoticed by Madeleine.

"What could possibly be wrong?"

She shot Shibu a warning glance and almost pushed him aside with her hips as she put the dishes in the sink. Then said, "Oh, sorry."

He replied with a look that was just as threatening but retracted it quickly in fear of Philip noticing their silent conversation.

"If you want have talk with your father, I can do dishes," Shibu offered.

"Thank you, but that won't be necessary."

This was said into the sink as she rinsed the dishes and loaded the dishwasher.

When she'd finished Madeleine left the room with teenage belligerence. As she did so she turned off the speakers, then went into the living room and put on rock music at a volume she knew would annoy her father. She strummed air guitar and mimed singing.

She was dying for a fag but couldn't have one until Philip was in bed. Last year she'd almost been caught as she hung out of the bedroom window.

She knew that Shibu was now receiving the subliminal story of her father's version of their family history. She knew too that her behaviour was making it more real. She turned the music down now, recalling how she had behaved in the previous year. Stomping and sulking and demanding that Julian understand how difficult it was for her, when all he seemed to do was present her with Philip's perspective. And now she realised that her behaviour, perhaps more than any other factor, had been instrumental in her downfall, had been the defining characteristic in Julian and Philip's collusion. She didn't want the same to happen with Shibu.

She was going to have to go to bed. She put on a professional smile as she popped her head round the kitchen door. "Goodnight, then."

"Bed already?"

"Gonna read for a while."

Shibu offered a pouty look, which made her worry that he was the one who needed rescuing now. But she was in no position to help him.

Predictably the book failed to distract her. Her father's voice boomed through the ceiling, like a distant cannon, and the words he spoke to Shibu seemed more portentous by virtue of their inaudibility. She was only on the fourth page when she heard Shibu retire to his room, almost twenty minutes later.

She overheard his phone call, which, although it was incomprehensible in Malayalam, was soothing by virtue of its tone. And in her memory she heard him talking lover's talk, and yearned for him. Every time she made love with him it was as special as the first time. It was like beer at the end of a long summer's walk. How was she ever to relegate him to the level of acquaintance?

Impatiently she waited to hear her father go to bed, so that she could sneak into the garden for a smoke, but there was no indication that it would be anytime soon and the urge was becoming an obsession. Soon, unable to stand it any longer, she dressed again and went downstairs, her intention being to fetch lavender oil and a burner to her room to hide the smell of tobacco, aid relaxation and help her sleep.

The lavender oil was in a drawer in the kitchen, the burner in the living room window, so avoiding her father was impossible. He was standing by the kitchen window, looking out into the frost-covered garden; the white wire dangling from his ear made it clear he was listening to his iPod. The sight of him disturbed Madeleine; so too did the open blind, because she liked to close the darkness out. It occurred to her that if she was really quick, and quiet, she might get in and out unnoticed, so she crept in behind him like a child preparing to steal chocolate from the Christmas tree. In the same manner she kept her eyes on him as she slid the drawer open and then closed again when she'd found what she wanted, but before she had time to leave, he turned around and saw her.

"What're you sneaking around at?"

"Not sneaking. Just fetching something. Goodnight."

Something in the interaction between them stirred a memory. It teased its way into the recesses of her mind: an ethereal figure, a whispery voice, a suggestion of something. Madeleine thought at first to pursue it, but then felt afraid and pushed it away. But an echo remained, the way a disagreement lingers in the room when the quarrel has ended.

"Can't settle." She held the bottle of lavender up. "This should help."

"Still into witchcraft, then."

Madeleine felt anger twist her stomach and wake her up even more, but she refused to allow it to show. "Goodnight, Dad."

Back in her room she lit the oil burner and then opened the window wide and exhaled smoke from her cigarette into the night air. She left the window open while she cleaned her teeth so that the room was stimulatingly chilly when she returned. Now she closed it, put the burner close to her bed and dropped a few drops of lavender onto her pillow.

A little while later, still feeling wide awake and charged by strong emotions, Madeleine picked up the small box she'd also brought from the kitchen drawer. She turned it over a few times in her hand before making her decision, because despite its necessity, and the relief it guaranteed, she always felt a little guilty doing it. Now, decision made, she took two drawing pins from the box and placed them up-turned hip-width apart on the floor, then simultaneously she pushed both of her heels down firmly on top of them.

After the phone call and the prayers Shibu tucked himself into his duvet, knowing sleep would remain elusive for some time but needing the duvet for comfort because the way the house felt now frightened him. It was a dreadful feeling, as if the house had suddenly become possessed by the paranormal.

Knowing a little about the relationship between Madeleine and her father, Shibu had expected that the atmosphere might be tense, quarrelsome, perhaps, as it had been when Tessa was there. Instead it was as oppressive as the first clouds of monsoon. And Madeleine's behaviour was as wild and wary as that of a captive tiger. Although he knew he was not the one responsible for the capture, he felt his own behaviour was tantamount to assisting with keeping the rope taut. His heart ached for her, because the more she thrashed and pulled against it the tighter the rope became, but he couldn't help her escape because in her gratitude she might devour him.

Shibu decided to spend the full five days' holiday in Reading.

Chapter Fifteen

When she came home from work Shibu had gone. The house rang with his absence. Silence could be full of peace or eloquence, but the silence that greeted Madeleine seemed ominous. She stood a while inside it, experiencing the accompanying emotions as a premonition of something terrible.

As she hung her coat up and changed from outdoor to indoor shoes, she strained her ears for clues as to Philip's whereabouts, and was satisfied he was out.

The empty house fired her imagination and she was visited first by the image of Shibu's youthful face, aged by fear and guilt over what they'd done, and then, just fleetingly, by the other. Tom, his open mouth formed in the shape of a scream and his round, staring eyes ringed in blue, each of which left the lasting impression of shock. Or of someone who'd changed his mind.

In the living room she riffled through her music collection looking for something strong enough to banish the images. She chose The Ruts and pogoed around the room to 'Babylon's Burning', as if she were still a teenager – the best days of a person's life, according to some. And in many respects they were, with the excitement of experimenting with new things and the making of new friends. Best of all were the gigs, to which she and Tom sneaked both themselves and the punk gear, changing their clothes and attitude as they sprayed their hair, pink, green and orange, and snorted speed.

Yet in other ways they were the worst of times. Philip's increased anger and Tom's quiet grief were constant reminders to Madeleine that, despite her efforts to fill all of her mother's obligations, she was a poor replacement for the absent Tessa.

Now Madeleine visualised the near future. Christmas Day. Though the day itself meant nothing to her, she felt more than a little bitter at the thought of spending it alone with Philip. She'd meant to work at the homeless shelter but delayed so long before asking that when she did, they had all the necessary volunteers in place. And now, the reason for her delay in contacting them, the reason for the current chaos of her life, had gone swanning off to Reading.

Momentarily she was angry with Shibu, as if he was the one to blame for it all. But maintaining anger at him just wasn't possible. It wasn't merely that she knew he didn't deserve it, she also understood that to express it to him was to court his rejection. She knew too, that the same risk was attached to the utterance of the other feeling; she must keep it in her heart and from her lips forever. But how she wished to shout it at a volume the world could hear.

Several times it had almost escaped in the midst of their passion; she'd had to seal it into silence with a kiss. And recently it had begun to slip into the spaces between the words of ordinary conversation. She could feel it pouring from her eyes and knew Shibu had seen it.

Yet, there were times when she felt he was equally beguiled. Like a pianist teasing the emotion from the music she could feel it in his touch, and she saw it softly manifest in the closing of his eyes at the climax of their union.

Thinking of him now, remembering him then, Shibu was becoming the only topic to occupy her mind. This was what she had been missing all those years, this, or more especially the loss of this, the generating force behind so many beautiful works of art. And if she could feel so lost and lonely knowing she wouldn't see him for several days, how would she feel knowing she'd never see him again?

She put the oven on. Not just in preparation for cooking but also to warm the kitchen because she suddenly felt cold. She wanted a cigarette so went to her room, fearful of smoking by the back door in case she failed to hear her father's return.

Something had changed. As soon as she opened the door she knew. The atmosphere in the room was predatory. Madeleine shuddered in response; cautiously she opened her underwear drawer to fetch the cigarettes from their hiding place, feeling like a child sneaking a biscuit. There was no way to be completely sure, of course – the drawer was just as tidy, the knickers in piles according to their colour and the bras on top as they should be – and yet, in the same way it was clear without counting them that there are fewer coins in the purse than expected, she knew.

Now she opened the door to her wardrobe and eyed the contents in an accusatory manner, then, as if expecting to find someone hidden between the clothes, she slid the hangers backwards and forwards along the rail. She picked up the book that was her bedtime reading and put it back down, then checked that the lock on the chest of drawers remained sound, feeling a little triumphant knowing he wouldn't have found the key. Her father's presence filled the room and filled her with disgust; she felt violated. Now there was another rule to add to the 'let's pretend' they played. Pretence was so much a part of Madeleine's life and psyche she knew the only authentic thing about her was her falsity. She was a genuine fake.

Madeleine flung the window open, knowing her secret was up but playing the game anyway. So many times she had tried to bend the rules or invent some of her own, but still they played the game Philip's way. And she liked Daddy's games no more now, than she ever had.

When Philip arrived Madeleine was in the kitchen preparing the meal, like an obedient wife. Even though she was expecting it, the click of his key in the lock made her jump. That sound was rapidly coming to dominate her. An anticipatory ear seemed always to be tuned to the door, and her liberty was as dependent upon it as if the key was in the hands of a jailer.

"Ah, smells good." Philip rubbed his hands together. "Good day?"

"It was okay. This'll be ready when you are."

"Shall I dish up?"

"No, I'll do it."

The last time her father had dished up he'd put the meat on top of the veg.

"Um, delicious. At least you're a good cook."

"Glad you like it."

"Doesn't look like you do."

"I'm not very hungry."

"That's not like you. Are you poorly?"

"I'm fine."

Madeleine forced a few mouthfuls down. Philip felt annoyed by her manner of eating. They didn't speak. Madeleine felt suffocated by the silence. She left the table and turned the radio on.

"Do we have to have this on while we're eating?" Philip turned it off.

"It's important to hear what's going on in the world."

"It's depressing."

The truth invariably is, she thought. "Even so."

"You can listen later."

They sat for a few minutes with empty plates. Madeleine's face rested in her palms, her elbows on the table.

"Can't you sit properly? You look like a sulky child."

She got up and started to clear the table.

"I'll load the dishwasher, only fair," Philip offered.

"Thanks."

"What're you up to tonight, then?"

"Visiting a friend."

"Anyone I know?" Philip paused in his task and turned to look at her.

"No."

"How long d'you think you'll be?"

"Don't know."

"A rough idea? I need to know you're safe before I can sleep."

That's fucking rich coming from you. "I won't be late."

As she fiddled about, getting ready to go nowhere, Madeleine was overcome for the second time that day by rage against Shibu. She needed the razor but couldn't risk it with Philip around.

The cold air hit her in the face as soon as she left the house and it stung her skin. It was almost as good as the razor; it sliced into her anger and calmed her into remorse. Poor, sweet Shibu.

Madeleine walked the streets for a while, enjoying the revitalising effects of the cold, and then she telephoned Sean. The persistent ringing culminated in his request for the caller to leave a message, but she didn't. Instead she phoned Carol. "Hi. It's been a while. Can I come round?"

"Sorry, hun, I've just agreed to a night shift. Tomorrow?"

"Yeah! Ta. Hope the night goes okay."

She scrolled through her phone, looking for Kumar's number and came across Julian's. She selected options and scrolled down to *delete contact*, but then pressed the back key instead and found Kumar's number again.

"Of course you can," he said in response to her plea.

"I'll be there in ten." She hurried her pace.

Kumar's house was smaller and more modern than Madeleine's. It was sparsely but tastefully furnished.

Sumayyia answered the door. Madeleine pulled her into a tight embrace. "Haven't seen you for so long, you look more like a woman and more beautiful every time. Where's that brother of yours?"

The more formal greeting, which Madeleine offered Beldiv, was due to his almost adult male status.

Kumar greeted Madeleine with a hug.

"It's great to see the children – not that they are really that anymore."

"Yes, makes a change for them to be here."

"You look so like your mum, Sumayyia. I hope you don't mind me saying so."

"Of course not."

"Are you really the little girl I used to push on the swing? And Beldiv, remember building that den in the woods?"

"Certainly do."

"Oh, um. Happy days."

"Come and sit down. Sumayyia can make you a coffee."

"White, no sugar, right?" Sumayyia asked.

"Wow! Perhaps it's not been so long, after all."

"You can have something stronger if you'd prefer," Kumar offered.

"Maybe later. I want my wits about me with you know who there."

"How's it going?"

"I'll survive."

"You're most welcome to come any time."

"Thanks. Just might take you up on that."

"You'll see Sean, of course?"

"Usually comes Christmas Day in the late afternoon when he's seen his mum. But he's all loved up these days, don't know if he'll have the time for me."

"I'm sure he will."

The message alert sounded on her phone. "That's probably him now, I'll check later."

"My friend is having a party at New Year if you want to come?" Kumar asked.

"Will he mind?"

"No, you can be my plus one." Kumar paused before continuing. "He's a postman, Julian might be there."

"I can't avoid him forever."

"When're you going to see your mother?"

"Twenty-seventh. Back thirtieth. So, not too much time with *him* on my own."

"Shibu working?"

"No. He took our advice and asked for time off. He's in Reading." Madeleine took a deep sigh.

"That bad without him?"

The question sent a shockwave through her. "I was thinking, not exactly that relaxed with my mother either. The party'll be something to look forward to."

The front of the house was in darkness when Madeleine returned, but she couldn't be sure if it was total; Philip might be still awake in his room or lingering in the kitchen. The creaky gate betrayed her. Over the threshold she breathed cautiously and moved quietly.

"Sneaking again!"

Madeleine jumped at the sound of Philip's voice. "I didn't want to wake you."

The landing remained in darkness, but she could make out his shape from the street-light's glow. "Told you I wouldn't sleep until you're in."

"Well, I'm here now."

"You going straight to bed?"

"More or less."

"Only I'm a light sleeper these days."

"I won't disturb you."

Although going straight to bed had indeed been her intention, Madeleine now felt the need to assert herself. Besides, the idea of sleeping in the house alone with Philip unnerved her.

She put the light on and then the kettle. The sound of running water made her oblivious to Philip's entry, so she jumped again when he said, "Thought I'd have a nightcap with you."

"Kettle's for my hot water bottle, not a drink."

"You smell of cigarettes. You've been smoking!"

Hardly a secret, you know, because you've been sneaking around my room, she thought. "Yes," she said.

"I thought you'd stopped."

"I had."

"Shame – so bad for you."

"Ah, well." She filled her hot water bottle and headed for the door. "Night, then."

"Maddie?"

"What?" She didn't turn to face him.

"I… I do worry about you, especially after… I worry about you, that's all."

"Thanks. No need, I'm fine." The genuine tone in his voice was suggestive of an apology, and Madeleine now realised that she feared this even more than she feared the status quo.

She hurried through her bedtime routine and into bed, where she kept one ear on her father's whereabouts.

It wasn't until she was setting the alarm on her phone that Madeleine realised she had forgotten to check the message. When she did, she was surprised to find Shibu's number instead of Sean's and she read: "*Goodnight Madeleine,*" as if it were a favourable horoscope prediction.

Chapter Sixteen

The Christmas morning hangover shamed her. How stupid she'd been to drink a whole bottle of red wine; now Philip would have more reason for disapproval, and her self-hatred would be underlined in bold type.

The distant church bells rang with an enthusiasm that matched the voice of a child she could hear in the street. Madeleine dragged herself from bed, feeling as if she'd left her head behind, and looked out of the window. A girl of about six or seven wobbled on a too-large bike to the encouragement of her mother. The sight of them filled Madeleine with envy. She might have been that mother years ago if she hadn't… She quickly arrested the thought. It too was a hangover from the night before when, seeing Carol's children's presents under the tree, she had been thrown into grief for the children she'd never had, and for the child she herself had been.

This was the emotion that drove her to hide behind the wine and the laughter. "Sing, Carol, sing a carol," she'd ordered, giggling like a teenager. But somewhere in the midst of 'Silent Night' the seeker found her hiding place and the tears flowed more freely than the wine. Pathetic! That's how it seemed now. She'd better ring later to check how Carol was feeling and if she needed to apologise.

From the bathroom there emitted the sounds of shaving; in the gaps between the splashing and the silence of concentration Philip whistled 'White Christmas'. There was nostalgia in the very sound of the razor, with the reminders of the men who'd shared her life, but more so in the song. It wasn't any particular memory; rather, it was the impression of every childhood Christmas. For Madeleine the sentiments expressed in the song were, like snow on Christmas Day, as much a fantasy as Santa Claus or the virgin birth, and for her the true colour of Christmas was grey. There was a knock on her door. "Bathroom's free."

Madeleine knew that was Philip's way of telling her he was ready to start the day. The knock produced an automatic programmed response from her body, which sent the core constricting in fear, while her extremities felt light enough to float away. It, and the hangover, impeded her routine, whilst the ghosts of Christmas past clung to her like leeches, and sucked away what little energy she had.

The smell of the cooked breakfast sent her running to the bathroom, but an empty stomach produced no vomit and left it aching from the retching. For several minutes she lay clinging to the porcelain, trying to calm her churning stomach. She knew to refuse Philip's offer of food would be unthinkable. Eventually she felt able to stand and cautiously made her way downstairs, where she flopped down at the table to find her breakfast waiting for her.

Philip was already eating his. "Too much to drink?"

"Yes." She scraped the beans from a piece of toast and took a tiny bite, deliberately avoiding Philip's gaze.

"Can't expect you to be much company today, then?"

"Sorry."

"I thought you'd long since stopped drinking to excess."

"I have. Just got carried away last night." She pushed her food around her plate like a fussy child, then, in the same manner, forced it down in tiny bites. Once her plate was clear, however, she did feel much better.

After breakfast they exchanged gifts.

"It's a trilogy," Madeleine explained, "set in the First World War, which I thought would interest you."

There had been a host of emotions at the time of purchase: excitement, because she loved to share books she was passionate about; disappointment, because Philip wasn't a person with whom she would enjoy that pleasure; and grief, for the relationship they could and should have had.

Philip scanned the back covers and nodded as if acknowledging her choice as a good one. He did the same with the CDs, over which Madeleine had experienced no emotion, their musical tastes having nothing in common.

She opened the wrapper on her parcel. Inside was a box and inside that a pair of high-quality red shoes, which Madeleine, somewhat reluctantly, loved. She tried them on immediately.

"Comfy?" Philip asked.

"Very, thank you."

"Pleased you like them. You have such strange taste in clothes I wasn't sure, but vouchers are boring, don't you think?"

"I guess so. Well, the shoes are great, thank you."

"You must be pleased with them, that's the first time I've seen you smile properly since I arrived."

"Sorry."

"Yes, so you've said several times now"

She almost said it again, but the words were arrested by Philip's next question.

"I suppose you've spared a thought for your brother?"

"Of course."

"D'you think about him much?"

"Yes."

"Does it still hurt?"

"Mostly. Sometimes not."

"Everyone says Christmas, birthdays and anniversaries are the worst, but for me it's every day."

There was genuine pathos in the words, which almost stirred Madeleine to sympathy. This was the emotion which underlined her inability to exclude their father from the funeral, as Tom had requested, and so, even in death she'd failed him.

"I've never been religious or understood why anyone was until then," Philip continued. "How I wanted to believe he'd gone to a better place! And pray for him, just in case."

Madeleine felt the flush of anger pink her cheeks at the suggestion of prayer. There would be no need for prayers if Philip had learnt to tame his devil.

Later, grateful for the time alone with her thoughts whilst preparing the meal, she was at last able to grant

Shibu an audience. All morning he had been teasing her consciousness, like a favourite song played on too low a volume; now she let him in, regretting only the lack of his physical company. She wondered what he was doing and if he spared a passing thought for her.

The message alert on her phone rang. It was Sean wishing her a happy Christmas and promising to visit in the early evening. His company would ensure a little lightness. And tomorrow she'd visit Kumar again.

Historically Boxing Day had always been the worst. On Christmas Day there was safety in dinner with the extended family, followed by a soporific television film. But by Boxing Day the veneer of goodwill slipped away and Philip, exhausted by overtime hours and distressed by spending over budget, waged war on his family. Madeleine wanted to slash holes in her new clothes, smash her stereo with a hammer, let go of the doll's pram and watch it speed down the hill into a stationary car. Anything but have to be grateful for and enjoy gifts, the money for which came at such a high cost.

In the confessional Shibu sat drenched in shame. He knew to what he needed to confess, but he feared God's representative on earth almost as much as he feared God Himself. And, in the deepest place in his heart, he knew that fear was not the only emotion which guaranteed his silence; the advice of the priest in the confessional was sacrosanct and must be adhered to. There was no need for Shibu to hear it in order to know what it would be, but if he didn't hear, well then… He thought quickly as he and the priest went through their preamble. The discomfort in his belly provided the perfect excuse. "I am guilty of the sin of greed," he said.

He left the confessional feeling no less guilty. He remembered the first time he'd been conscious of feeling that particular emotion. It was in response to the look of disappointment in the eyes of his favourite teacher, which came with the realisation that Shibu was amongst the boys who taunted a younger pupil. The disenchanted, questioning glance rendered punishment unnecessary, but Shibu would have given anything to exchange rejection for reprimand. It was this that he feared most from God. And that on the Day of Judgement He would demand Shibu look into his own soul and question himself.

And if he were to do so right now, the only thing of which he could be sure was the contradiction between what he wanted and what he believed to be right.

As they headed back towards the house Shibu became irritated by the excited chatter of his cousin, as he enthused about the service having been delivered in Malayalam, and he wished to go back to church and make a proper confession.

Chapter Seventeen

The train pulled out of the station with Tessa running alongside waving at Madeleine. It made her feel like a child, or, to be more precise, that her mother wished to reinstate the child. It was, in Madeleine's opinion, Tessa's response to guilt. Wishing to allow her relief from this, she waved back with more enthusiasm that she felt. She didn't always feel so well disposed towards her, but it had been a good stay and over the years Madeleine had come to realise that Tessa was as much a victim as her children in many ways.

If she compared her young self with her mother at the same age it was even possible to imagine that she would have been the same. She had, after all, almost accepted Gary's marriage proposal despite knowing the volatile nature of his passion. And it was true that there were times when loneliness had led her to regret that she had not, if only for the sake of the children she would have had.

Yet, over all she considered she'd made the right choice in that respect. Because she understood only too well the cyclic nature of abuse.

"Please try to forgive your daddy." She remembered her grandmother's sobbing plea. *"It's what he learnt, you see. When Granddad came back from the war, he wasn't the man he used to be. He was a stranger – angry, so angry. But what could I do? He'd been fighting for his country. How could I leave him? In any case it was different in those days, women just didn't do that."*

The occasion was her third stay with her grandmother, on whose doorstep she arrived post-midnight, her back bearing a rucksack and her soul a far bigger burden. And, as she lay with her head in her grandmother's lap, feeling only half of her actual fourteen years, she absorbed the news in disbelief. True, she remembered times when Granddad had shown signs of irritation, but nothing more. Before the cancer, he ran around the garden with Tom playing football, counted while she skipped, directed her with a wink towards Tom's hiding places and he was always at their school plays.

Yes, she was right not to have had any children; it was a small heartache when compared with others.

She indulged herself a little now with Etta James and Norah Jones on her MP3 player, and inevitably her melancholy mood brought her back to Shibu, to whose company she could soon look forward. It would be different now they were no longer lovers, but it would be fine. Better than his not being around at all, and it would help her when it was time for him to leave. She'd behave professionally towards him, like the landlady she was supposed to be.

Shibu was sitting at the computer. He was dressed in jeans that fitted tightly around his calves and a shirt that emphasised the shape of his forearms. Madeleine's stomach lurched.

"Hi," she said, "good Christmas? Uh huh, that's good. Where's my father?"

"I don't know where he."

"Well, he'll be back soon enough for sure."

She made a cup of tea for herself and a coffee for Shibu, then took her drink to the bedroom while she unpacked her case. Despite all she'd told herself, she kept one ear tuned to Shibu's whereabouts and her mind strayed, either back in remembrance or forwards in anticipation, each of which enjoyed equal airtime. So it was that, because she knew he had turned the computer off and was heading for the stairs, she could time her exit from the bedroom to intercept him at the top of the stairs. Yet, suddenly she felt predatory and stepped sideways to allow him past, offering an apology as she did so.

Shibu, however, stood still long enough for the two of them to engage in eye contact. Before either of them had the chance for analysis they leapt into an embrace and urgent kissing.

"Your father?" Shibu's breath on her neck was like a warm breeze.

She led him away from the top of the stairs and into the shadows, where they resumed kissing, each one so deep it reached Madeleine's solar plexus. Shibu's hands strayed from her back to her breasts; in the same instant she turned the handle on his bedroom door and pulled him inside.

"Your father?" Shibu asked again, without showing any indication of stopping.

"We're safe in here."

Hands were inside clothes; then they were naked and exploring each other with mouths, tongues and genitals, hungrily and yet slowly, savouring the experience. Satiated, they lay awhile.

"I'd better go." Madeleine was pulling her clothes on when she heard Philip come in. "Shit!"

"Madeleine?" he called up the stairs. "Maddie, you home?"

Fear constricted her throat; although she knew to reply was the sensible option, she was afraid he'd know where she was. A second later Philip came up the stairs, knocked on her bedroom door and called her name again.

"What we do now?" Shibu's question was quieter than a whisper.

Madeleine put a finger to his lips and to her own. Nervous hearts pounded in their ears and each of them worried about the volume of their breathing.

Now Madeleine heard Philip open the door to her bedroom. "Madeleine, you in here?" And as she heard him go in, she felt a flash of rage, which grew as she sensed him rustle through her half-unpacked case, then open and close her dresser drawers.

The pad of his feet across the landing was terrifying. Shibu saw his future flash before him, Madeleine her past. Then there came a knock on Shibu's door.

"What I do?" The words were mouthed.

"Answer him."

Another knock: "Shibu?"

"Yes, sir?"

"Have you seen Madeleine?"

"I saw, but I don't know where she now."

"Okay."

They resumed guarded listening. "He's gone up to the attic. Quick, get dressed. We'll go down together and I'll pretend I've just come in."

Shibu was dressing in time with Madeleine's instructions.

They hurried down the stairs like naughty children. Madeleine felt as afraid as she had when forced to play this as a child, pretending to Mummy she'd been downstairs all the time.

Shibu felt sure they were discovered and his reputation, as well as his soul, was damned. He headed for the kitchen, whistling, then opened a cupboard door and slammed it shut. Madeleine grabbed her coat and shoes as she quietly exited the house, put them both on and, a few minutes later, re-entered in the opposite manner. It coincided with Philip's descent from the attic, "Ah! Where've you been?"

"I just had something to do." She didn't try too hard with the lie, because even if he knew he had no evidence to back it up.

"What did you have to do?"

"Does it matter? An errand for someone."

"Why're you always so secretive?"

It's a lesson you taught me years ago, she thought, but said, "It was nothing important."

Philip sighed. "I thought we might go out to eat tonight – didn't think you'd fancy cooking after travelling. My treat, of course."

"Okay. What time? Guess I'd better start getting ready, then."

"While you do that I'll go and chat with your lodger."

Madeleine longed for time with Shibu, feeling in need of some reassurance and the need to offer him the same. She was also more than a little worried that his conscience would give him away.

Her concern was misplaced. Now that he had regained his composure Shibu played his role in the manner of one who was well rehearsed.

In the shower Madeleine felt comfort in the warm water flowing over her.

She was certain that Shibu's fear in the face of almost being caught would reignite his decision to stop. As she ran her hands over her breasts, washing them, her mind strayed back to his touch; his fingertips and lips spoke much more honestly than his tongue. Needing to see him she hurried from the shower, but as she was adding the final touches to her preparations, she heard Shibu's bedroom door close and knew the opportunity was lost.

In her assumptions Madeleine was all but correct. However, Shibu's renewed resolve was born less of their near-miss than it was of his growing need for her. The forbidden fruit now tasted as bittersweet as opium to the addict, and it countered every argument, reasoned or superstitious, against the continuation of the affair. It was only Madeleine who could relieve the craving, because it was only her he craved, yet, it was only this that sent him into despair. These were the feelings he sought to rationalise and conquer while Madeleine and Philip ate their meal.

And, while they ate, Philip wrestled with irritation at his daughter's habit of portioning off each item to be eaten in isolation from any other. It was, in his opinion, neurotic, and a trait he considered to be inherited from her mother.

He tutted and sighed but didn't say anything. He was under no illusions as to how uncomfortable Madeleine felt in his company, but at least she continued to see him. Tom, in doing what he'd done, had condemned him, but Madeleine's continuing to see him offered proof enough that his parenting hadn't been so bad. Tom was weak. Like his mother.

Madeleine made the bites smaller and ate slower, her eyes twinkling with defiance.

Philip felt his temper rising. Still he didn't risk an out-and-out accusation but instead said, "Funny thing is, I had a feeling you were home when I got back this afternoon."

"You saw me come in." Madeleine found holding his gaze was fine as long as no direct lie was involved.

"Yes. You seem to have a close relationship with your lodger."

"We get on well."

And there the game ended: stalemate.

New Year's Eve Shibu got up at his usual time for work and crept around in the hope of leaving before either of the other occupants arose.

But Madeleine's need was the opposite, so she was waiting for him when he arrived in the kitchen.

"Morning," she said.

"Morning."

"Are you okay?"

"Of course."

"I just wanted to check after... well, you know."

Shibu's reply came in the form of an alarmed glance in the direction of the ceiling.

"He can't hear us from upstairs."

"Maybe he come down."

"We both know he knows. Don't worry, he'll keep pretending that he doesn't."

"How you can be sure?"

"We play this stupid game, he and I. Confidentiality is guaranteed because neither of us trusts the other. It's like mutually assured destruction."

"What means this?"

"Two countries point their nuclear bombs at each other to ensure neither of them uses them. Anyway, you can relax; if it comes to war, I have the bigger bomb."

Shibu looked puzzled.

Madeleine sighed. "I just needed to see you. I've been worried about you."

"Just I tell to you, I am fine."

"Good. See you later then." She hesitated, wanting to kiss him but didn't.

After he left, she went back to bed, buried her face in the pillow and cried. But she too had her job to go to and the time was getting on. Although work was the last thing on her mind Madeleine was also grateful for it, because it would spare her from another day with Philip and keep her mind from Shibu.

As it turned out only one of those was true, as Shibu hardly left her thoughts.

She returned to a house that was full of the sound of Coldplay; although Madeleine was pleased that her father was listening to the CD she'd bought him, she was irritated by it too. There was only one more day of his company to endure and then she could play her own music again. When he saw her Philip stopped singing along and turned the volume down; by way of greeting he said, "Can't understand why you don't like these guys."

Madeleine didn't answer; they had had the discussion before. She checked the message that had just arrived on her mobile; it was from Kumar, asking if she was still going to the party.

"You going out tonight?" she asked her father.

"Are you?"

"Yes."

"Not much point in my staying in, then. Don't suppose your little Indian friend is likely to celebrate?"

"Don't suppose he is."

Madeleine took a long time over getting ready, hoping to delay long enough for her father to be the first to leave so she could review the situation with Shibu, but he showed no sign of hurry. For a long time she sat in her bedroom listening as Shibu came in, showered and had his meal.

Still Philip showed no sign of leaving, so she devised a plan; she'd go for a walk around the block and then return; if Philip was still there, she'd pretend to have forgotten something. With this in mind she left her phone in the bedroom, fearing if Philip saw it he would hang on and wait. When she came downstairs both he and Shibu were chatting; the relaxed nature of it made Madeleine feel like an outcast.

"I'm off, then. See you both next year," she said. The words were accompanied by a giggle. Neither man showed more than a passing interest at her departure.

Fifteen minutes later she returned; Shibu was at the computer.

"Hi, forgot my phone."

He didn't acknowledge her.

"Has Philip gone?"

"I think he upstairs." Shibu's gaze remained fixed on the screen.

Madeleine's throat constricted, along with her stomach, and hot flushes tinged her cheeks.

"Shibu. Shibu?"

"What?"

His eyes remained fixed on the screen.

Tears pricked her eyes and her bottom lip quivered, and Madeleine felt as if she was being watched as she used the toilet. She covered her shame in politeness.

"In case I don't see you later, Happy New Year."

Now he did turn towards her, but ever so slightly, and quickly he returned his eyes to the computer. "Oh. Same to you."

She hesitated, lowered her head to her hands, stroked her brow, then went to get her phone.

She was alerted by the closed door, being sure she'd left it slightly ajar. Anger and fear set her heart at a fast pace and unlocked another memory. *Just making sure it's closed properly.* As he moved away from it and towards her, she felt herself shrink in size and drift away from her* *body.* In the present she turned the handle as quietly as she was able; Philip jumped when he saw her.

"What're you doing in my room?"

"You left your phone."

"I know, that's why I'm back." Madeleine experienced a rare feeling of power. "That still doesn't explain why you're in my room.

"I thought I heard it ring."

"And?"

"And I was going to answer it – thought it might be important."

Madeleine picked the phone up and glanced at the screen; there was no record of a missed call.

"Must've been your little friend's, I guess. Well, see you later, have a nice time." Philip's tone was cocky. He hurried from the house.

Once again Madeleine checked the contents of her drawers and cupboards. Once again there was no physical evidence, but she knew what he'd been doing with her clothes. She pulled out the drawer and threw all of her underwear on the floor, then gathered it up and put it in the washing machine.

Shibu was in the kitchen now, eating and fiddling with his phone; earphones in place, he paid no attention to Madeleine. His face wore a pout. She made no attempt at communication; she'd had enough humiliation for one day. Madeleine felt like a child watching her mother drive away without her.

A few minutes later she sat on the wall outside the off-licence, having purchased wine for the party, scrolling through her phone without purpose. As if she were a teenager, and in a mood to match that age, she made her way to rendezvous with Kumar.

The party was still quite quiet; standing in one corner of the room was Julian.

Kumar put an arm around her. "Okay?"

"Fine. Thanks."

Julian looked at them and away so quickly Madeleine wondered if he'd even seen them. Feeling a mixture of relief and regret she too turned her attention away, but it was no use pretending. His voice was audible above all others and, because she sensed his gaze kept drifting her way, it was necessary to make a conscious effort not to look in his direction, all of which meant Madeleine's mind was somewhere other than on the person to whom she talked, and so she accepted the need to acknowledge him.

She approached him person by person, hoping to create the image of natural progression and offering him the chance to back out, but he didn't; when she reached him she said, "Hi, how are you?"

"Not bad. You?"

"I'm good." She took a sip of wine. "Haven't seen you about for a while."

"Changed my round."

Madeleine wondered if she was the reason, but she didn't ask.

"You're here with Kumar? Are you and he…?"

"No. No, just both of us free tonight. What about you? Living back home?"

"No. Still have the room; still see her most days, though, nothing much has changed."

"Boys okay? Good." Now Madeleine took a deep sigh, feeling relieved that the ice was broken. "Guess I'd better get back to Kumar, catch you later."

It would have been fine if she'd left it there, but at the bottom of the third glass of wine she found the deal of Shibu's making and the fourth was infused with nostalgia. The midnight chimes urged a new start, but 'Auld Lang Syne', with its talk of remembrance, reinforced the sense that for her nostalgia was all there was. She stood between Kumar and Julian as they sang, her voice clear and strong despite the wine and the tears in her heart. They joined hands; Julian's felt strong and familiar, Kumar's reassuring. Yet for Madeleine there was no comfort; in that moment the future looked so empty that the past was where she desired to be.

Perhaps it was this. Or perhaps it was that, loosened by alcohol, Julian was more relaxed, so much so he danced and held her close. Most likely it was simply too much wine; whichever was the case it led Madeleine to answer in the affirmative when Julian offered her a nightcap. "That's okay with you, I suppose, Kumar?"

"I guess. You'll see she gets home safely, Julian? I'll get your coat, Madeleine."

As he was helping her into it, he whispered, "You could have a nightcap with me."

"You could come with us. Hey, Julian, Kumar can come too, can't he?"

He sighed heavily. "S'pose so."

"It's okay," Kumar said. "Just stay safe. I'll call you – soon."

Madeleine was in a haze, as deaf to the body languages of both men as she was to her own sensibility.

She and Julian walked hand in hand. The hand Madeleine held was the right size, but there was no flow of energy into her palm.

Almost as soon as they were in his living room Julian pulled her into an embrace. Her head was low on his chest; she couldn't tuck it neatly under his chin. She accepted his kiss, but his mouth was thin and hard, not full and soft, and the taste was of bitter beer, not dry wine.

Now Julian was telling her how much he'd missed her and how sorry he was that he'd called her a whore.

Yet that was exactly how she felt now. How could she do this to him again? How could she stop now that it had gone this far? His hand was on her thigh and his fingers were stroking the most recent wounds. "Oh dear God, oh my honey, your poor, poor legs. Is this because of me?"

Suddenly she came to her senses and pulled away. "Julian, stop!"

"What? What'd I do?"

"Nothing! I'm sorry. I just can't." She sat up and adjusted her clothes. "I have to go."

Julian's demeanour immediately changed. "You're going? You think it's okay to leave me like this?" He grabbed her hand and pushed it into his groin, so that she felt his erection.

"Of course not." She struggled to her feet, feeling nausea rise in her stomach. She held on to the door frame to steady herself. "I shouldn't have come. I don't know what I was thinking of. I'm sorry."

"You're sorry. Big deal. You're always sorry."

Wobbling on one leg Madeleine hurried into her shoes, grabbed her coat and headed for the front door.

Julian barred her exit. "Please don't go, Maddie. I meant it when I said I've missed you."

He knew she hated being called Maddie and it brought her closer to her senses, but she didn't say any more to him for fear of making the situation worse. She was already dialling for a taxi. "How long? Never mind then. Open the door, please, Julian."

"Don't go. Let's do it just once more. We can be friends."

"No. I'm sorry. Please move away from the door."

"You can't walk, it's too late."

"I'll be fine."

"Let me walk with you."

"No need, really. Please just move out of my way."

The desperate look in his eyes sent a message to her psyche that spoke of her own need for the other man. *Bitch, whore*, she heard in her head. *How can you do this to him a second time?*

"Do you enjoy fucking with my feelings?" His tone scared her. The look in his eyes was determined. He would have what he wanted. Knowing she deserved what was coming she braced herself. But then, suddenly, he moved aside.

There was a second's shocked hesitation before she moved for the door, but once out of it, Madeleine increased her pace. As she was hurrying along the corridor towards the stairs Julian called, "Happy fucking New Year to you too," then slammed his door shut.

Chapter Eighteen

Madeleine's sleep was constantly interrupted by grief: for Shibu, for Tom, for the woman she should've been – and by regret on Julian's behalf. In the morning the same emotions greeted her; they punctuated the nausea and headache of her hangover, each of which ensured there would be no yoga today. Besides, it was late, almost eight-thirty.

She ran a bath, lacking the energy to stand in the shower. The heat upset the delicate balance of her current condition and made her vomit. She turned the taps on hard to prevent Philip from hearing. Dizzy, sick, headachy and full of self-loathing. What a way to start the New Year! Her teeth and the bathroom received a minimal clean because what Madeleine needed right now was food.

When Philip came down she was lying on the sofa, a plate of toast in one hand and the washing-up bowl in the other.

"Another hangover?"

"It was New Year's Eve."

"Even so! It is a hangover, I suppose, and not something else?"

"Like what?"

"A grandchild for me?"

"At my age?" Madeleine knew a better response would have been one which suggested it was impossible for another reason, but she couldn't be bothered to play games with him anymore.

"It wouldn't be unheard of."

The question took her back – back to the time of her pregnancy. Perhaps it had been too early, the baby gone too soon, but she hadn't felt sick, only strange and scared. The old regret was tainted by another now, that she would never be a grandmother either. She wondered about the future and tried to imagine herself as an old lady, living alone in this house. Where would she find the money for repairs? And who would come to break the monotony of everyday life?

Madeleine thought fondly of the summer afternoon teas she and her grandmother had shared in the garden, and her visits to her other nana in the retirement home. Without any family there would be only one person on whom she could rely, and it looked as if he would soon be less available. Thinking of Sean reminded her he was due to visit that afternoon; she hoped the hangover was gone by then and that Philip would be too.

Even while he was busy Madeleine was often on Shibu's mind, but in the quiet moments she was the main occupant of his thoughts. It disturbed him to find reminders of her in many of his daily tasks: Edith's coconut shower gel and Arthur's classical music were the most significant, but hardly less so Barbara's slight over-emphasis on the S when she said his name, in almost the same way as Madeleine did. He was annoyed with himself for failing to banish her.

Anger inflamed superstition and he imagined himself bewitched, feeling for the first time that he really understood the power of Eve. Madeleine's temptation was no less. She seduced him with her singing and her dancing and even with the yoga, which was not as it seemed. Under the guise of a spiritual act there was sexual allure. It wasn't just that she kept her body toned, the better to trap her man, but also that she had beguiled him with it, and the memory of her in the Virabhadrasana refused to leave his mind.

Of course, Shibu knew in reality this was all nonsense. Madeleine was only to blame in as far as she accepted his advances, and if she had been a young Indian woman he could have tamed his lust by marriage, which was what God required of him, he was sure. But marriage for the sake of it was not the answer; he should love his wife too, and he didn't love Madeleine. Did he?

So, what did he feel? Although it was tinged with guilt, when he was with her he felt alive. It was like waking his senses with a rich spice. Without her he was restless and dissatisfied. But this wasn't love, was it? This was merely the result of so much intimate time together, the satisfaction of a desire so long repressed, the addictive nature of sexual attraction.

The question remained on how to proceed. The stay in Reading, and especially his behaviour upon returning, had impressed upon Shibu the depth of his involvement. In his heart of hearts, he knew the cause was lost; as long as they remained under the same roof all he could hope for were occasional reprieves. He considered once more the possibility of moving out, but it would be hard to find somewhere as nice, especially at a price he could afford.

Philip left a little before midday. He was hardly out of the door before Madeleine, now feeling very much more herself, was cleaning to the usual accompaniment. She had only just finished when Sean arrived, around whom she threw her arms and then burst into tears.

"Hey, babe, what's up?" He held her close and rubbed her back.

Through the cracks in her heart ran Shibu. "It's such a relief to be rid of my father, that's all. Plus – I did something really stupid after that party."

Over a cup of tea she told the full story and Sean, of course, said all the right things.

"You were keen to salvage something and got a bit carried away with it, that's all. At least you stopped short of doing the deed."

"Only just! And he was quite angry. Can't really blame him."

"I'll bet in the morning he was just as glad as you that you didn't. Unless he wants you back."

"He said he does, but that's not what I want."

"And you've made that quite clear."

"I could have made it clearer if I'd behaved differently."

"You were drunk."

"And upset."

"Because of Philip?"

"Yes. And Shibu." She hadn't meant to say that.

"Shibu? What's he done?"

"Nothing. Nothing at all, except be Shibu." She knew there was tenderness in her voice.

"Are you telling me…?"

"I've fallen in love with him."

"Ah!" He didn't say that he'd guessed as much.

It was such a relief to say it, but Madeleine was scared too. "I shouldn't be telling you this, he wouldn't like it."

"So, you haven't just randomly fallen for him? There is more to it?"

"We've been getting it on for a couple of months now. I shouldn't be telling you this."

"Come on, you know I'll be discreet. Sounds like you need to talk."

"Oh, God, yes!"

The story culminated in more tears, more hugs and an immense feeling of relief.

"So, you finally fell!"

"And how? But it's all wrong, of course. Trust me to mess this one up too."

"What's wrong about it?"

"I'm the wrong race, the wrong creed, the wrong age. I'm just wrong."

"Those are his issues and they didn't stop him in the first place. They're not insurmountable; it would be difficult for him, true, but if he really wanted—"

"He doesn't, though." When said out loud the words hit her like a punch in the chest. "He doesn't want me in the same way I want him."

"That hurts, yeah?"

"I was madly attracted, I really thought it would be okay."

"And now?"

"My head agrees with him. We have to stop! My body is crazy for him, like never before."

"And your heart?"

"I want whatever makes him happy; he's such a beautiful person I don't want to spoil him. But for myself, I just wish I could keep him near me. And we could be the way we are now forever."

"Certainly sounds like love."

"Yes." Madeleine's voice drifted off in a dreamy tone; her consciousness followed. When she returned, she said, "Thanks, I needed that. So, you and Aileen?"

"Guess I'm in love too."

"I hope she is too?"

"Think so. It's early days, though."

"You're not bothered about the kids anymore?"

"No, they seem cool with it. And it's rapidly getting so we couldn't stop if we wanted."

"It's very addictive, isn't it?"

"Yep! It's also the best high. Cocaine never was this good. I tell you, I'm so grateful too; let's face it, they haven't exactly been queuing up."

"I don't know why, you're one of the loveliest guys I ever met."

"Let me see if I can guess who the other one is. No, seriously, you've never fancied me."

"You're my friend, my best friend."

"Exactly. I'm everyone's best friend, never anyone's lover – until now – whoopee. Hey, sorry, that was—"

"Fine. It's fine, you deserve no less."

"I could say the same for you."

"Yeah, well." Madeleine sighed. "It was good while it lasted. I'll probably be able to celebrate that someday. For now, I have to try to keep a bit of distance."

"We're getting a bit slushy here one way or another, let's dance."

When Shibu came in they were still dancing. He tried not to mind the way Madeleine shook her breasts at Sean as she danced.

The music still reached his ears in his room and the image of them dancing taunted him. In the dance was remembrance of her breasts brushing against his bare flesh, and cascading hair falling into his face.

In denial of his feelings Shibu telephoned his friend and laughed exaggeratedly loudly at every witty comment, just to let Madeleine, and himself, know he was feeling fine.

But she didn't hear him. In Sean's company she was almost able to keep her consciousness with her physical self. Sean stayed the night.

"You can have Philip's room," Madeleine told him.

"You sure?"

"Perfectly! He's hardly likely to come back. It's about time I put a stop to his control. And anyway, he spent half his time in my room."

"What?"

"Every time I was out he went rummaging around in my stuff."

"Bastard!"

When she retired to bed Madeleine gave a gentle tap

on Shibu's door. He didn't answer, so she didn't call out the 'goodnight' she'd intended.

Shibu wasn't asleep. He was lying in a foetal posture with the duvet and a pillow over his head, but the matters he wished to banish seemed instead to be intensified: Madeleine and himself in a lover's posture, she and Sean shaking their bodies at each other like shaman casting spells, the contradictory feelings in his heart.

In a half-sleep Madeleine made herself a promise: she would do her very best to make sure she did nothing to tempt Shibu out of his chastity.

And so it was that their interactions changed. Flirtatiousness became contained within the rules of formality, like dancing a minuet. In the same manner they continued to share everyday tasks and do favours for each other, but apologies followed every accidental breach of personal space.

Yet, sometimes Madeleine couldn't help but advance, even if only slightly, when the ache in her stomach was too much to bear. Then she might stand a little too close behind him as he worked on the computer, feeling him stir under the breath that teased his neck. Or pause before vacating the doorway, or brush his hand in exchanging goods.

Shibu, burdened by the weight of both their emotions, retreated further. He began taking his time over the last-minute duties at work and then walking home via town; he'd peer into shop windows or, if the weather was too cold, stroll around the supermarket. At home he called up his cousin on Skype and talked for hours. He even returned to attending church, although still he kept the big confession from his lips.

Mostly Madeleine recognised the behaviour for what it was, but sometimes she became afraid; that he didn't love her was a fact within the bounds of her acceptance, but that he might not even like her filled her with dread.

On those occasions she often couldn't stop herself from focusing on him. Perhaps she'd have his coffee ready in the cup with only the water to add; she'd find it necessary to have a conversation with him concerning the rent or the washing, or there would be a special offer on that she was sure he needed to know about. Then, if Shibu gave her something beyond the bounds of everyday politeness, no matter how small, a particular kind of smile was all it took, then she would feel reassured and the ache would lessen. Yet, at other times he would barely interrupt the telephone conversation and only offer a shrug or monosyllabic answer, and then Madeleine felt wretched.

She came in from work and cleaned until almost midnight, then drank herself to sleep on wine. On her days off she cleaned the already spotless house, unable to concentrate on yoga, and, when none of this made her feel any better, she slashed at her legs with the razor. Sometimes she cried – into her pillow so Shibu wouldn't hear.

But sometimes he did. The image of her sobbing face disturbed him; he pictured peeling the tear-fixed hair from her face and brushing the tears gently away, but he knew what the result of that would be. Instead he selected music on his phone, plugged in the earpiece and wrapped the duvet over his head.

Twice a day, on his knees beside the bed, he prayed, his eyes closed hard against the distractions of the outside world. In the same position he masturbated, this time senses on alert, afraid equally of the consequences of ignoring his need and of Madeleine overhearing him. His desire seemed never fully satisfied and he felt himself a base creature of little worth.

He recalled an earlier time with shame: his barely more than teenaged self aroused by the glimpse he had caught of his sister's developing breasts. To the sexual act he had confessed, but not to the object of his fantasy, for fear of the priest's promise of eternal damnation.

He was no better now than then. It seemed to him that he was become someone whose lust had conquered him and, furthermore, a person who chose to ignore the hurt of another human being. He was no more worthy of God's love in this state than he had been as Madeleine's lover. What was needed now was guidance from a priest. This Sunday was his day off; he would rise early enough to go to church and this time he would confess.

On the same Sunday Madeleine got up early herself, as she'd vowed to get back to doing yoga.

Although the music drifted into his sleep it didn't disturb Shibu. But when he awoke and heard it he knew she would be practising her second Surya Namaskara, which didn't give him long, and he would have to be quiet so as not to disturb her in the Savasana.

The morning erection was proving obstinate. He beat it away in the shower with fierce jets of water, but it had already made him late so that by the time he reached the kitchen Madeleine was already there. Although over her leotard she wore her baggy grey jumper, which reached almost as far as her knees, and thick woollen socks right up to the bottom of her calves, memory, and the remaining parts of body that were more exposed, were enough to reignite Shibu's lust. For a second he was angry with himself, but soon the other emotion dominated. She had just boiled the kettle.

"You're up early, going to church?"

"I don't think so."

"Coffee?"

"Yes, thank you."

"Porridge too?"

"Okay, thank you."

He hovered close as she cooked it and closer still while she served it, close enough for her to hear arousal in his breathing. It sent her heart racing. She sat down opposite him. They ate in silence, each of them keeping their eyes on their breakfasts, each of them occasionally looking up to make sure the other was still doing so. Suddenly, overcome by his feelings, Shibu grabbed Madeleine's right hand and began stroking her fingers.

"You're turning me on."

He turned her hand over and rubbed her palm with his thumb.

Madeleine took hold of his other hand and they guided each other to standing and then into an embrace. She raised her eyes and then her mouth towards Shibu. They kissed, long and slow, like always.

"Let's go to bed," Shibu said.

Chapter Nineteen

Afterwards they lay with their limbs locked around each other, Madeleine's head tucked neatly under Shibu's chin. "What changed your mind?"

He didn't answer. Her question scared him. He didn't want to lie to her, and he was no longer sure what the truth was.

"Well, I'm glad that you did." She kissed the hand she was holding. "Are you?"

"I did it, didn't I?"

His heart was full of contradiction. He felt guilty on God's behalf if he did, and guilty on Madeleine's behalf if not. And he was so full of the two of them there was no room to decide what he felt on his own account.

"Are you regretting it again?"

"Little bit, but… is nice, I know I do again."

Madeleine wanted there to be no regret but knew she desired the impossible. It gave her an inkling into the emotional response her own shame had provoked in past lovers. She propped herself up on one arm and looked Shibu in the eyes as she asked, "Is your problem with God or with me?"

"Little bit both."

Now she looked away. "Why with me?"

"I worry to hurt you."

His concern for her was reassuring.

"I'm doing what I want. Just be sure you are too."

"I sure today, but tomorrow maybe not."

"I want you big time, but only if you want me. Promise me you won't do it just for me."

"I promise."

Madeleine lay back down and tucked herself into Shibu once more; they remained there for some time in silence. She drank him in, committing him to somatic memory by exploring him with her fingers and toes; she inhaled as he exhaled, making his breath her own. She wanted to make a cut in each of their hands then join them together and feel Shibu's blood flowing in her veins. She wished that she was younger and the circumstances different, because she desired to conceive his baby; in that way they could share their genes and he would never be fully lost to her.

The ticking of the clock in the hall, the gurgle of the water through the radiators, the very distant hum of electrical equipment, these were the noises Shibu concentrated on, because the synchronised sounds of their bodies disturbed him.

Madeleine was calm again, for the time being. She knew one day it would be over, but so long as it was one day, and not this day, she could cope. All she wanted was to savour every moment with Shibu. Sometimes she pictured her future, a year, ten years, thirty years from now; every imagined scenario was punctuated by sweet recollections of Shibu. Not only was he her first love, but he would also be her only love; she wanted to never feel about anyone else like she did about him for fear of tainting it. It mattered, sometimes a lot and others only a little, that her feelings were unrequited. It mattered more that Shibu be comfortable with himself and so she sought ever harder to keep her true feelings from him and, in so doing, protect him from any sense of obligation.

In this she failed. It was visible in her face and discernible in her actions: the way she ironed his clothes and folded it in neat piles, cooked curries too hot for her pallet, shopped for him on the way home from work, and especially in the way she surrendered her body to him, whenever and however he requested it. Her efforts to help him find a way to extend his visa were, they both knew, as much for her own sake as for his.

"What if you did another course?" she suggested one evening as they were lying on the sofa cuddling and discussing their days at work.

"I can't do, level four is very costly."

"Is it only the money that stops you?"

"Mostly."

"Mostly? What else?"

She was the what else. "No nothing, only money."

"I could borrow it from my father."

"Thank you, but I don't want debt to your father."

"It'll be to me. You can pay me back whenever."

"I don't know. I need to think."

The offer was tempting; currently the return home would leave him still in considerable debt. The uncle who had secured the loan for him had told him not to worry – there were arrangements that could be made – but still he felt burdened by the responsibility. A financial debt was a big tie, but if he accepted Madeleine's offer, he would only be transferring it, not ending it. There was undeniably some appeal in the idea of living for two more years with Madeleine. Coming from the cold into the warmth of her embrace was as homely as an after-school snack and he loved to share the experiences of his day with her. But he was concerned that if he stayed, their need for each other would grow deeper. Then, like a drug, they would become each other's habit instead of each other's high. Besides, he needed a wife soon.

His cousin was pushing him to stay. He sent details of a level four course in London and offers to secure a loan from the bank. Shibu calculated the cost and compared it to returning home in debt. If he could find bank work in another nursing home it would be the best financial option, but he would need it to go undetected for at least a year. With just one job, and a debt to either his uncle or to Madeleine, there was barely any difference between going and staying. This being the case, the decision on which was the most appropriate changed according to how he felt with regard to his personal circumstances. So, without one hundred per cent commitment, he applied for the level four course and an extension to his visa. In six weeks, his destiny for the next two years would be decided. In his mind he passed the responsibility to the Almighty, trusting to be guided by an act of fate.

Yet on that same God he turned his back, choosing instead the comfort of his earthly relationship. Daily Madeleine became more like a wife. It wasn't only in the way she looked after him, and it wasn't only the sex that made them close; there were the conversations, often held in bed as the night closed around them.

One time Madeleine asked him, "What's the best thing you remember from your childhood?"

Shibu was puzzled. "Everything was good. There was one or two bad thing, of course, but mostly was good."

"Okay. What's the worst thing you remember then?"

"When my mother go to hospital to have my sister I felt very scared and lonely."

Madeleine sighed, understanding his emotions only too well and wishing hers were limited to a single event. "Are you close to your sister? I guess you miss her then? I know that feeling."

"What happen your brother?"

"Told you, he died."

"I know, but what happen?"

Shibu had a way of asking direct questions, which were, by their very nature, hard to ignore, but in any case, she longed to tell him because the loss of Tom formed an integral part of her character, and she wanted Shibu to understand who she really was. Her persona was like a house built on shaky foundations. With Tom's death she'd bricked up all of the windows. Only now was the mortar beginning to soften. But she understood that Shibu possessed both a chisel and fresh cement.

"He killed himself."

"Oh!" Shibu remembered again Jobin dying in his father's arms, as Madeleine recounted the details of Tom's death.

"He was living in London. He did his degree there and then never came home. Partly because he loved it, but mostly because he didn't want to see our father. He used to phone me most days and we'd meet once or twice a month. He got these terrible depressions, when he couldn't get out of bed for days, then he wouldn't phone. But he'd always respond to my calls, even if only to say, 'I'm okay, Sis', but that was all that was needed. Not this time, though, obviously! There was no answer for three days and his girlfriend at the time had just spectacularly become his ex so refused to go and check on him, which meant I had to. I took the day off, went to his flat, found him there, dead."

The conviction that there was something wrong had been growing over the past few days. She stood outside the door to his basement flat. The curtains were open; they were closed when he was depressed or away. His bike was left uncovered, despite the rain. Madeleine trembled inside – surely he wouldn't have... She took the spare key from inside the electricity metre box. The air was still and the silence terrifying. Madeleine crept her away along the corridor, feeling sick.

The bedroom door was ajar; she inched it open, turning her head away when she saw the foot dangling from the bed. No, no. She closed her eyes and lowered her head as she pushed the door fully open. The first thing she saw, as she opened her eyes, was the empty clingfilm box on the floor. She heard the click, click of the stereo arm and knew it would be The Verve. She glanced slowly up from the naked foot to suffocated face. She was frozen to the spot. She didn't scream; she didn't cry. She swallowed her solid breath then turned and left.

The door to the neighbouring flat was opened by a middle-aged woman. Madeleine sat staring into space while Tom's neighbour fussed over her with tea and called the emergency services.

What Madeleine felt then was the sense of the inevitability of it all. In some ways it was almost a relief; every depressive episode on his part brought the fear of this on hers. Now those years of apprehension were closed, and along with them the book on her life, but a sadder, bitter sequel was only just beginning.

There was no suicide note and no definite motive, so the coroner recorded an open verdict. If not suicide then murder; it could only be one or the other and the coroner was keeping an open mind.

Only Madeleine knew that it was both. Only she had the evidence that would convict both his murderer and accomplice, each of whom sat crying copious quantities of tears. She had the power to vindicate Tom's death, as well as to comfort the guilt-ridden Beth, whose last words to Tom had been accusatory. But she never said a word. Neither did she try to prevent their father's presence at the funeral, despite recalling how several times Tom had said, "If I die before you and him I want you to promise to keep that bastard away from my funeral." And she had said, "I will." But she had no energy for a fight.

Madeleine tried to maintain a relationship with Beth, but, like any that is based on obligation, it soon became unsatisfactory for them both.

"Why he do this?"

"He didn't have the best of experiences growing up. Neither of us did."

"But you're okay. You're still here."

"Sometimes I wish I wasn't."

These were words which frightened him; suppose his leaving made her want to die?

"I don't like it when you talk like that."

"I suppose it's impossible for you to understand?"

But it wasn't. Sometimes he felt guilty enough over what they were doing to want to end his life.

"In my culture is very big sin."

"Only God has the right to end life?"

"Yes."

"Well, I have no fear of your Christian God. If there is one and He is full of love He'll forgive me. If there is nothing, then there's nothing to fear."

"You not afraid of die?"

"Of course, everyone is, but sometimes life is more scary."

Shibu's gaze was intense and so full of tenderness that without thinking it through she said, "If you were with me, I wouldn't be afraid. With you I feel so peaceful."

"Then maybe I come and hold your hand when you die."

If that were the case, she could more easily bear the loss of him in the meantime.

"You'll probably have forgotten about me by then."

"I'll never forget you. How I can forget you? You were my first lover."

He'll never forget. That's something. "Then be there."

"If I can I will, it's my promise to you."

In that moment, Madeleine looked so vulnerable, and so beautiful, Shibu didn't think he could ever leave her.

Yet the God who resided in his conscience was never far away, and soon the voice which spoke to him of eternal damnation echoed back from where Shibu had hidden Him.

As usual Madeleine was in the process of making his coffee when Shibu arrived in from work, and, as usual she rushed towards him, but he held his hands up in a commanding manner. "No!"

Although she always half-expected it, the effect on her body was hardly less than the impact of hitting a wall and it responded in the same shocked manner, but she took an inward side-step to compose herself.

"It's over again?"

"Yes. I sorry. We be friends from now, not lovers."

"Okay."

She felt weak and tired, and so tried to lighten things. "Don't s'pose you want a nice, friendly blow job, then?"

Shibu stuck his bottom lip out and clenched his fists. "Umph!

"Come on, Shibu, you know that was supposed to be funny."

She went to touch him, but he shrugged her away. Now she felt angry, with him and with herself.

She sat down opposite him. "We can manage this without falling out, can't we?"

Shibu shrugged. "You don't take what I say seriously."

"Is that what you think?"

He shrugged again. "I don't like when you make joke about it."

"I was protecting myself. I don't want it to end; it's been so lovely."

"Maybe for you."

"What?"

Although he hated himself for what he was saying Shibu wanted to hurt her enough to make her stay away from him. "You heard me."

"You're telling me it wasn't good for you?"

Shame made him want to erase his words with deep caresses, but he had to keep her away. "Was okay."

Madeleine swallowed away the tears and checked the bitter response that sprang in an instant to her lips. "Well, I'm sorry. Clearly you enjoyed it less than you appeared to."

She left the room to compose herself. She knew he couldn't possibly mean it; the intimacy was always so much more than merely physical, and even on the merely physical he could hardly pretend it was just okay.

When she heard Shibu ascending the stairs she felt a sudden panic. She hurried after him, but he had already claimed sanctuary by locking himself in the bathroom.

Although she was hungry she postponed eating to wait for him, pacing from her room to the landing and back again like a caged tiger. Madeleine was standing in the doorway of her bedroom when he emerged, wearing a towel around his waist; they exchanged suspicious looks, as if they were prisoner and guard.

Shibu felt helpless in his role, like the habitual criminal who knew no other way to survive. He knew his only hope of salvation was in avoiding her. With this in mind he took his time over dressing and then telephoned his cousin. His avoidance of her was unfair, he knew, but he had proved himself incapable of maintaining a friendly relationship with her. He followed his phone call with a prayer, hoping to gain not only strength but also advice. But Madeleine's rage was seeping under the door like poisonous gas, and he began to fear the effects of it would make themselves known as more scars on her legs.

He went down to the kitchen. "Did you eat yet?" he asked.

"Yes, I was getting the message you didn't want to eat with me."

"I had phone call to make."

"Um!"

Far from being a safe boundary, the tense atmosphere was wrought with danger; charged emotions so readily displaced themselves in unpredictable ways. "Frankly, Shibu, you insult me with your refusal to talk to me."

It felt wonderful to have an excuse to attack her.

"I wasn't refusing, I was making phone call."

"Which couldn't have waited until we'd eaten?"

"I don't want eat with you every day."

"It was okay when you wanted to fuck every day."

"Don't swear at me. I don't like swear."

"Well, I don't like being ignored."

"I told you I wasn't ignore."

"I don't believe you."

"Now you call me liar?"

"Yes."

They stood staring at each other for several seconds, but then they both realised the tension was diffused.

Madeleine took a deep sigh. "Hey, I'm sorry for getting angry."

"Is hard be friends and not do sex."

"I know."

"I want, but, I scared."

"I know that too." Madeleine rubbed Shibu's shoulder, intending it as an offer of support; the next moment they were locked in an embrace.

Chapter Twenty

This time Madeleine's equilibrium didn't return. Daily the status of the relationship between Shibu and Madeleine changed; sometimes they parted in the morning as lovers but met in the evening of the same day as friends.

When high on love Madeleine's eyes, hair and mood were shiny; when low on loss they were dull. She worked with either maniacal efficiency or on automatic without any enthusiasm at all. When she and Shibu were lovers she slept peacefully; when not, sleep was interrupted by longing. Yoga left her empty of energy; her feet lost their rhythm, her voice its song. The unpredictable nature of the relationship was reminiscent of her childhood, when evenings and weekends were governed by Philip's capricious moods.

Her morning routine took longer now because counting failed to provide a clear enough boundary, and sometimes it even took a knock on the door from Shibu to halt her. "Coming." The word, and the automatic response from her body, took her back to the era in which the behaviour had its routes. There was no question of making Shibu late for work, so Madeleine vacated the bathroom before she was ready and learnt to accept the permanent knot in her stomach and throat.

Madeleine vented her spleen with cleaning: cupboards were emptied of tins and scrubbed, drawers were tidied and bags filled for charity shop removal, shelves became bare and windows sparkling. The smell of bleach permeated the house, reminding Shibu of the cheap hostels he'd stayed in.

The behaviour disturbed him because he knew he was to blame. God spoke harshly to him, reminding him of the requirements of heaven and of its alternatives. He was a bad Christian whom God would forsake because no matter how hard he tried, even if sometimes he succeeded for days, in the end his lust always beat him. He wanted to lay the blame at Madeleine's feet, but her acquiescence to his whims made it impossible and he knew if he stood any chance of conquering himself he must first conquer her. Sometimes it seemed easy, when she made him late by staying so long in the bathroom, or obsessively scrubbed the kitchen around him as he ate. But often he felt compassion at the need this behaviour identified, and increasingly he feared that she would do herself some serious harm.

This is what he felt now as he lay beside her, coaxing both of their bodies towards sexual union, in which he was lost to both himself and God. Yet as soon as it was over the worries returned, so, when Madeleine kissed him and thanked him and asked if he was okay, all he wanted was to escape. Sometimes her tenderness made him so angry he wanted to shout at her to shut up, or even hit her so that he could say, "Look, God, you are more important than my desire." Instead he pushed her away as gently as he could and returned to his own room.

It was no more than seconds before she was there behind him, touching him as he stared out of the window. "You okay?"

"I need to sleep."

"Why not with me?"

"I want sleep here."

"What're you feeling?"

"I don't know."

"I'm sorry." She turned him around and slipped her arms around his waist, but he remained rigid. "I'll leave you to sleep, then." She tilted her mouth towards his.

"No."

"What?"

"Kiss only for sex."

"What?" '*Whore*', echoed back from the distant past, and the jangle of Julian's coins from the recent.

"Please go."

"Kiss me first."

"I already tell to you, kiss only for sex."

"You bastard!"

"Don't call me that."

"Then don't treat me like a whore."

Shibu had got what he wanted: in her eyes, from which love usually shone, there was anger.

Madeleine stood a while longer in silent shock, her nakedness making her feel all the more vulnerable.

Finally, she returned to her bedroom feeling bitter towards him, disgust towards herself and hoping that the morning would bring a change of heart.

But it didn't, and neither did the evening. It was over a week before Shibu shared himself with her again, first with a softened mood, then with a touch and finally with his body. And for the same length of time he acquiesced completely, so that every chilly evening was warmed by intimacy.

It was nearing the end of February; although the days remained dull the nights were getting shorter and optimism was edging its way back into the air, but Madeleine felt so tired. It was most likely all the ups and downs with Shibu that were to blame. Besides, she still felt hormonal tension even though the pain seemed to have subsided; yet, there was a nagging doubt as she counted the weeks on her calendar to check. And she was right: it had been six weeks since her last period.

There was no cause for alarm, she told herself; some irregularity at her age was probably to be expected and she'd only failed to use her cap once or twice.

She went upstairs, stripped to the waist and looked at herself in the full-length mirror, face on and then sideways, then she scrutinised her breasts. Everything about her looked exactly the same; she was being stupid; how could she be pregnant? She was pushing forty-three. But then, surely, she was too young for the menopause too? She remembered hearing there was a correlation between the age of the mother and daughter, but she had no way to know how old Tessa had been because they didn't talk about that kind of thing.

Although she detested herself for it Madeleine skimped on vacuuming and dusting; she didn't even properly clean the kitchen and bathroom, not only because she lacked the energy, but also because the chemical smells were so intense.

When she'd finished, she dug out her medical encyclopedia and, even though she was certain she knew them, looked up the early signs of pregnancy. Some breast changes were likely, it said, and feeling sick; well, she had neither of those.

Back downstairs she emptied and reloaded the washing machine. She started hanging the washing on the dryer under the bay window but, becoming distracted once more by the question of pregnancy, abandoned it half-done to look on the internet for the oldest mothers. All listed were in their fifties, but all except one had been artificially assisted. She typed in pregnancy in forties and was at first reassured to read the statistics on how much fertility declined with each passing year. Then she came to the advice on how to maximise your chances, all of which she did: eat a healthy diet, take vitamin supplements; yoga was even included in the list. This was ridiculous, she finally decided, there was an easy way to clear the matter up and then she could settle in to what she should be doing.

Now Madeleine gave her teeth a quick clean, grabbed her coat, hat and gloves, slipped on her boots and walked into town to the nearest chemist. Half an hour later she was back home with the pregnancy test. She took it to the outside toilet, finding it necessary to hide despite the fact there was no one in the house, but also so that she could smoke while she waited. So sure was she of the negative result that the single blue line announcing her pregnancy seemed as unreal as an end-of-the-world prophecy. For several minutes she stood staring at it, the cigarette in her other hand burning down until it almost burnt her fingers. She discarded the pregnancy indicator underneath piles of existing rubbish in the outside bin, went into the house, poured herself a pint of water, drank it down in one and waited until she was sure it had reached her bladder. Now she returned to the outside toilet and repeated the test with the second indicator. Again, a clear blue result over which there could be no argument.

When it too was safely deposited at the bottom of the bin Madeleine lit another cigarette, this time taking long, hard draws on it, which made her giddy. What the hell was she to do now? She remembered the conversation with Shibu. *"Suppose I did get pregnant?"*

"My family and my community cast me out."

Then there was no question about it: she'd have to have an abortion, and Shibu must never know. Again she recalled his words: *"This is very big sin."*

If she acted fast it wouldn't be so bad; no need for sedation and unpleasant procedures like the last time. This time there would be no quarrels, no threats nor marriage proposals. She'd make an appointment first thing on Monday morning and by Friday it would all be over.

Over before it had properly begun, just like the relationship. Yet she hardly dared to use that word to describe what there was between herself and Shibu. A relationship from Shibu's perspective was about lifelong commitment and love, neither of which he intended for her. There was irony in the fact that the one time she embarked on an affair she knew to be temporary, she could have stayed with it forever. The one time she could have done without falling in love, she had. And the only person she had ever loved was the one to whom she lied.

Suddenly Madeleine felt cold and tired and alone. She went upstairs and climbed into bed, pulling the duvet over her head. She couldn't help but think back to the earlier time. Weeks of indecision and arguments with Gary, which culminated in her fourteen-week termination, followed almost immediately by Gary's departure from her life. The grief she experienced was not for him; she had long since decided it needed to end, because the cycle of violence followed by sex was rapidly wearing her down. The grief was entirely for the child. Her body ached from the absence for weeks, and her heart and soul sometimes still did. But it probably wouldn't be so bad this time; it was very early on. She shouldn't have done that damn test. If she'd just gone to the doctor and asked for pills she wouldn't ever have known for sure.

Fucking Shibu; this was his fault. His emotional games made her slack with the contraception and his pathetic beliefs prevented her from bearing his child. But then, what about her wishes? Why was it always on his terms? No, she would not, could not, abort another child. Yet, then she imagined Shibu's face contorted by fear, and, as she thought of the consequences for him, understood she had no choice. Now she wept from the pity of it all.

Madeleine lay cocooned in the duvet aware of the time ticking away; it reminded her that the same applied to her life; a year in time was no more than a second on the universal clock. Normally she would have been feeling excited at the prospect of Shibu's imminent return, and when she heard him come in she knew she should get up, but she didn't want to see him. She heard him moving around the house, the pauses indicative of the fact he was looking for her. She sensed him standing outside her door, listening, and silenced her breathing, aware of the irony, because it was usually she who was the listener.

The sound of the shower offered some respite. She tried to force sleep upon herself, but the embryonic life inside her was too loud. Instead she indulged in a fantasy – she was giving birth, pushing her baby into life while Shibu mopped her brow – they were walking hand in hand along the street, he carrying their child in a sling. The biggest delusion of all was Shibu's beaming expression, for she knew the news of pregnancy would wipe the smile from his face forever. And the reality of it sent her hurtling into a future in which the family portraits were only of the three of them: no aunts, no uncles, no paternal grandparents. And uniformed observers would mistakenly view the photograph as representing three generations. Now she imagined herself as sixty, seventy, if she was lucky eighty, and the still relatively young Shibu, with only his son as family, resenting her very existence.

Yet, how she wanted to have his baby! Something of him to keep for herself forever; the pity of it broke her heart. If only there were some way she could go through with the pregnancy without him ever knowing.

Yet, she was forgetting her genes. She lacked confidence in her ability to break the cycle of abuse and had no wish to inflict on her child the self-hatred she had to live with herself.

Madeleine sensed Shibu's presence outside the door again and responded to his tentative knock with an invitation to enter the room.

"Oh, you already waiting me?"

His skin was shiny from the shower, his eyes seductive in his eagerness and his full mouth looked wet and tempting.

"Actually, I'm not feeling that great."

"What happen?"

What's the matter? she corrected in her mind, but didn't verbalise it. "I'm just really tired."

"You want me leave you sleep?"

"I'll be down for some food soon."

Shibu sat down on the bed and brushed the hair from her face. "I think maybe you ill."

"Only a little, I'll be down soon."

"You want for me to cook you?"

The image conjured by the words, and his genuine concern for her, warmed Madeleine and brought a smile to her face; she did love him so much.

"If you don't mind, that would be nice."

Chapter Twenty-One

Ten-twenty Monday morning Madeleine was in the doctor's surgery. "I'm pregnant," she said emphatically, then, after a pause, "I can't have it."

"You don't sound very sure."

"Two positive tests, but still a bit of a shock at my age."

"I meant about not having it."

Madeleine was surprised at her transparency; she hung her head as if ashamed. "I'm old, circumstances are wrong."

"Nevertheless."

Madeleine didn't answer.

"When was your last period?"

"The end of December."

"Then it's very early, early enough for pills."

"I know."

"I'm going to refer you to the clinic." The doctor was typing into the computer as she spoke. "They do things thoroughly, including checking that it's really what you want." She glanced up at Madeleine, who looked away from the gaze. "So it might require a couple of appointments. Um, the earliest appointment I can get you is for Thursday morning."

Madeleine felt a rage boiling up inside her. She didn't want to do this, but because she had to she wished it would just hurry up and happen; there was work and Emily to consider too. "Okay," she said meekly.

On the way down the street she bumped into Shibu as he made his way home with his shopping. "Oh! I thought you at work today."

"I am, had to do something, on my way back now. See you later." The chance meeting felt portentous, but of what?

To Emily she said, "I have another appointment Thursday, sorry." She offered no further explanation. "I could take it as my day off if it's easier."

Madeleine smoked her lunchtime cigarette a little guiltily, feeling it a denial of her pregnancy despite the circumstances. As if it were a punishment she was overcome by nausea. If smoking was going to do that to her, perhaps she should take it as an opportunity to quit, she thought, but hardly enough time – it would be gone by the end of the week. Instinctively her hand lowered to her abdomen, which she rubbed now, only in part in response to the queasiness.

Over the road the postman whistled along to the tune from his MP3 player as he posted letters through doors, reminding Madeleine of her lunchtime rendezvous with Julian. She felt unaccountably sad at the thought and, as a wave of nostalgia swept through her, she wondered how she would have reacted to a pregnancy by him.

With Thursday secured as her day off she returned home, wondering what to expect from Shibu. She approached him cautiously. "Have you missed me?"

"Of course," he said, as he pulled her into an embrace.

They shared a meal then a bath; Shibu sat behind Madeleine with his hands on her breasts. "Aw! They feel nice today, round and hard like apple." He played with her nipples, which irritated her, so she pulled his hand away. But immediately she worried that it would be an excuse for him to call a halt to their affair, so she kissed his hands then returned them to her breasts.

In bed with him Madeleine went through the motions and forced her body to a climax. The post-coital cuddle felt so natural that Madeleine had to remind herself how nothing was ever normal for her. She buried her head in Shibu's chest, felt him relax as he stroked her hair and knew that in that moment he felt safe. Feeling so close to him made it necessary to fight the urge to tell him of her pregnancy. Instead she played it out in her imagination, worrying slightly that her thoughts were loud enough to hear, as in her mind she said, *You're going to be a father*, to which he responded with a whoop of delight. In reality she said, "Night," then, "Sleep well."

The scan was her first shock. "We like to make sure of the dates so we can offer the safest method."

"I know when it was."

"I expect you're right, but we like to make sure."

The first thought to enter her head was, *Can it do the baby any harm?* She could hardly ask that under the circumstances. The second was that it made it all too real.

"Yes, the size agrees with your dates."

"How big is it?"

"About the size of a pea."

"It doesn't look like a baby yet, does it?"

"No."

The skin on Madeleine's belly, where the gel had been, felt dry, as if to mark the spot. She sat in the waiting room, feeling as ashamed as if she were in court for murder. Once was forgiveable, but twice? But she had no choice; to go through with the pregnancy would mean she was going to have to tell Shibu and she'd had this conversation with herself several times now. Unless? Suppose he never knew? If he didn't get the visa, for example, or if she asked him to leave, then maybe – how stupid, she was never going to do that. Whichever way she looked at it there was only one option and she wished they would just hurry up and give her what she'd asked for.

"Madeleine, come through." The doctor was Asian, which seemed like another omen; she was getting very superstitious these days. "So, how are you in general? Is your health good?"

"Very." All of the questions she'd already answered should have told her that.

"I'm not rhesus negative," Madeleine said in response to the blood test, remembering the explanation she'd had the first time around.

"It's routine, we check for STIs too. Your blood pressure is lovely, better than the average thirty-year-old's."

"I look after myself."

"The pregnancy is in its very early stage so we can induce the abortion chemically. That's generally the best option at this stage, but we can discuss the other options if you like."

Madeleine flinched at the word 'abortion'. "No, thank you."

"And you're sure it's really what you want?"

She was slow to answer. Too slow. So that the doctor continued, "Sometimes other people influence the decision, but it must be *yours*."

"It is."

"My nurse said you were asking questions."

"I'm interested, that's all." Then, without intent she blurted out, "The father doesn't know; he can't ever know."

"Is that why you're here?"

Madeleine didn't answer.

"Do you need to think about it?"

Now, she swallowed hard. "I've already told your nurse and my doctor. I know what I want – I'm forty-two, not fifteen."

"Okay, then." The doctor got up and took a packet from the medicine cupboard. "You take this now." She put a single tablet into a pot. "In two days' time you come back and we insert misoprostol into your vagina. We see you for a check-up two weeks after that." Now the doctor passed the pill pot to Madeleine.

She took the pot but couldn't bring herself to take the pill. She wanted to ask, *What happens if I take this and change my mind, will I have done any harm?* What a ridiculous question if she was really sure! "What does it do?"

"It blocks progesterone, so that the lining of the womb breaks down; sometimes it works on its own, but we give the misoprostol to make sure. It makes the womb contract and ensures the pregnancy evacuates."

Such a clinical explanation, Madeleine shook the pill pot. "Can't I do it at home?"

"We like you to take it here."

Now Madeleine sighed and choked back the tears. One small pill was all it took to end a life; she wished it could be a cyanide pill to take her own. She put the pot down. The doctor moved it out of her vision. Perhaps because of her ethnicity Madeleine said, "He's Asian, he's young; the father."

Not even a flicker of emotion crossed the doctor's face. "Only you can make this choice, Madeleine."

"How long have I got the pill option?"

"It can be used at any time, but obviously the more advanced the pregnancy the longer it takes, so we don't normally recommend it after twelve weeks."

"And then?"

"The vacuum method is the safest and quickest."

"Oh, God!" She put her hands to her face then pulled at her hair.

"I think you need to talk this through, Madeleine. Let me see when the counsellor is free." The doctor got up and left the room.

In the few minutes she was alone Madeleine sat transfixed, her body rigid, her arms crossed, and she remembered the feelings that followed the first abortion. Alienated from herself she felt sub-human and deserving of every negative label Gary threw at her. She was even grateful for his fist in her face, as it wrought the punishment she wished upon herself. While Gary made public her abasement, into her thighs and stomach she etched the hidden message of self-contempt. Guilt and grief killed her soul, while her body insisted on remaining alive if only for Tom's sake. How would the post-abortion trauma be this time? A million times worse, she knew.

There had been no love for Gary, no desire to share his genes. She was afraid for Shibu if she continued with the pregnancy but afraid for herself if she did not. And, at the centre of it all was the most important individual in the equation, the pea-sized life which was relying on Madeleine for its very existence.

"Madeleine," the doctor's voice was very gentle now, "can you come back this afternoon?"

"Yes, thank you."

Finally, being able to talk was such a relief. "I'm pregnant by a man who's almost young enough to be my son, Asian and Catholic; I can't go ahead with it; it would be disastrous for him. And I'd make a rubbish mother anyway."

"There's a lot to unpick there. The age of the father, his religion, his ethnicity and your feelings regarding your ability to parent. I wonder which is the most significant of those?"

"All of them."

"Then, which one would you like to start with?"

"Shibu. He must never know. I'm wrong for him. His family would cast him out."

"So, you haven't told him because you believe you're wrong for him."

"I am. He'd be devastated."

"You think he'd be devastated. That's a strong word. What d'you think he'd do?"

"Marry me, probably."

"And you don't want that?"

"I'd like nothing more if it was because he wanted to, but I don't want to be anyone's obligation. He'd resent me his whole life."

"So, you feel you can't have the baby because the father will marry you and then resent you?"

"Yes."

"How would it be for you to refuse his marriage proposal?"

"Then he'd resent me for bearing a bastard."

"It sounds like you're really afraid of his resentment."

"I am."

"How would he feel about you having an abortion?"

"He won't ever know."

"I see. So, the abortion is because you want to protect yourself from Shibu's resentment?"

The words hit Madeleine like a rush of freezing water in the face. "My God! I never – I thought it was about protecting him."

"And would that be okay?"

"Yes."

"But protecting yourself is not?"

"Well, now I'm wondering if that's what I am doing."

"It sounds like you're saying if the abortion is to protect Shibu that's okay, but if it's to protect yourself then it's not."

Madeleine thought for a while before replying. "I

guess that is what I'm saying. But actually, there's no way to protect me."

"Do you want to tell me more about that?"

"I want a baby and I want Shibu's approval."

"So, you feel you have to choose between the baby and Shibu's approval?"

"Yes, that's it exactly."

Now Madeleine began to cry, at first lightly, but then copiously as the counsellor said, "It sounds like his approval is very important to you."

And she eventually replied, "Yes, it is."

"It sounds to me, Madeleine, as if there is a lot more for you to explore, but we are running out of time; would you like to come and see me again?"

"Can I come whether or not I have an abortion?"

"Of course."

Back with the doctor Madeleine said, "I need to think a bit more. If I decide to go ahead… with the… to not have the baby – what do I have to do?"

"Phone for an appointment."

"I don't need to see my doctor first?"

"No."

"I want to make another appointment to see Sarah."

"Okay, the receptionist will do that for you."

At home, deflated, she lay on her bed. Although she was neither tired nor cold Madeleine crawled under the duvet and sought sleep simply for its oblivion. As she fell towards it she contemplated how terrible it would be to suffer sleep deprivation and have no peace from thought, but when she awoke, it seemed as if there had not, in fact, been any. She was angry with herself for still being pregnant, and yet relieved that she was. One thing was for sure: if she was going to have an abortion it had to be in the next five weeks; she couldn't bear the idea of a vacuum being used. It seemed so violent.

The first child was defined by violence: passionately conceived in Gary's apology for his ferocious fists, vehemently defended by him in his desire for control, and finally vacuum sucked from her womb. Never had she doubted how the violence would have continued. The best she could have hoped for was an injunction to keep him away, but not before her bruises had damaged her child's soul and fine-tuned her own abuser's genes. But there were no such genes in Shibu, and if Madeleine could control her own, she might yet raise a child as gentle and beautiful as him.

This thought filled her with a longing to be held and reassured by him. And she had no doubt that even without his love, if it wasn't for his fear, she could rely upon it. Perhaps she should just tell him? Didn't he have a right to know, after all? He would be scared, of course, but she could impress upon him that there were no expectations on her part. Even just thinking this she felt better, so much so she was almost cheerful as she prepared to cook Shibu a chicken tikka masala, because it was his favourite meal.

There had been a message from God. The conversation was intended only for the ears of the confidant and Shibu had only overheard it because he was sent on an errand to the store room, which was how he knew God wanted him to hear.

The manager's office door was slightly ajar but he couldn't see the occupants, although he knew who was talking because he'd already heard his colleague's compassionate leave was over.

"He made a death-bed confession about an affair that happened years ago."

"Your poor mother."

"Indeed, she's devastated. She said it was even worse because he claimed the woman meant nothing to him, which insulted her all the more. I was really angry with him. Yes, for the affair, but especially the confession – why tell her after all these years?"

"Was he religious? Then I guess he was worried about God and wanted to make it right with Him."

"Well, I think he should have kept quiet and taken his chance with God."

Chapter Twenty-Two

It was nearing nine-thirty and there was still no sign of Shibu; even if he'd been shopping he should have been home by now. Madeleine rationalised, there'd been a problem that had kept him at work, but in the back of her mind were two worries: he'd found another place to live and gone without telling her; he'd had an accident and was in hospital, or worse. Who, she wondered, would be contacted in that event? The realisation that it wouldn't be her made clear her position in the hierarchy of Shibu's significant people.

She was on the point of checking whether his things were still in his room when he arrived. "Oh, there you are, I've been worried about you."

"Why you worry?"

"In case something bad had happened to you. Anyway, it hasn't, so that's okay."

"I don't want you worry about me."

"Sorry, couldn't help it."

His tone made it more than clear there would be no comfort from him tonight and this was not the time to tell him of her pregnancy.

She was really hungry and beginning to feel sick, but Madeleine waited, feeling she was at least entitled to eat with him.

He took his time, knowing what she was doing and wishing to delay contact with her as long as possible. The British priest had been too soft on him, he knew, with his assurance that God would forgive him, and his mildly offered advice to find another address as soon as possible. But Shibu was sure that a priest from his own culture, in whom he had more confidence to accurately report God's opinions, would have had more to say on the subject.

He knelt and prayed, mumbling the words of the Lord's Prayer out loud, hoping that the echo of them in his head and ears would quieten all other thoughts and he would hear directly how God wanted him to proceed.

Despite her own needs Madeleine dared not interrupt Shibu's prayer, which was audible from outside his door as she poised ready to knock. Hearing it recited out loud took her back to a time when she performed the same ritual herself. Nightly her childish voice uttered words that were incomprehensible to her and sought a listener whose form was no clearer, until maturity and the experiences of life convinced her there was no one there to hear.

Suddenly Madeleine was overcome by nausea and ran to the bathroom to vomit, but an empty stomach produced nothing other than pain. Now, afraid for her child, she went downstairs and forced food into her stomach.

Shibu heard her retching but didn't believe it was real. She was, in his opinion, seeking to enlist his sympathy, which he was in no mind to offer. So, he telephoned his cousin in Reading and feigned good humour.

His laughter excluded Madeleine as surely as had the mocking of her classmates, who had ridiculed her for hiding in the cloakroom to eat her lunch.

Into a plastic container she put the curry intended for Shibu. The kitchen looked filthy. And she felt miserable. She picked up the book she was reading, but, though each individual word made sense, the overall meaning was lost. She put it down and turned to her usual comfort, stopping due to the lateness of the hour, not because the house looked clean.

Feeling dirty herself now, and to help her relax, she decided to have a bath. She scrubbed herself, as if the hurt she was feeling was on her skin and there was a possibility it could be washed away. It was hard for her to stop, and when the water cooled to a temperature that was uncomfortable she topped it up and continued scrubbing. A nicotine craving finally called her to a halt.

As she stubbed out the cigarette Madeleine made the decision to make that her last: if she continued with the pregnancy she wanted to give her child the best chance, and if not, then no matter; it was time she stopped anyway. She was about to screw up the packet to put it in the bin but didn't; instead she put it on top of one of the kitchen cupboards, which she could only just reach in her bare feet, pretending to herself that out of sight was out of mind. She shut and locked the back door and went to bed.

Shibu was still awake. The cleaning had stirred him and the accompanying emotions produced alertness. Initially he was angry that she should be vacuuming at that time of night, but soon he felt remorseful knowing what was behind it and that he was to blame. Hunger too was preventing sleep, but he was afraid that if he got up to eat, Madeleine would hear him and come looking for reconciliation. Now he was angry again: with Madeleine for presuming to cook for him as if she considered she had the same entitlement as a wife; with the priest for his mild-mannered telling-off that offered Shibu no relief from self-punishment; and with himself that he should be in this mess.

After about ten minutes, and fairly sure Madeleine would have fallen asleep, Shibu risked the kitchen. There remained a faint aroma of curry, which almost tempted him into submission, but, keen to reassert control, he chose instead to cook himself some toast and eggs. Every part of the process seemed noisy in excess so that he feared Madeleine's arrival at any second. With this in mind he left the dirty dishes in the sink, feeling some satisfaction that in the morning they would bear witness to his night-time feast, and Madeleine would understand it as a renunciation of her love. Yet, once back in bed his mood towards her softened and he got up, washed and dried the dishes and left her a note: *"Sorry, my cousin brother was talking a long time. See you tomorrow."*

In the morning internal clouds kept the light from Madeleine. She felt sick, of body and mind, and had to drag herself from bed.

Shibu's angry with me, already, she thought. *I wish I could have this baby, but how can I?*

Then she found his note.

Oh, he does care, doesn't he? He's scared. She poured cereal into a bowl and made tea; the smell of the tea was acrid and she ran to the outside toilet feeling she would vomit, but although there was much retching she wasn't sick.

She forced her breakfast down, chewing slowly and resting her head on the table between each mouthful.

Won't be long before Shibu notices at this rate. I'll tell him later. He needs to know, of course he does. Maybe it'll be okay. I won't make any decisions on what to do until I've spoken to him. But she didn't really believe it would be okay.

In the shower, she washed and rinsed and scrubbed, finding at the end of every number sequence the need to add another ten. Now she was late for work. She took the packet of cigarettes, removed one only, slipped it into her bag telling herself one at lunchtime and then one in the evening and she'd quit altogether at the beginning of next week.

Shibu was unexpectedly home when she got in from work. His conciliatory mood both reassured and annoyed her; she was tired of pandering to his whims but could never stay angry with him. And then he offered an explanation for his hiding.

"Yesterday I go to confess, I tell to priest about us."

"And?"

"Priest say God will forgive to me. But I think He won't if I keep do."

"We've been here many times, Shibu."

"He tell to me I should find new address."

The idea terrified her. And yet. His moving might make it possible for the pregnancy to go unheeded by him. "That might be for the best."

This wasn't the response Shibu expected. Another unexpected feeling soon followed, rejection.

A trace of it flickered across his face.

"It's hard to be friends when we've been lovers," Madeleine said.

Shibu nodded in agreement, because he knew she was right. And yet. He felt disappointed. He was hoping at least to have to fight with her a little.

"So, if you hear of anything—"

"I'll let you know, of course." Madeleine sat down, because she felt suddenly too tired to stand. She felt tears coming.

"I'll see you later," she said, in as composed a tone as was possible.

In the safety of her room the tears came in a torrent. She fought to keep them quiet. But Shibu heard the occasional sob. It left him feeling reassured she did still want him, afraid and wanting to comfort her. But he knew where that would lead.

They avoided each other for the rest of the evening. Madeleine imagined how to keep her baby hidden from him. It would be only proper, she thought, if, when he first moved out, they had the occasional coffee and chat. Then, once the baby was showing, she could avoid it without causing offence. Yet, how ridiculous! Of course she must tell him; he had a right to know. Was she proposing to hide his child from him once it was born?

What a fucking mess, she thought. *All the years I've regretted not being a mother, and now I'm going to be it all feels so wrong.*

She buried her face in the pillow, as if wishing to suffocate herself. She wanted to die, yet she wanted to live, like never before.

Chapter Twenty-Three

For a while Shibu was almost content. He'd done right by God, Madeleine said she was okay and the Punjabi man from the shop said he could get him a room within a month. He changed his routine. Leaving earlier, coming in later, eating only snacks in order to avoid the kitchen.

But then the house became quiet. Near silence began to hurt his ears, which strained for clues to Madeleine's state of mind. His stomach became tense from hunger, and sleep eluded him.

It was several days since he'd seen Madeleine, sitting still as stone, staring at nothing, as if she were a corpse. He heard her only from behind the bathroom door, where the sound of running water became heavier and continued for longer, making his escape all the easier.

This morning he was late because he'd fallen asleep again after switching off the alarm. It was too late to wait. He hurried his wash and shave, not only because he needed to leave, but also because he knew Madeleine would soon be wanting the bathroom.

As he opened to door, she barged her way in, offering a grunt by way of greeting. The sight of her shocked him. Her skin had become pallid and beneath her eyes were dark circles. Was it his decision to leave that had caused the change in her? How could he move out if that was to be the result?

Her face appeared in his mind many times that day. This time it generated feelings of compassion and remorse.

With that encounter the depression that had stalked Madeleine for days, finally won. Her routines were the battlements that kept it at bay. But the look in Shibu's eyes just then shattered the ramparts and allowed her old enemy in. In his eyes she'd seen blame. And it reminded her of the earlier time, when she'd seen the same look in Tom's eyes. That time when he'd echoed her 'no' with his own. That terrible time she could never forget. She accepted culpability then; she accepted it now. She, almost old enough to be his mother, and the person responsible for keeping a roof over his head had failed in her duty towards him. Just as she'd failed in her attempt to keep Tom safe.

Why hadn't she just conceded? It would hardly have made any difference. Once more, twice more, a hundred times more. After the first time what did it matter? And if she had yielded, if she hadn't vehemently persuaded Tom to follow her lead, then perhaps he would still be here.

Madeleine dragged a comb through her hair; the force of it wrenched her head backwards and left loose hair behind. She reviewed herself naked in the mirror, detesting her round breasts for the femininity they represented and wanting to cut them off. She detested too her vagina for being the seat of her desire and the entrance to her womb, the very thing that defined her as a woman. Shibu was afraid of her. How much more so when he became aware of the evidence of their actions growing inside her? Self-hatred, self-disgust, responsibilities to which she could not rise left her with only one solution.

She gathered together the necessary tools, but only when she heard Shibu leave did Madeleine feel it safe enough to climb into the empty bath. She turned the blade over between her fingers and hovered for a second over her wrist, but now, like before, she knew that cutting an end to her life was not the solution. Then she needed to stay alive for Tom, this time for Shibu, if not the foetus. Imagine how he'd feel when the coroner announced she was pregnant? Yet, just like before, the inner critic accused her of cowardice.

The first time came back to her:

She sat in a bath full of bubbles, orange-scented candle in the window; the event that generated the need, hardly more than a week old. She'd do her wrists, though she knew the neck would be better, but that would take more courage than she had.

She took the razor from the packet. Fear coursed her veins, making her feel sick and her hair stand on end, but she was sure it would pump the blood out faster. Remember to cut length ways, *she told herself. She hovered over her wrist, feeling dizzy and hot. She took a deep breath and moved the razor closer, but the fear of death was greater than the guilt. And then she imagined Tom facing Philip alone and was afraid for him too.*

"Fucking coward! Fucking selfish little bitch!" she said under her breath as she sliced into her thigh instead. The pain was so intense she cried out.

"You all right in there? Tessa knocked on the door as she asked.

"Fine, water's a bit hotter than expected."

And after the pain came release.

That was where it began. She failed in her attempt to kill herself, but the pattern was set for regular ritual suicide.

From inside the black cloud Madeleine watched herself going through the motions of life. It made her sluggish, made her late, made the morning ritual longer every day and the evenings longest of all. She was cold, so cold. She longed for someone to share her pregnancy with. And she needed to talk to someone. Sean was the obvious choice, but they had seen little of each other in the past couple of weeks, his new love kept him away, and Madeleine didn't want to dampen his happiness with her misery. So, Carol then, or Kumar. He might be the best person to help her understand the cultural implications. And yet, it didn't feel right that anyone should know before the father. Although all the likely consequences were terrifying, Madeleine now wanted to tell Shibu.

True to his word, the Punjabi shop keeper soon had a vacant room. Shibu went straight from work to view it.

It was a disappointment. The bed and the wardrobe were single, the bedding old. The grass in the back garden was long and it was, he was now being informed, the responsibility of the tenants to maintain it. In the kitchen he noticed there was grime on the cooker, and in the bathroom, there was mold. The all-inclusive rent amounted to fifty pounds more than he paid now.

Although he told the landlord he'd think about it, Shibu knew he would never make that room his home. Yet tolerating the atmosphere in his current one was barely any better. Still he knew that restoration in that one was possible. He hurried home.

Madeleine was sitting at the kitchen table. She sat straight and stiff like the portraits he'd seen of nineteenth-century women in British history books.

"Hi," he said, in a conciliatory tone.

"I need to talk with you," Madeleine replied, in a business-like tone.

"What you want talk about?"

"Something important, so don't be in a rush."

"I have phone call to make and shower to take."

"Then after that."

Madeleine quickly left; she didn't want to be forced into it until she was ready. She waited in the lounge, and, as she did so she rehearsed the words and imagined her response to each of his.

Shibu was sure she was going to issue him with a deadline to move out. He could hardly blame her, he deserved no less, but the very thought of it panicked him, and that emotion troubled him too. Separation from her was what he wanted. Wasn't it?

He took his time in the shower, then cooked his first meal that week. Madeleine came back into the kitchen just as he was putting his dishes into the dishwasher. He turned and saw that her resolve had lessened; her eyes wore the more familiar look. He felt both grateful and ashamed, and a sudden need to rescue her. He rushed towards her and scooped her into his arms.

Madeleine returned his embrace and sighed deeply as she buried her face in his chest and cried, but into his neck she whispered, "Shibu I can't do this anymore."

Her refusal fuelled his desire. Her tears, his guilt. "Why you can't?"

"It's hurting me too much. Tomorrow you'll tell me no again."

"I sorry, I promise I never say that again."

"Don't promise me anything until I've said what I need to."

"You can tell to me after. Let's go to bed."

Madeleine knew that the news of the new life would be the death of their affair, but perhaps she could enjoy him just once more. Shibu was afraid of an ultimatum that would ensure there would be no chance to do this again.

The wounds on her thighs confirmed for Shibu that rescue had been necessary. He stroked them gently and whispered a verbal apology to her and a mental one to God. Now Shibu felt convinced that if He knew about those wounds, as surely He must, God would understand and Shibu be forgiven.

Madeleine lay a while in the afterglow rehearsing the words in her head; the fear of utterance was the cause of her delay, and the delay the cause of Shibu's falling asleep.

Chapter Twenty-Four

The sun was just breaking through the curtains when the alarm rang; Shibu stirred, stretched, turned it off. Becoming aware of the empty space beside him he remembered where he was and the promise he'd made. Immediately he felt self-contempt. He couldn't even pretend to blame Madeleine this time. In surrendering to himself he was finally forced to admit that his desire for Madeleine was bigger than his duty to God, or to his community.

He closed his eyes against the light, but with them shut his conscience seemed closer. He whispered an incantation: "Please guide me, oh Lord. Show me how to obey, without hurting her." Shibu listened with an open heart. The answer came as an impression, soundless, formless, yet real. *It's too late to spare her.* Recoiling from the knowledge he turned onto his side and cradled the pillow for comfort. It smelt of Madeleine.

Perhaps I should marry her, he thought. *Should I, would that save us both?* he silently asked. His cousin had even suggested it, only a few days ago, as a means to gaining a visa. Shibu had felt insulted on Madeleine's behalf.

Yet, if he were to marry her his family and friends could be told that was the reason, and he could pretend the love had grown from that circumstance. *"The love comes later,"* he'd always been assured, on the subject of arranged marriages. And he had considered this a likely result of prolonged intimacy. In that case, were his confused feelings regarding Madeleine part of that process? Sometimes, especially in the midst of their sexual union, he felt such a great affection for her that it terrified him. Yet at others he despised her with equal passion. Were such contradictory feelings a natural part of the lover's experience? He wished he knew. He wished there had been others before her with whom to compare, and yet he wished too that there had been no one at all and his virginity was still intact.

His family would never accept her, he knew; they, like he, desired an Indian wife for him, one that understood his customs, and her duties. And, if he were to remain unmarried much longer, they would be finding him a suitable one as surely as they had provided for his childhood needs. And Shibu wanted children. He'd decided on three, maybe four. For that reason, never mind all the others, he couldn't marry Madeleine.

Madeleine's touch on the door handle came with just enough warning for him to feign sleep as she entered the room. He was aware of her watching him between each of her everyday actions; it inched him deeper into his acting role.

When he heard the clunk of the letter box a couple of hours later, he realised he had fallen asleep again for real. He wondered if the letter regarding his visa would be amongst the morning's post and felt nervous as he checked. When it wasn't, he experienced a combination of relief and disappointment.

The morning nausea was a shock. It wasn't just the fact of it, but the intensity too. Madeleine hurried from bed to the bathroom, where she retched so violently she wet herself. She turned the taps on hard to prevent Shibu from hearing, as the heaving continued to rock her body without any sign of subsiding. She felt disgusted with her incontinence and wanted to shower, but every time she stood up a big wave of nausea sent her back to the floor.

She ran a bath, all the while keeping close to the toilet bowl as she continued to vomit bile. She drank water then vomited, but at least her stomach hurt less, so she drank some more and vomited again. Now she climbed into the bath, but the movement produced more nausea, and it was the same with washing: every time she moved she was sick. If this was going to happen every day it would only be a matter of time before Shibu realised her condition without her needing to tell him.

Now Madeleine sat in the kitchen wrapped in a towel, forcing down a piece of dry bread, but after two mouthfuls she was sick again. She lay with her head on the table while she forced food down. Just as suddenly as it had started the nausea stopped, so that now she was able to eat some cereal and drink a whole glass of water. The mere idea of tea or coffee reviled her. The retching had made her hot but now, recovered, she felt chilly and sufficiently well as to risk the bedroom.

She opened the door quietly and was relieved to see that Shibu was still asleep. He looked as peaceful as a child. In her mind's eye Madeleine pictured their child lying beside him; it was a beautiful scene. The pregnancy was reaching its tenth week; she was going to have to tell Shibu soon.

On her way to work she automatically took a cigarette from the packet, but even the thought of it made her feel sick. *Good*, she thought, *if I'm going to have this baby I need to quit.* She screwed up the whole pack and tossed it into the bin that was awaiting collection. There were other things she would have to change too: cutting herself was one, and facing up to her past was another. At lunchtime she'd make another appointment with the counsellor.

It was a week before Madeleine could obtain an appointment with Sarah, but she needed to talk now. She felt like a teenager as she sat flicking through the numbers in her phone. She hovered over Kumar's name, knowing he would be a good person in whom to confide, but her default person was Sean.

"*Hi, really need to talk, please come around soon,*" she wrote.

He visited the next day.

"I'm pregnant," she told him in the tone she'd practised for Shibu.

"Jesus! That's a surprise. Congratulations?"

"Should be, you know I'd love to be a mum, but…"

"But?"

Madeleine told Sean all of her fears.

"You won't be a bad mother, quite the opposite. Being aware of the issues'll make sure of that and the counsellor can help you sort them"

"I hope so, but Shibu…"

"What do you want from him?"

"Everything! Nothing!"

"What d'you expect then?"

"I told you, an offer of marriage that I can neither accept nor refuse."

"Why can't you accept?"

"I don't want anyone to marry me for duty."

"You sure it would be?"

"Positive."

"Why can't you refuse?"

"It's a sin to breed bastards."

"And what about what you want?"

There was no need to reply; she'd said it all.

"You sure he couldn't love you? It wouldn't be easy, but if he really wanted—"

"Exactly! If he really wanted. He'd have to really want me, and really love me."

"When you going to tell him?"

"Today, I guess."

"I think you should wait a bit. Be one hundred per cent sure of what you're going to do so that you don't falter in that however he reacts."

"That ain't going to happen."

Sean hugged her. "Then, why don't you put the whole thing to Shibu exactly as you did to me?"

"I guess, but I'm terrified."

"Most things are worse in anticipation than they are in fact. And that'll probably turn out the same for Shibu too if he tells his family."

"If?"

"Well, he wouldn't necessarily have to, would he? He might choose to bugger off back to India and ignore it."

Madeleine shrugged. "That option had never even occurred to me."

"No? You seem to think he's the one without choices, but in actual fact both you and he have options. The only one without is the little person himself."

The expression 'little person' was so emotive it seemed deliberately chosen. One of Sean's talents was that he always changed Madeleine's perception of things; it was the very reason she often chose him as confidant. Now she thought of all the times and ways that Sean had rescued her, right from the time of their very first meeting when his arrival next to her on the bus had saved her from fear that she would choose the wrong stop.

"You look like you've found a pound and lost a fiver," *he observed after the customary hello.*

"Concentrating, not sure where to get off. D'you know the area? I'm going to Victoria Road."

"Well, you're in luck because that's where I'm going too, which number? I'll show you exactly where. What're you up to, visiting friends?"

"My mum just moved there."

"Ah!"

When the visits to Tessa became regular there were frequent encounters between Madeleine and Sean, but it wasn't until some months later that they exchanged telephone numbers and made an arrangement to meet at a gig.

"I have a boyfriend." Madeleine worried there might be an assumption behind the invite.

"Thought it likely, but hey, I'm good at being mates with girls."

And then, when she was single, she loved him too much to risk it.

There was something about Sean compared to other men. He was so easy to be with, so honest, so accepting. He was the first person she ever told her story to. For a long time, he was the last.

In the present he said, "Don't worry, you'll be a great mum. And I for one envy you, I'd love a child of my own."

"Couldn't you and Aileen…?"

"She doesn't want any more; fair enough, she's done all that." The pause that followed was less than comfortable. "Are you up to dancing?"

"Oh God, yes! How I need to dance."

But in the middle of it she felt sick and had to sit down.

"Is there anything I can do?" Sean asked.

"You could heat up the dinner. I don't think I can do it, but I know I'll be better once I've eaten."

The sight and smell of the spaghetti sauce was disgusting and made her heave.

"Come on, hun, you need to eat." Sean held a forkful out for her. Madeleine took it, chewed it, swallowed it and then ran to throw up. After that happened three more times she felt better and managed to eat the rest.

A few minutes later she was absolutely fine. "I guess that's a lesson to me then? I mustn't allow myself to get hungry. At least this'd stop if I had an abortion."

"Don't think that's gonna happen."

She stood to do the washing-up.

"Let me. I know how to do it to your liking," Sean said.

"No, it's okay, you're my guest."

Madeleine washed the dishes, rinsed them, put them in the dishwasher. She sprayed the work surfaces and tiles with anti-bacterial spray and washed them down. She did the same with the cupboard doors and the windowsill. Now she took a clean scourer and more spray and scrubbed the cooker and microwave, before starting on the outsides of the fridge and washing machine.

Sean's hand was on her shoulder: "That's enough, babe."

"The floor's dirty."

"It's fine – Shibu's going to be here soon and make another mess. Let's dance some more."

"Actually, I think I need to sleep, sorry."

"Don't be." He kissed her forehead. "I'll be in touch, yeah? Phone if you need me."

She went to bed and that's where she was when Shibu returned. He was puzzled by her absence. He checked the hall; her coat and shoes were there. Surely, she wasn't avoiding him? He tapped on her bedroom door before entering.

"What happened?"

"I'm not feeling too well."

"What I can do for you?"

"Nothing. I'll be fine. Just need to sleep now."

There was no reason to, yet Shibu doubted the sincerity of her words. He closed the door and went back downstairs, feeling lost.

She was sick the next morning. The noise of the bath running drowned out the sound. On the internet she read a tip. Eat a dry biscuit before getting out of bed. Well, that'd only be possible if she stayed in a separate bed from Shibu.

The queasiness persisted throughout the day. Twice, when serving customers, she felt it creeping up from her stomach to her throat and had to sit down until it subsided.

"You okay, Madeleine?" Emily asked. "You look a bit peaky."

"A little too much wine last night, sorry." She didn't want anyone else to know before Shibu; besides, she hadn't fully decided on having it yet.

She walked home slowly. At the top of town sat a young man with a cap in front of him. Madeleine rummaged in her purse for a pound, but the act of leaning forward to give it to him brought a rush of nausea with it, so she squatted down beside him. The young man took it as an invitation to talk.

"Don't want you to think I'm spending your money on drink or drugs. I want to get enough for the night shelter."

"You spend it on what you like. It's your money now, not mine. I chose to give it to you, and you choose what to spend it on."

When she felt better Madeleine continued her journey home thinking back on her conversation with the homeless man. She had said it herself – it's all about choice. She had chosen to sleep with Shibu, and he with her, and Sean was right: it *was* his choice how he behaved. She'd tell him after dinner, and at the weekend, when he'd recovered a little from the shock, they could properly discuss it.

She started to cook a curry, but the smell of the spices and the feel of the raw chicken made her sick. She sat down and ate a biscuit.

Feeling relatively well, she cooked herself mash and beans, chewing each mouthful as if it were a plate of hemlock that condemned her to death. Afterwards she felt much better, so she washed up and tidied the kitchen, but this brought the sickness back. She went for a lie down. Then, hearing Shibu come in, she dragged herself downstairs. He was wearing a pensive expression.

She approached him, put her arms around him and kissed his cheek. He responded with a cautious hug.

"I wasn't feeling well enough to cook," Madeleine told him, hoping he would ask why.

He shrugged. "It doesn't matter, I can do. You have the flu?"

"No, not flu. Actually, I really need to talk with you." Madeleine's tone was rather more guarded than she had intended.

"I have important phone call to make to my cousin brother."

"Can't it wait?"

"I had letter, it say my college under investigation."

"Why?"

He shrugged. "They say not real college."

"What?"

"I don't understand, but I speak to my cousin brother."

"Okay, then after that."

"Okay."

Shibu suspected he didn't want to hear whatever she had to say. The same was true of his cousin's words now, who told him bogus college equalled bogus qualifications. His cousin had mentioned some time ago that some of the colleges were under suspicion. Shibu had worried at the time but quickly forgotten about it. Now, hearing this, his worries were resurrected; it would make a visa extension so much more unlikely. He sighed heavily, feeling weighed down by it all. Perhaps it was meant to be, he thought. This was the sign he was looking for. Suddenly he really wanted to see his family.

He couldn't be bothered to cook so he ate chips from the chip shop. He ate them sitting on the wall outside. He sat at one end, a group of teenagers of mixed gender at the other. With his coat collar up to his ears and his hat pulled down to meet it, he was fully able to understand why they eyed him with suspicion from time to time.

And now he had to go and face whatever the issue was with Madeleine. He thought he'd appeased her, but there was always something with her.

But when he got back, she was in bed again. He considered waking her, but it seemed cruel when she was clearly unwell, and besides, he had enough to consider for one evening.

Chapter Twenty-Five

For the third day in a row Shibu returned from work to find Madeleine in bed. The disappointment he experienced in response perplexed him; in the shower he thought it over. Could it be that she was now trying to avoid him? If so, he should be grateful, but instead he felt rejected and lonely. She seemed different lately. She was quiet, always lying around, and she hadn't cooked for him in days. He'd grown accustomed to her ways, in which there was a crazy kind of security, but with all of her habits changed he had no idea what to expect.

She was in the kitchen when he came down. She looked heavy-eyed and about her there was an air of irritability; Shibu was about to ask her if something was wrong, but then she said, "Hi, darling."

And it angered him. "Don't call me darling."

"What?"

"Maybe you forget and call to me in front of someone."

Madeleine sighed. "I call lots of my friends darling."

Now she sat with her head in her hands, which stirred Shibu's guilt, so he softened his tone and said, "Just I prefer you don't call to me. It sounds very intimate."

I don't know what we are if not intimate, she thought, but said, "Okay. Whatever you say." She raised her eyes towards him in a manner of resignation.

"How'd your phone call to your cousin go?"

"He say some of the colleges are not registered. Mine might be one of them."

"Really?"

"That's what he say and that's what my letter say. Is scam? Is that right word?"

"Yes, scam. This is where you pay money for something but don't get what you expected to get."

"Yes."

Madeleine's hands fell instinctively to her belly, which was where she felt the impact of his words. "So, what now?"

"I think my visa be refused."

Madeleine put her left hand to her throat and swallowed.

"Is there anything you can do?"

"I don't think so there is."

Her mind was a flurry of differing scenarios and her heart a tangle of mixed emotion. "Is there anything I can do to help?"

"I don't think so there is."

Madeleine wondered if he would accept it if there was, or whether this was the perfect excuse to escape, but she didn't ask. Weariness overcame her.

"I think I'm going to have to go back to bed, actually."

"Is very early."

"I'm very tired."

"You still not well?"

"Not ill. Just tired."

"You want me come too?" He considered it conciliatory.

"I think I'm too tired, sorry."

He found her lack of interest disturbing because it was so unlike her, and, like a belligerent teenager who only wants the very thing he is denied, he found it made him want her all the more.

Shibu hurried his dinner and then went to Madeleine's room.

She wasn't sleeping. She was thinking, at least as well as she was able to considering the fog that surrounded her. The likelihood that Shibu would soon be leaving felt like a stay of execution. Madeleine's emotions changed from hope to fear and back again, by the minute.

The knock on the door was so quiet she wasn't sure she'd heard it, so, instead of calling out she got up and opened it.

"I came see if you need anything," Shibu said.

"A cuddle, I need a cuddle."

She allowed him into her bed, and then into her, but she couldn't make the connection. He climaxed quickly, she not at all. Afterwards she said, "Sorry, darl, sorry, I'm just not feeling great today." They pecked each other on the mouth. Shibu got up. Madeleine went immediately to sleep.

Alone with himself Shibu felt self-disgust. What was happening to him? For weeks he had been trying to free himself of Madeleine, but at the first sign she might no longer want him, he desired her more. And she was ill; she deserved some peace. He tried to pray but found there was no one there to hear him. Perhaps he was even beyond God's rescue now.

The sex hadn't even been that good. It felt routine, as if he and Madeleine had already become each other's habit. If that remained the case it would be easy to resist.

But the next time the fire was back.

Afterwards Madeleine lay with her head on his chest; in her imagination she heard the tiny heart beat from inside her echo through the strong and steady one to which her ear attended. Shibu was twisting a strand of her hair around his forefinger and she found it comforting. She formed the words 'I'm pregnant' in her mind and took a deep breath in preparation to tell him.

Shibu felt the emotion in the fingertips of his right hand, which brushed Madeleine's breast. He sensed a readiness in her and believed she was about to tell of her love for him. In anticipation he pulled at the twist of hair, as if trying to drag the thought from her mind. He eased himself away from her and, pushing himself up on one elbow, looked her in the eyes and saw the love there. Shibu put his forefinger to her lips. "Shush!"

"What?"

"Don't."

"Don't what?"

"Say it."

"You don't know what I'm going to say."

"I see it in your eyes."

"What? What d'you see in my eyes?"

"That you love me."

"That wasn't what I was going to say."

"Your love make me feel guilty."

"I don't want you to feel guilty."

"I see you love me. I don't love you."

Even though she knew it, hearing it said so directly put jagged edges on her heart. "I can do without your love, Shibu, as long as you respect me."

"How I can respect you when I do sex with you?"

"What?" His remark was like a hand that clenched her throat and made sure she couldn't cough up the words she'd been about to utter. "You don't respect me?"

"How I can?"

She got up and pulled on her knickers and top, hearing again the accusing voice echo back from the past – 'little whore'.

She said nothing as she headed for the bathroom and ran a bath, into which she climbed, hoping to wash herself clean, not only of him but of the past, and bring the warmth back into her body. He didn't love her, she was used to that, but his lack of respect shamed her to the core.

Madeleine took a deep in breath and slid under the water. A thousand images flashed in her mind. Shibu looking so content in the afterglow, gazing fondly at her, trying so hard to please her, in bed, in life. He couldn't mean it. And yet, he must. She released her breath as she came back up to sitting. Her hair was heavy under the weight of the water, her heart under the weight of Shibu's words.

Shibu knew his words had wounded her, it had been his intention, but the second they left his mouth he regretted them.

275

Now he was afraid she was cutting herself. He got up, went to the bathroom and put his ear to the door. He heard the sound of weight passing through water, but it told him nothing other than that she was in the bath.

He knocked on the door and called out her name.

"What?"

"Will you be long? I need to go toilet."

"I'll be two minutes," she called in a cheery tone.

She dressed before going onto the landing, feeling ashamed to be naked in front of him.

"There you go. Night, then. See you tomorrow." She gave him a peck on the cheek.

She cultivated a firm resolve to never let him into her heart or body again.

Reviewing himself in the mirror the next morning Shibu felt ashamed of his own reflection. His physical features had changed little since he came to England, but the man inside was very much changed. He worried that his family would see and reject the imposter who posed as their son. How he wished he could stop what he'd started. How he hated Madeleine. How he desired her. How he wished to make her hate him too. How he wished to be forgiven.

And forgiveness came second nature to Madeleine, so before long they collided in a passionate embrace. But, forgetting was harder and she wanted to honour her promise to herself. Yet, she wanted reconciliation, so she chose words that would keep them apart without animosity. "I have my period." The words left her mouth before she'd considered the consequences.

Shibu, who was always glad of that information, should have taken it as the opportunity to withdraw, but instead he said, "You could use your mouth." As was her habit, Madeleine obliged.

His stroking of her breasts, and his arousal, evoked the same in her and left her feeling frustrated. Serve her right for her weakness and her lie, to which she was going to have to admit when finally forced to announce her condition. And then he would have double cause to hate her. From the past there echoed a sardonic laugh.

As soon as he was relieved of desire Shibu felt so full of self-contempt he wanted to die. It would be easier to give himself up to God now than have to live in anticipation for fifty more years. He felt the finger of the Lord pointing in his direction and imagined the accusing voice cast him out. He heard, too, the gleeful laugh of the devil, confident in his victory.

Madeleine approached him for a kiss.

"No." He put his hands up. They stopped Madeleine as surely as a brick wall.

"A kiss reassures me."

"Of what?"

What could she say? His affection? He'd already told her he had none for her. "That there is something more than just sex between us."

"What else there is?"

For a second Madeleine was stunned into silence but, recovering herself, felt angry enough to say, "Well, if it's only sex you owe me rather a lot of money."

"You think I treat you like prostitute?"

The anger in his eyes terrified her. It reached to the

277

deepest part of Madeleine's psyche and laid unending loathing at her feet. She couldn't bear it if he hated her.

"No. No, course not, I'm sorry. I'm sorry." She touched him on the shoulder.

He shrugged away from it. Her acquiescence disgusted him. She hadn't even enough self-respect to put up a proper fight. He left the room.

Madeleine stood staring at the door, hoping Shibu would walk back through it and offer her something, if not an apology then at least some sign of friendship.

Earlier that very day she'd been on her knees vomiting, her body forced into submission by biological changes for which Shibu bore fifty per cent responsibility, but from which their mutual inhibitions had so far kept him safe. His ignorance of the situation angered her now, and in that moment, she hated him, though she hated his God even more. A God who cared only that Shibu had given into temptation and not at all that he wounded her so often and so deeply. A God who would refuse their offspring entrance to heaven as long as no marriage took place. This God was contemptible, and she wanted to smash the symbols of His religion. To burn Shibu's Bible, rip the rosary to shreds and scream, "That's what I think of your fucking God." But then, almost immediately, she relented and wanted to comfort him and tell him she understood. Poor, sweet Shibu, how he must be suffering!

She didn't believe that he would refuse to ever kiss her again; he'd threatened it before, but he always came back for more. She could live without their ever having sex again, but not without his kiss. It was so gentle, and in it there was a different story to the verbal one.

Alone in his room Shibu's contempt shifted from Madeleine to himself. How could he, a Christian, be so cruel? God must surely disapprove of this as much as He would their affair.

A few days later they met on the landing, Madeleine was heading back to bed for five minutes to recover from the vomiting.

"Just I go to work, now," Shibu said. He pulled Madeleine into him, lifted her face towards his and kissed her softly on the mouth. "I hope you have good day."

Later, he came up behind her and put his arms around her. "I think you put weight on since you stop smoking."

Madeleine's heart rate increased and she felt a trickle of sweat on her brow; she should tell him now and she braced herself in readiness.

Shibu's hands were on her breasts and he said, "These are bigger too." He gave her breasts a gentle squeeze in emphasis and licked her neck, then turned her around to face him and kissed her deeply.

She pulled away gently. "Wait, I—"

Shibu silenced her with ever deeper kisses. Soon they were one, the boundaries of their bodies blended, and Madeleine felt his soul whisper a reply to hers. They moved slowly, in perfect unison, and climaxed at the same time. Madeleine's whole body responded with a soft sigh. Shibu collapsed on top of her; his breath warmed her neck and his heart echoed through her chest. She nuzzled into his face and felt for his mouth, but suddenly he pulled away, out of her and onto his feet. "Okay, goodnight!"

"You're going?"

"Yes." He grabbed his clothes and headed for the door.

"Don't leave me, Shibu, not yet. Please."

He didn't answer but hurried out of the room. Madeleine lay for a moment in shocked silence. Recovering a little she rose, wrapped the duvet around herself and headed to Shibu's room. When he didn't respond to her knock she walked in and sat on the bed. He was facing the wall with the duvet over his head.

"It's not fair that you treat me like this, I only asked you to stay for a while."

He didn't respond at all.

"Speak to me," she demanded.

"Go, please." Shibu spoke from beneath the duvet.

"I want to talk, explain how I feel."

"I know how you feel. Now go. This my room."

"You were just inside my body and now you want me out of your room."

Again, there was no answer.

Madeleine was grounded by humiliation. She pulled Shibu's duvet away slightly and touched his shoulder. "Shibu, I—"

He sprang up and turned on her. "Go, I said. Get out!"

"Okay, okay." Madeleine raised her arms in submission and dragged herself from the room, feeling as if she must uproot her feet from the floor in order to do so.

Shibu tucked himself up again, wishing to cocoon himself in the womb of his duvet. This time they'd lost themselves in each other. And he had felt himself on the edge of a religious experience. They would never be able to part if this continued.

Back in bed Madeleine lay still. There is the stillness that comes from contentment, and then there is the stillness of death. Madeleine lay so still she was hardly breathing.

Chapter Twenty-Six

Afterwards Madeleine felt two things: humiliation and grief. She knew her self-respect could only be maintained by distancing herself from Shibu. But, from habit, and from desperation to regain his approval, she pandered to his every whim.

Shibu felt two things in response: ashamed of himself, contemptuous of Madeleine, who reminded him of a neighbour's dog from his childhood; beaten and starved the stupid thing cried outside the door to be let in. Madeleine uncomplainingly acquiesced to all his requests and Shibu felt utterly miserable in her company.

Then the Home Office letter arrived.

Madeleine felt so unwell that morning at work it was necessary for her to sit down at frequent intervals.

"I think you need to see a doctor," Emily told her. You've been ill a lot lately."

"I'll see how I go on." She rose to serve the custom coming through the door; it was Kumar wishing to purchase echinacea to stave off his daughter's advancing cold.

"We're sold out, expecting a delivery, could be this afternoon."

"Okay, I'll come back then."

"Why don't I bring it when I finish? Save you the bother."

"That'd be good. Thank you. You okay? You don't look as if you're feeling that great yourself."

"I'll be fine. Thanks, though."

She sat back down and took deep breaths.

The delivery arrived just before closing. Madeleine took it straight to Kumar's.

"Tea," he offered.

"Could I have hot water, please?"

"Of course, but you never refuse tea."

"I'm off it. Off a lot of things." She paused only for a second to consider her words. "I'm pregnant."

"Wow! How'd that happen? No don't answer that." Kumar laughed. "I meant – New Year's Eve?"

"God no, it's not Julian's. But hey, on the subject of New Year's Eve, I owe you one massive apology."

"You owe me no such thing."

"Thank you for being such a good friend, Kumar, but I definitely do. I was so wrong going off with Julian like that. I was, Kumar, I was. It was unfair to you and unfair to him, I don't know what the hell I was thinking of."

"It was a combination of alcohol and loneliness, I think."

Madeleine burst into tears.

"Hey! Hey!" Kumar pulled her into an embrace, which felt so secure it sent Madeleine into a volley of wailing. Kumar waved away Sumayyia, who'd come to check when she heard the tears, and sat Madeleine down.

"Do you want to talk about this?"

"It would be kind of useful, in complete confidence, of course."

"Naturally."

Kumar's shock at discovering the father was unspoken yet clear. His support was honest and non-judgemental. Madeleine returned home with renewed conviction that she would never tell Shibu about the baby. Kumar's opinion was that Shibu's fears regarding the reaction from his family and community were probably not exaggerated.

Shibu was sitting at the computer. He stood up when she entered the room. "I have some news," he told Madeleine.

It was early evening, late March, the sun was strong for the time of year; Shibu stood by the window and was cast by its light into the leading role.

"The visa?" Instinctively Madeleine's hand gripped her belly, as if a sentence was about to be issued on two lives.

"Yes. I heard yesterday, but I didn't want tell you."

"You're going?"

"Yes, they refuse to me."

A tear crept into Madeleine, of sorrow and relief. "How d'you feel?"

"Will be difficult to pay back money I owe, but will be good to see my family."

She wanted more, a hint that she would be missed, even if only a little. She felt like she'd been put in a glass room with Shibu on the outside.

"When're you going?"

"They tell to me I must go before the end of April, but I think I have holidays to come, so maybe sooner. Tomorrow I speak with manager and she can tell to me my leaving date."

"Any point in an appeal?"

"I don't think so there is." As far as Shibu was concerned the refusal was influenced by God. He had a sudden inkling of himself back home in India, a changed man, but a man indeed, without the woman who had made him that. There would be some need for readjustment for sure.

"Well, I'm going to miss you, Shibu."

He didn't reply.

"If I can I'll borrow Kumar's car – drive you to the airport."

"Thank you."

Suddenly without intending to, he said, "My cousin brother think I should marry you for visa."

The words were like a shower of confetti; they both tickled and irritated.

"And what about you, what d'you think?"

"I think maybe it work. If you want means we can."

Shibu's proposal, in her imagination, was one born of duty to his unborn child; this one had a tone of indifference. Her refusal was supposed to be stoical; this one would be matter-of-fact. Under the imagined circumstance it would be to assert her independent

285

motherhood, under the current one to protect it. The irony of it all produced a cynical laugh, for which Shibu had his own interpretation.

"I don't blame you for feel like that, after all that happen, just I think maybe—"

"Maybe what? Maybe I'd do it just to help you?"

If it weren't for the pregnancy that's exactly what she would have done.

"I'd like to, Shibu, but… if we had sex after a ceremony, I'd be your real wife in every sense of the word, even in God's eyes. You wouldn't be able to stand that. And if we didn't, we'd have to live under the same roof in a way that convinced everyone else we were a real couple. I couldn't stand that."

Shibu nodded. He was surprised by Madeleine's words, which sounded all the more rational because they were so unexpected. He had predicted she would be only too pleased to marry him and he would have to wrestle with self-reproach when he changed his mind and backed out. In truth he was more than a little hurt by her refusal.

Madeleine approached him. "Can I have a hug?"

"No, I don't think so."

Madeleine felt like a child starved of parental approval; in her solar plexus a hole had already begun to open that only he could fill.

"Shibu, what did I ever ask of you?"

"What you mean?"

Shibu saw her pain and felt culpable. He wanted to take her hurt away, but he was afraid of the consequences.

"All I'm asking for is a hug."

"We have hug you want sex."

"So might you. You just asked me to marry you, for God's sake."

"I don't like you use God's name like swear."

"No? Prefer fuck? That would be fitting, since that's what you've been doing to me."

They stood gazing at each other in mutual anger and agony.

"You know what I think, Shibu? I think it's you who is afraid about sex, afraid in case you can't stop yourself, cause you know what, I don't want the kind of sex we've had lately. I only want it if you'll stay with me after and hold me and kiss me."

"This for proper relationship."

"What?"

"You speak like we were boyfriend and girlfriend."

"I speak like there was something a bit special between us."

"For you, maybe, not for me."

"Well, fuck you, you bastard!"

"Stop swearing at me." Shibu charged upstairs and slammed into his room.

"Don't treat me like a prostitute, then," Madeleine yelled up the stairs.

In a rage she ran after him. Shibu was standing staring out of the window. She took a deep, calming breath. "Hey, sorry. Can I talk to you, please?"

"No, no more talking. This second time you say I treat you like prostitute; I think this your problem – maybe that how you feel about yourself."

Madeleine felt like she was standing naked in the window displaying herself.

"Why exactly did you start sleeping with me, Shibu?"

"Just I need to know how sex feel."

"And that's not treating me like a prostitute?"

Shibu shifted his gaze, from Madeleine to the floor.

"What about now, after all these months?"

"Now it become habit."

It was like being pelted by nails. "You bastard!"

For a second there was silence. They were like the last two people standing on a battlefield of bodies, eyeing each other with suspicion.

"So, I could have been anyone?"

"Yes, was because of circumstances; because of our sharing home."

"I don't believe you."

In her memory Shibu pushed her hair back from her face and planted a gentle kiss on her mouth; his eyes were full of her.

"You call me liar?"

It was like a stake had penetrated her head and fixed her to the floor. A dark chasm opened inside of Madeleine, into which she fell, and at the bottom she found the experiences of her past. She stifled her tears. But then there came another memory: *his arms around her as they lay in the afterglow – his voice soft and happy. "Thank you, thank you."* And with it came grief so profound the tears exploded from her in a wail.

It frightened Shibu. "Please, I need you go now."

Madeleine was unable to speak. Both she and Shibu rocked backwards and forwards under the weight of her tears.

Then he said again, "Please go."

Madeleine found her voice and her rage. "I'm going," she said with vehemence, and pushed him backwards onto the bed, then she stormed out of the room.

Shibu lay for a moment. Then he stood up, intending to leave the house dramatically and walk his anger away, but as he did so he glanced out of the window and saw Madeleine in the garden. At first he felt his outrage vindicated by her behaviour, as she kicked the tree and then the shed door, which now she thrust open. But when she emerged with an axe Shibu felt suddenly panic-stricken. It was the sound of shattering glass that sent him running down the stairs and into the garden. When he got there, Madeleine was smashing the garden mirror.

"Why you do this?" Shibu demanded.

"This is just the start. I'm going to smash every mirror in the house so I don't have to look at the image of the whore anymore."

"Good idea!"

Shibu was about to leave her to do just that when she moved towards him with a large slither of glass in her left hand. He stepped back from her, unsure as to which of them her ill intent was directed.

"What you doing?"

She said nothing but took another step towards him, and he another step back.

"What you going to do?" Anger gave way to fear now. His mind was full of her crucified legs.

Still she didn't answer, as she took a step closer.

"Put that down, Madeleine, please. I don't want you hurt yourself."

"Course not – it'd be another thing on your conscience."

"Put it down, please." Still he couldn't say what he knew he should.

"Don't worry, I'm not about to kill either of us, it's going in the bin."

She was calming down now and feeling sad rather than angry; inside her the tiny life seemed to be crying too. She looked Shibu long and hard in the face.

"I'm sorry," he finally said.

"For what? It was the truth, wasn't it?"

He didn't answer for fear of having to examine feelings he was himself unsure of.

"That's what I thought. It's okay, all my life it's been the same, since as long as I can remember. Men want me for sex then they hate me and blame me for it. First Philip, then all the rest—"

"What?"

"I thought it was different with you, but I was wrong."

"What? What you say about Philip?" The words had hit him like a blow to the chest.

"I said he was the first."

"Your father had sex with you?"

Of course, he should have known that's what it was.

"He didn't penetrate, if that's what you mean? No, he was too clever for that. Nothing so aggressive that we couldn't rightly accept the blame, nothing so visible as to evidence his crime. We, Tom and me, we had to relieve his desire with our hands. He liked us to tie him up and blindfold him, so that he became the *victim*."

"No, please, no."

Shibu saw Jobin's dying face reflected in Madeleine's gaze.

"Oh! You don't like to hear it. You don't like the truth."

"I'm sorry."

"What for? Why be sorry, you have no feelings for me? But he, Philip, our father, *loved* us apparently. I expect you're thinking, well, they couldn't have objected that much or they wouldn't have done it—"

"I wasn't thinking that—"

"That's exactly what he used to tell us, so, one day, at my suggestion, we said no. No, I said with confidence. No, Tom said, just as I'd directed him. So, what d'you think he did? Our father, with his erection that we wouldn't relieve?"

"I don't know, I don't want to know. I'm sorry, so sorry." Shibu was crying now.

"He forced it on my brother, that's what he did."

"No! No! Stop!"

"Not me. I could have lived with it. But my little brother. I should have helped him, but I couldn't. I couldn't move." Madeleine's tears sounded other-worldly.

Shibu wanted to comfort her, but he was afraid of making things worse. And he was too ashamed to look at her.

Madeleine slumped down on the step and let her hand relax its hold on the glass. Shibu picked it up and put it in the bin. Then he edged past Madeleine and out of the house.

She experienced his exit as if she were an insect he was repulsed by.

Shibu walked without any idea where he was going. He thought back to Christmas and Philip's pleasant conversation. *I couldn't understand what Madeleine's problem was*, he thought.

He walked along the river, and being there reminded him of home; he wanted so much to be there now. And then he remembered Jobin and the day he'd realised why she'd chosen death. The overheard conversation, in which his mother and her friend were so engrossed they didn't notice him come in. "Intimate, they say, her and her father," he heard his mother say, and Shibu was so shocked he gasped. All three looked at each other, but no one ever acknowledged that he'd heard.

Just then his attention was caught by squawking: a drake was mounting a female so forcefully that her head kept submerging. Instinctively, Shibu picked up a stone and threw it at the drake.

Madeleine saying that she hated herself. Her crucified legs, the way she separated the food into piles on her plate. Somehow it all made sense now, although equally none of it made any sense at all.

Her words came back to him. "*Don't treat me like a prostitute.*" Then: "*Men want me for sex, then they hate me and blame me for it. I thought it was different with you.*"

Have I done that? he asked himself now. *Did I blame her? Did I treat her like a prostitute? I need to speak with a priest.*

At the door of the church he hesitated, then turned and walked away, feeling too ashamed to seek forgiveness. He went back to the river; it was almost dark now. Again he remembered Jobin and her dying face. The sin of suicide seemed nothing compared with the sin he'd committed against Madeleine, and he wished he had the courage to slide down the steep banks and end his own life. He didn't know how he was going to survive another minute in her company, or how he would ever be able to look her in the eyes again.

For hours Madeleine lay languidly on the sofa, one ear tuned for Shibu's return, her heart full of remorse. She should never have told him. In using her deepest insecurities as a weapon, she had finally defeated him, but, in common with all wars, there were only losers. The repugnance she felt for herself had been mirrored in Shibu's gaze, and she knew all chance of gaining his respect had been lost for certain. How could she ever resolve her feelings of self-disgust now that she had generated the same in him? How could she bear his child, when knowing that his loathing for her was greater than her own?

Shibu crept into the house a little after midnight, walking in a whisper as if afraid to disturb the molecules in the air, but, though the house remained in darkness, Madeleine called out into it, "Is that you, Shibu?"

"Yes."

"You okay?"

"Yes."

He ran into his room and shut the door noisily so as to make his need of solitude clear.

He got up at six, washed and shaved in the washbasin of the outside toilet, then left without tea or breakfast and wandered the streets until he could go to work.

Chapter Twenty-Seven

The quiet and the stillness were what woke Madeleine; it was as if the house was holding its breath. The ginger biscuit stuck in her throat on the way down and again on the way up a few minutes later. In the bath she rubbed her skin until it was the colour of a sunburn; she chewed each mouthful of her breakfast fifty times, then once, twice more; she brushed her teeth until her gums were sore. She arrived ten minutes late at work.

She waited until midnight but Shibu didn't come in.

An awareness of him penetrated her sleep – the shower running, the light breaking – but not enough to rouse her. She ate the ginger biscuit, pulled on her clothes, was floored by nausea at the top of the stairs, which sent her hurrying to the bathroom. In the midst of the vomiting she heard the creak of the gate as he left.

She phoned in sick to work and waited all day for his return. She ate just enough to stave off sickness and sat at the table in silence, or paced the house. Again, there was no sign of him by midnight. This time she woke hourly in anticipation of his return. Then she slept through the seven o'clock alarm and woke not knowing whether or not he had been home.

Another day of work was missed, another day wasted in staring at the wall. This time Shibu returned at his usual time, said, "Hi," then, "Goodnight," and refused to open his bedroom door to her pleas.

In her bedroom Madeleine cried desperate tears which Shibu heard. Guilt bade him go to her, but shame bade him not. He buried his head in his pillow and prayed for death to come.

Madeleine felt like she was suffocating. Without his forgiveness she was bound to die. She gathered together the necessary tools and crept into the bathroom, but even as the water was running Madeleine knew she couldn't do it. Not now, with another life to nurture. She pulled the plug, put the razor away, went downstairs and wrote Shibu a note.

"I'm so sorry to have burdened you with the problems of my past, please find it in your heart to forgive me – I can't bear to think of us parting on bad terms."

She put it under his door and fell into her first sound sleep for days.

This time sorry induced not contempt for Madeleine but for himself. It was he who should be begging for forgiveness. In self-disgust he ripped it up and threw it into the bathroom bin, then left the house in search of a priest.

On her hands and knees as she was throwing up, Madeleine noticed the paper in the bin. She took it out to check, then screwed it into a ball and threw it at the wall.

Work was harder than ever as she battled not only nausea but the sickness in her heart. As lunchtime approached Madeleine made the decision to go home and sit it out for as long as was needed. She must speak with Shibu. She would wait in his room if necessary.

"I don't feel at all well, Emily. I think I'm going to have to go home."

"Promise me you'll go to the doctor?"

"I will."

Madeleine didn't expect to find Shibu so easily. He was sitting at the computer.

"Shibu, I've been desperate to talk to you. Did you read my note?"

"Yes." He kept his eyes on the screen.

"We can't go on like this for another month; we have to speak to each other."

"Two and one half week, not month."

"You've booked your flight?"

"Just I do now. April fifteen. Is Sunday, is morning flight."

What Madeleine felt more than anything was relief. "Heathrow? Okay, I can drive you."

"If you don't want means my cousin brother can do, he already tell to me."

"No, I'd like to."

"Then, thank you."

"But please can we be friends again?"

"When we stop being friends?"

"I thought – what I told you the other day – I thought that had ended our friendship."

"No." He wanted to explain, but equally wanted to forget.

"I thought—"

"Please, I don't want to discuss anymore."

"Still friends, though?"

He turned to look at her. "Of course. You are my intimate friend."

Intimate friend. And she sighed out the breath she'd held on to for days.

Peace was maintained by keeping their interactions friendly but formal, like work colleagues nearing the end of a project.

Once, when their eyes met, Madeleine saw the depth of his shame. It was an emotion so familiar to her that it made them kin.

At the airport Madeleine said, "Can I have a hug now?"

There was only a second's hesitation before Shibu grabbed her and hugged her close. Her coconut scent teased his nose, but most of his awareness was on her breasts as they squeezed into him on her in breath, then away on each exhalation. One day this space would be filled by a legitimate wife. Into Madeleine's back he said, "If I invite you my wedding will you come?"

"If I can." She felt so safe in his embrace. It was impossible to believe it was lost to her forever, and agony to imagine another woman in his arms. To lighten her load she said, "Don't forget you promised to come to my funeral."

Shibu laughed. "If I'm still alive."

He pulled away, turned and walked through the gate; just before he walked out of sight he turned again and waved. His last impression was a flash of orange and red, as her dress spun like a flag when she turned and hurried away.

Madeleine made it back to the car before she cried.

Shibu turned his face from the stranger in the seat beside him and looked out at the clouds drifting by. His heart was full of remorse as silently he asked himself, *Why didn't I tell her I didn't mean it? I should have told her I'm glad it was her.*

There would be many Keralan sunrises and sunsets, and there would be Valsa, before it ceased to be a daily refrain.

Chapter Twenty-Eight

Without him she was like a shadow. It was like being alone on a dark ocean in a fishing boat. There was no music, no desire, except for him. She lay for hours with the duvet over her head to shut out the light, or sat staring into space, a film forming on her cup of tea. The phone went unanswered, the housework undone. She felt cold, so cold. She had insufficient energy to stand in the shower, so she sat in the bath, staying there in a trance until the water went cold and rubbing her rounding belly.

To Emily she said she was too sick to work. To Sean, "I just want to be on my own for a while."

"Okay, I'll give you two weeks, then I'll be round."

It was no longer morning sickness that made it difficult to leave her bed but the dawning thought, *He's gone, he's gone.* But then, sometimes, and increasingly so, the bulge in her belly lent some comfort and relieved her loneliness.

A re-run of her life in the past few months kept her awake at night and allowed no peace in the day; she recalled him saying, *"Just I never try before I need to know what it feel like.*" But then, there was the tender look in his eyes, the way he stroked her limbs, and said, "*Thank you, thank you,*" after she surrendered herself to him. And best of all: "*You're my intimate friend.*" Grief made her listless. Anger provoked cleaning.

She was squatting, washing out the cupboard that used to be Shibu's when she felt it. It was such a small sensation that at first she wasn't sure, but then, yes, there it was again, it was definitely a movement. Automatically her hand lowered to her belly; as it did so she felt the confirmation of the movement against her hand. There was a flash of excitement and just for a second she was neither angry nor grieving; if Shibu had given her nothing else at least he had given her this. As if it had only just dawned on her, Madeleine now realised she was going to have to tell people.

Her mother was first.

"Sorry to do this over the phone, but there's something you need to know."

Tessa squealed with delight, then said, "Who's the father?"

Madeleine said, "That's not important, the baby's mine," without being sure of her motives. Philip could wait a little while longer, because he would be the hardest to tell.

She went back to the doctor, who smiled approvingly and made the necessary appointments.

Carol went with her for her twenty-week scan and held Madeleine's hand when she cried in response to seeing the foetus.

"D'you want to know the sex?" the radiographer asked.

"No, thank you, I like a surprise."

Outside she was overcome with grief and had to sit on the wall to recover.

Carol rubbed her upper back and asked, "What is it?"

"My heart is broken," she sobbed.

"By the father? He doesn't want to know?"

"I haven't told him."

Still Carol didn't ask who he was.

But then, with the scan picture to make it more real, she knew it was time to tell Philip and he said, "Pretty little Indian boy, I presume. I knew you were in that day."

Yeah, well, I knew you'd been in my room, she thought.

"He's back in India, you say – nothing like making things hard for yourself. Hardly the most appropriate person to father your child."

"I hope you're not going to lecture me on sexual propriety."

There was a prolonged silence before Philip replied, "Well, congratulations. I'll get to meet him at Christmas, I suppose."

It was late May when Tessa came to visit; over lunch, which they ate in the garden, Madeleine announced the parentage of her baby.

"Why didn't you tell me in the first place? Did you think I'd be shocked?"

"Aren't you?"

"A little."

"His age?"

"Well, yes. But more the fact he'll never know."

"We'll be fine without him."

"Don't you think he or she has a right to their father?"

"People aren't always better off with two parents."

"Most fathers are not like yours, Madeleine." Tessa's face was flushed, despite the air being cool enough to urge them back indoors. "You will let me be a proper grandmother, won't you?"

"Of course, why wouldn't I?"

"I hardly deserve it after…"

"It was a long time ago, Mum, time to move on."

"But that day – you know, the day I came in to—"

"Don't, Mum, please." The door opened in Madeleine's memory, on to the scene to which her mother returned. Madeleine was still in the process of cleaning up the carpet where Tom had been sick. Philip was crying. Tom was locked in his room. And into silence from which he never fully returned.

Now, Tessa was crying. "I think I knew, yes, I knew what he used to do."

"Stop it, Mum, please."

"I should've told someone. The social, the police. Why didn't I tell someone?"

"You just didn't. None of us did what we *should* have, that's the way it is with these things."

"And then I left you with him, for God's sake."

"Mum, it doesn't matter anymore."

Truth was, that was the worst – nearly grown up, but not quite enough. Not enough for Tom, who couldn't be left alone with Philip, but just enough for Madeleine to take over her mother's role.

"I intended to get somewhere big enough for all of us, I didn't want to leave you with that monster."

"Mum. It's okay – really, I'm okay." Now, feeling more than a little awkward, Madeleine put her arms around her mother. "It's okay, really."

"You should hate me. I do. Tom did."

"No, he didn't. He hated Philip but not you."

"She's weak, Madeleine, she's the one who should've helped us, instead she fucked off and left us; she can go screw herself for all I care."

Those were Tom's thoughts on his mother, but she didn't need to hear them. When the emotion was becoming too much to bear Madeleine said, "The baby's coming between us already." And they both laughed.

To Sean she said, "I've asked Carol to be with me when the baby comes because I know she won't let me give in and have loads of medical stuff unless it's absolutely necessary, but I'd like… d'you think Aileen would mind if you were with me too?"

And Sean said, "Babe, I've been dying to ask if I could."

To the counsellor Madeleine said, "I need to learn to like myself. I don't want to pass any of this screwed-up stuff on to my child. D'you think I can do it? D'you think it'll be okay?"

And Sarah said, "I'll be with you while you're learning."

Sean held her when she rocked and moaned through the pain. Carol cradled her head when she cried for Shibu, and they both encouraged her when the midwife urged, "Push, Madeleine, push that pain away."

And, the instant she held her daughter in her arms she knew it was going to be just fine.

Madeleine was feeding Jasmine when the Skype call came. She disconnected it quickly, then, when the baby was settled, called him back.

"Sorry about that, there's a problem with my phone; I'm on the computer now so should be okay. Anyway, I can see you better this way. You look great. How'd you feel?"

"Good, thank you. I just called to wish you Happy Christmas and New Year."

"Thanks. You too." Shibu was dressed in a sarong; he wore a broad smile that made his face look as warm as the day behind him.

"How Sean? How Carol and Kumar?"

"Fine, we're all just fine."

When the call was over Madeleine felt the tide of grief rising; she took a deep breath in as the wave hit her full on, then breathed out hard and let it wash over her – just as Sarah had taught her.

Christmas with Philip was easier. It wasn't just the baby, whom he seemed to genuinely enjoy, but the freedom from him Madeleine was beginning to achieve.

"Would you think about prosecution?" Sarah had asked.

"I did think about it, especially after Tom died, but no. I've always been too afraid. And now it seems too late, like it would be about revenge rather than justice. Anyway, it's not any easier for him this way. He probably lives every day in fear that I'll do exactly that."

"What about the potential danger to your child?"

"There won't be any. I'd never leave him alone with any child. I never have."

304

New Year's Eve Kumar came to visit and she told him about the call from Shibu.

"I never thought I'd get to this stage, but now I prefer not to talk to him."

"That's easier for you?"

"Much."

"There will be times when being on your own is hard, though."

"No doubt, but I'm resourceful."

"Indeed you are. Will you be alright financially?"

"I've got my jewellery-making, I'll get some benefits, thought I might take up child-minding."

Kumar was sitting with his elbows resting on the table and his hands in prayer position; he rubbed them together then tapped his mouth with his fingers, cleared his throat and placed his hands on the table. "This might be the wrong time to ask, but I'd be very honoured if you would marry me."

The shock was like being knocked over on the beach by a huge wave. Tears filled Madeleine's eyes.

"Oh, sorry, I'm sorry," Kumar said.

Madeleine reached across the table and touched his hand. "There's no need to be, that was such a beautiful gesture."

"It wasn't a gesture, I meant it. I know you would never feel about me like you did – do, about Shibu, and I know I don't have too much to offer you, but well, Jasmine would have a father from the right cultural background and I would be able to provide for you both financially. And in time, who knows – maybe—"

Madeleine squeezed his hand tightly as she cried,

"You're right, it is the wrong time to ask, but you're very wrong about having nothing to offer, you're a very fine man. I couldn't marry you now despite that, because my heart still belongs to Shibu, but, if you could give me more time then maybe."

"I'll give you as much time as you need."

"I don't know how long that'll be. Maybe too long, maybe never."

"I'll take that chance. I don't mind being second best."

"I promise you that if I marry you, you won't be that."

*

Two years later there was Valsa. Madeleine sat through the wedding ceremony without understanding a single word, and afterwards with their English-speaking relatives hearing stories of a childhood she could barely comprehend. When her gaze caught Shibu's he smiled and lowered his eyes only slightly, and she saw that his shame was now small.

At arrivals Jasmine ran towards her. Madeleine picked her up, squeezed her and kissed her all over her face; Jasmine screeched with delight.

"How was it?" Kumar asked.

"Fine. It was actually fine."

Later they sat drinking wine and eating the meal he'd cooked for the two of them.

"Did it hurt seeing Shibu with a wife?" Kumar asked.

"I thought it would, but, no." Madeleine sighed and felt a lifetime's pressure released. "D'you still think you could marry me?"

"What would you say if I asked?"

"I would say, yes, please, because we're two fine people who deserve to be happy."

Epilogue

Jet lag, apprehension, but most of all Jasmine, prevented proper sleep. As soon as she'd opened the door he knew. Her hair was like Madeleine's but the rest. Davinder's face came into his mind. But for the hair, and the softer female features, she could be his eldest son. But then, he must be wrong. Why would Madeleine not have told him?

Oh, a million reasons, he thought, remembering how it had been then. Eventually thirst drove Shibu from bed well before dawn.

His behaviour, as he crept along the landing in the dark, fearful of waking the only other inhabitant of the house, was so reminiscent of that earlier time he felt himself transported there. Madeleine's presence pervaded everywhere; it was as if she was a ghost already. As he inched his way down the stairs Shibu expected to be startled by her presence, real or phantom, at every stage. In this frame of mind, he opened the kitchen door

308

cautiously, then jumped and gasped out loud when he saw Jasmine sitting at the table.

"Sorry," she said.

"I didn't expect you to be up."

"Couldn't sleep. You neither, I guess."

"No, too many thing on my mind."

"Then, please sit. Shall I make you a coffee? It is decaf. Okay, water it is."

They were sitting opposite each other, peering over their drinks and through their inhibitions.

"I thought she'd outlive me," Shibu said, "all that yoga. And such a strong spirit."

"She's done pretty well."

"How's it been for her? The illness, I mean."

"She's been comfortable – most of the time."

There was a pause. Shibu took a deep breath. "I have to ask about your father, Jasmine."

"Don't you know?"

"I think so. Not Kumar?"

"No."

He nodded. "Why she didn't tell to me?"

"She thought it was for the best."

"I'm sorry. I should've been here for you. And for her."

"You have no need to be sorry. I had plenty of love, not only from my mother, from Kumar. And from Sean."

"When she tell to you about me?"

"Always. I always knew. She used to say, 'Your father would never have chosen to leave and if he could be here, you would know he loves you. When you're old enough to understand I'll explain it all.'"

309

"And?"

"I did understand."

"Thank you for that."

"I'm very glad you're here now, though."

"I had promise to keep."

"Well, thank you for that too." She paused, took a deep breath. "I'm very glad to meet you, of course, but if you want to go home and forget me, I'll understand."

"And if I don't?"

"What about your family in India?"

Shibu remembered that he had felt terrified, but he couldn't really connect with it. He imagined being home and telling his wife. His children. His stomach churned and his throat tingled, but no deep chasm opened up before him. There was no accusing finger pointing from the sky. Valsa would be hurt, no doubt, but they were solid; they'd survive. Anyway, it was the right thing to do.

"They will have big shock." He reached out his hand; Jasmine did too and they closed their fingers around each other's palms. "Yes, will be big shock, but I will explain."

"You have three sons, I believe?"

"Yes, you my only daughter."

For several minutes they sat in silence. Then Shibu asked, "Are you married? Ah! Good. Do I have grandchildren?"

"Yes, one of each."

"Then, I look forward to meet them." He patted Jasmine's hand as they released their hold on each other. "We have much to talk about, but for now I think we need sleep, to be fresh for Madeleine."

"How long will you stay?"

"Until the end. I promised."

"I don't think it'll be more than a few days."

"She'll have a nurse? Good." He stood up and looked at Jasmine with satisfaction for a second or two.

"You are beautiful. Like your mother."

*

Shibu whispered outside the living room, into which Madeleine's bed had been moved. "Have you tell to her I'm here?"

"No, I thought it would be better not to. One last surprise before she goes."

Schubert was playing as he entered the room; although he remembered neither the name of the piece nor the composer, Shibu recognised the music and the memory evoked the same emotions as those from the past. He sat down on the chair next to Madeleine's bed; she was lost in the music, her eyes were closed, but when he picked up her hand, she opened them.

"Shibu? Is that you? You came."

As Shibu patted her hand tears came to his eyes.

"Of course."